Lightning See(
By Nathan McGra...

****

******

Also by Nathan McGrath:
Nanopunk
Magic. A Rough Guide

******

Chapter One

Seven years old. His birthday. Jules, his sister, had taken him to
the most hi-tech lab in Europe. They said so on TV. Mum
brought him here last. Dad said to be strong. He walked slowly,
sliding his hand along the edge of the bench, the memory of
Mum heavy on his heart. Alister turned and peered back.
Beyond the door and the glass walls, his father was fast asleep.
Poor dad, all alone.

 Motion-sensitive proximity lights bloomed into glowing
pools of soft yellow, and he passed deeper into the lab.
Occasional bursts of colour and the quiet bustling of machines
busy in the shadows, blinking, talking to each other, doing stuff,
changing things. His electronic jungle.

Over the long table, eight big screens hung side by side.
Coloured lines flowed across them through shapes that expanded
and shrunk on a pale silver grid. "Wow." Alister's spirits lifted
as his eyes adjusted to the gloom. His gaze darted over the
parade of objects: beakers, electronic devices, rows of test tubes,
and skinny glass tubes that swirled a shiny liquid into and out of
shoebox-shaped computer screens. Strange, small metal cubes
and cones wired to crowds of little displays that blinked numbers
at each other. The lab had never looked so bright and busy.

Then he stopped. In the middle of the cluttered table, a glass
beaker stood on a charging mat surrounded by little magnets like
a magical treasure protected by tiny soldiers. A digital scale
beside it blinked 333 ml. The liquid inside seemed alive,
sparkling with gold, blue, green, and red flashes.

Something pulled him towards it. Gaping at the swirling
colours, he slid his hands from his pockets and touched the
table's edge. The patterns of flashing colour echoed something
inside him, familiar, comforting.

He slowly reached over the instruments and a circle of
magnets until his finger hovered over the surface of the beaker.
The liquid bobbed up against the glass. Alister gasped, his face
beamed when a little wave chased his finger around the surface.

He had to; he just had to. He pursed his lips and touched the
top of the liquid. A thin, slow stream of flickering rainbow,
warm and lacy, reached up and curled around the tip of his
finger. He stirred the liquid and smiled. The number on the

2

digital scale flashed and changed.

He stared open-mouthed at his warm, dry finger, dipped it in deeper, and gently swirled it for several seconds, lost in a daze. A fuzzy, bright sensation danced up his arm and spread through him. The digital scale beside the beaker blinked rapidly down from 300 ml. It hit 250, and a ping brought Alister around. The number continued to drop.

Standing motionless, Alister stared at his finger, took it out of the liquid and shivered. Why was their lab always so cold?

"Woah." His head spun for a moment. The thermostat clicked, and the heaters hummed into action, raising the temperature in the lab by five degrees.

Back in the office, he pressed the big green button and went out into the bright, open hallway. It had stopped snowing, and beams of sunlight merged and spread like wide curtains across the snow-covered city.

The sofa squeaked when Alister jumped beside his dad, who shifted and woke up. "Oh, I must have dozed off."

A phone began to beep softly in his dad's pocket. His dad pulled it out, and Alister craned his neck towards the flashing particle-detector app.

"Hey, nosey!" his father slid it back into his pocket.

"All those funny lines and dots looked like a picture of me, Daddy."

***

The metal door slammed shut with a heavy clang that shook through him and dragged him out of a deep, clumpy sleep. Every part of him hurt; his head a crowded mess of thoughts and voices. He let them gargle and rumble in there and hoped they'd settle. Then, one of the voices, coarse and angry, jumped out from the rest, startling him.

"Let's start again, who are you?"

"What? Was that me? Is someone there?" he croaked and tried to clear a painfully dry throat. He tried to sit up, and pain snapped across his shoulders and back. He slumped forward, and a burning sensation ran round his wrists. "Okay, pain is real." The tight pressure around his head turned out to be a blindfold.

A soft, hollow, distant boom rattled the chair he was strapped to, and the thin, metal legs banged on the concrete floor, agitating dust and grit under his bare feet.

The voices in his head faded away, leaving only the sound of two men arguing. More sounds took their places around him. It sounded like he was in a small room. From over to the left and right above him came the hiss of small pistons and occasional creak and clang of pipes knocking against metal rings.

The argument stopped, and a hard punch snapped his head sideways, dislodging fragments of memory and thoughts that rose to consciousness. He didn't know which were real, made up, or belonged to someone else. Someone else? How was that even possible?

A blow to the other side of his face knocked those ideas out of the park.

A glob of warm blood mingled with some stale muck that must have collected in his mouth while unconscious. He swallowed. Spitting it out might land somewhere, leading to more lousy karma punching his face.

"I said, what's your name?" the voice barked.

"Okay, hang on," Why was he so cheerful? A thin line of warm blood trickled escaped from the side of his mouth, made its way down his chin and dripped onto his bare thigh. "Wait, am I naked?"

"Your name," the voice almost shouted.

"Alright." Behind the blindfold, his eyes darted left and right through the dark. "No, sorry, I got nothing. How about you give me a clue?" He clamped his mouth shut, shit.

"He's lost it. Just shoot him, Krish," the other voice said. "I told you this was a waste of time." The click of the safety on a rifle punctuated the end of the man's snarl. The click initiated the hiss of a fusion rifle's priming chambers, and the sound joined the other noises. He recognised the sound. It was an old M40-n fusion rifle. The mix was wrong, but he wasn't going to tell anyone. Hopefully, it would blow up in the guy's face if he pulled the trigger on burst. Now, that would be funny in a gruesome way. How did he know this?

Before he could stop himself, he said, "Don't I get a last wish?" He scrunched his face as soon as the words slipped out. "Oops."

"Shut it." the first, deeper voice spoke away from him.

"What, and get on the wrong side of Plotinus? Not a chance. I want a name, Yossy. What did you inject him with this time?"

"Uh," Yossy stammered, "I thought it was that truth drug, sodium thio something or other."

"Thiopental sodium," he murmured.

"Yossy, that finished yesterday. Show me the bottle." Something smashed against a wall. "You idiot, no wonder he's high!" Krish shouted and then snarled into his face, "Where's that cloaking body armour you were wearing?"

Cloaking body armour? That would be so cool. A cold, round metal ring pressed hard against his temple, forcing his head back. Warm, foul breath and splats of saliva hit his face. Krish was a smoker of some pretty rough stuff.

"And how did you get past the security cameras?"

"The what?" he tried scrabbling together enough sensible thoughts to put in some kind of sentence that made sense. There wasn't much to work with.

"Talk," Yossy said, "now, or I'll start breaking bones."

He could tell Yossy meant it. He concentrated on not saying anything stupid. "I don't remember anything…my memory's gone…that's the truth…All I remember…is something…about an airship, a crash." And a red-haired girl.

A big hand grabbed his chin, the thumb and fingers digging into his cheeks. "The body armour, where did you hide it!"

'How can I talk?' came out as, "Oa, ca' I 'awk?"

The hand let go, leaving a thick ache. He dragged in a deep breath, "Dammit, I don't remember, alright? I swear I don't; if I did, I'd tell you," he lied.

A voice crackled, probably from a walkie-talkie. "Perimeter breach, all units report to level 9."

"I'm not carrying this thing around anymore." One of the guys said.

Something dropped onto his bare lap, and the blindfold tore off his head. Sketchy blurs of human figures followed by wiry ripples that trailed and faded moved through a misty haze. After a few seconds, the images sharpened to form two figures dressed in thin, loose-fitting brown and grey leather combat outfits. Both men carried nano-steam fusion rifles. He even knew the make and model type.

"Look through that list," Krish said. "One of these people is you. We'll be back."

"Isn't this cheating?" He winced and bit his lip; thank God they're leaving.

The men left, and the door clang on the worn metal frame rang hollow through the cell and spaces between the cells inside him. Pistons and valves hissed overhead, the shifts in pressure making pipes clang against their metal clamps. Muffled sounds, gurgle, rush, and churn of liquids; gasses being pumped and shunted seeped into the cell from beyond the walls.

Up to his right, bubbling plasma, sizzling with sparks, rushed through thick glass tubes linked to copper and steel pipes that split off in different directions through the walls and ceiling. Behind all this, or maybe coming from somewhere in his head, was a different sound, like classical music bubbling out of a poorly tuned radio. Whispering tones of intangible messages that resonated through his thoughts.

This was all insane. He just needed to come down from this weird high and get some sleep.

The tube of light on the ceiling flickered off and on annoyingly until it finally got a grip on a steady glow, and the misty haze cleared away. He was in a bare room. Lines stretched along the walls; the remains of shelving were long gone. Grey and pale-blue patches covered the floor, and a bundle of clothes lay in the corner. The place must have been a cleaner's storage room. Behind him, over to one side, a plank with straps leaned on a chair. Beside the chair was a hand basin attached to an old iron frame bolted to the wall. A scaly, dark-brown hose hung from one of the taps. A pile of grubby towels lay by the corner that sloped to a drain. A small metal table with a syringe and several bottles stood in the opposite corner. A plastic bottle lay on the ground, the last thing Yossy must have injected him with.

Apart from the clipboard on his lap, he was naked, his olive-brown skin covered in dust and bruises. Ropes snaked around his wrists and ankles and bit into his flesh when he moved.

As he wasn't going anywhere, he scanned the list of names and seat numbers. None of them rang any bells.

His head began to clear except for the barest tingling in the back of his mind; something creeping through his nerves— trying to make connections – with what?

He was still thinking about this when his face warmed and a

weight lifted from his shoulders. A radiant, golden light bloomed through the cell, and he closed his eyes.

A soft breeze and crisp sea air replaced the cell's musty, dry smell, and he opened his eyes. A beach stretched into the distance on either side of him; a glittering sea reflected an almost cloudless blue sky. He could feel the sand under his feet and smell the refreshing air and cool breeze.

A figure glided down from the sky, and he cried out and almost fell backwards on the chair as the being settled in front of him. Big, spiky black hair; black leather jeans; thick black leather belt covered in runes made of tiny metal studs; black T-shirt under a collarless biker's jacket; and pure hallelujah, glory-be, sleek, white, feather wings.

"This is most unusual." the punk-angel said.

Speechless, he stared at the vision.

"You really shouldn't be here," she, or was it a he, said, "you should go."

Another golden glow bloomed around him, and when it faded, he was back in the cell. Okay, apart from almost total memory loss, he was either drugged out of his skull or some kind of a nutcase. He tried hard to work his memory back and remembered something about a crashed airship: a red-haired girl.

Explosions thumped through the cell, shaking it like a drum. Screeching alarms blasted away the thoughts he was trying to piece together and drowned out the whispering symphony of background sounds. Around him, pipes clanged even louder, and dust billowed into the air. Then the lights went out, and the room fell into darkness. Crumbs of concrete, powder, and dirt settled on his skin and caught in the blood and phlegm in his mouth.

He coughed and spat out a coarse globule as chalk-drawn surroundings emerged through the darkness. Built-in night vision, really? What is this?

The sirens died to be replaced by a vicious gunfight ripped through with hollow shouting and screams that echoed off distant walls. He twisted his wrists and winced in pain, "Bloody ropes."

Someone banged on the door, and a woman's voice called out. "Is someone in there?

"Yes, get me out," he cried.

"Okay, hang on."

"I'm not going anywhere."

Muffled voices and sounds from the other side, "Stand to one side away from the door."

"Stand aside?" He shouted, "How…" His eyes widened in shock at glowing red spots around the lock and hinges, "Aw crap!"

Grunting, he shifted his weight, lifted one shoulder over the back of the chair, and, leaning over, fell sideways to hit the floor. A second later, the metal door exploded out of its frame and shot across the room, close enough for him to feel the snap of air as the thing missed him by inches and smashed into the rear wall with a deafening crunch. More dust and chunks of plaster and concrete sprayed out and splattered over him.

"What the hell?" he cried out.

"Hey, Blue," a woman stepped into the doorway and, looking over her shoulder, called out to someone retreating across a metal walkway, "Go easy on the gel next time."

Another woman's voice farther away said, "Sorry, Magpie."

The light snapped back on. Magpie, a tall, lean black woman with a firm, slender face and dressed in lightly armoured urban combat gear, clicked the safety of her assault rifle and hitched it over her shoulder. Her outfit's gold, navy, and burgundy tones changed as the light danced over it. Some kind of responsive camo gear seemed built for speed, not strength like her.

She touched her earpiece, "Idris," She smiled, "I found one adult male, butt naked." She looked from him to his surroundings, her eyes stopping at his clothes. "Doesn't look like he needs any medical. I'll take him with me, Magpie out." She touched the earpiece again. "Well, well. Least you're in one piece, apart from the circumcision."

"Hilarious," he murmured, mesmerised by the activity of the Nano-steams in the rifle's chambers. The sounds were smoother; she clearly looked after the weapon. Something in him was tuned into the hypnotic harmonics of the unstable particles curling through the weapon's thin lines of brass and Nu-iron veins. Time seemed to slow as he listened to the barely audible crackle of energy in the cobalt steams generated in the ammo canister. A phrase, a memory of a woman's voice, his mother's perhaps, "The timeless symphony of physics." He'd done something a long time ago in a lab.

The energised particles spiralled up against the link valves of the tubes emerging from the cooling vents under the barrel, urging it to open and allow fusion with the gently whispering silver steams in the conductor piston. The nanosteams yearning to mix and feed the fusion bursts into the firing chamber.

Magpie snapped her fingers in front of his face, "Hey."

"What?" Time returned to normal speed.

"Let's get you out of here," Magpie knelt behind him and slit the ropes binding his wrists. He rolled onto the floor and turned away from her to untie the cable around his ankles. Quickly grabbing what looked like a pair of long swimming shorts from the pile of clothes in the corner, he put them on.

Magpie crossed over to the table and poked the instruments and bottles with the muzzle of her rifle. "You must have really pissed them off."

"Yeah." He peeled a T-shirt from the pile of clothes and put it on. "What the—?" The T-shirt and shorts, made from the same fabric, moved, adapting to fit comfortably around his chest, arms, and legs. His flesh tingled when the material sizzled over his skin and then squeezed out the dirt underneath to create a small, muddy stain on the floor. He put the sweatshirt on over the T-shirt and picked up the jeans, standing up to put them on. He was taller than Magpie by several inches. That would make him around five foot ten or eleven.

Magpie turned to him, "What's up?"

"Nothing."

"You're a bit stiff."

"What? Oh, yeah. Feels like they had me strapped to that chair for hours. Think I'll be okay, though."

"Good." Another explosion echoed, stretched and faded. "They're pulling back from this sector." Magpie crossed to the door and stood with her back to the room, weapon at the ready. Standing in the way of the cavernous gloom outside, the colours of her outfit continued to shift between the light of the cell and the shadows beyond.

He rubbed his eyes and shook his head.

"They sure beat you up, didn't they?"

"Yeah, I think there's something inside me numbing most of the pain. It's giving my head a boost. I think I'm a bit high."

"Lucky you." With slight turns of her head, she continued looking out across a dark expanse.

A new bruise from the fall spread along his arm. His ankles and feet were caked in stuff he'd rather not think about. Using one of the damp towels, he wiped away as much as he could and started to dress. The tightness in his muscles made putting on the crumpled, dusty clothes a struggle, but he managed. A pair of navy denim jeans, a thin black thermal-weave hooded sweatshirt, or so the label said, and a dark-grey-washed canvas jacket. He found his socks inside-out beside a pair of faded black and red trainers. A red headband, probably what they'd used to blindfold him, lay on the ground.

Magpie spun into the room and crouched down when gunfire rattled past them.

"What the hell was that?" Magpie spoke into her mic', then after a pause, said, "Okay, well done, I'll be out ASAP." She turned to him, "Come on, pal, we don't have much time."

"Alright, hang on." He went through his pockets—no wallet, no phone, nor any kind of ID. He splashed water over his face, swilled some around his mouth, and spat it out. He couldn't resist a few gulps, and then he directed the water at his feet and began to hose away the dust and dirt, rubbing between his toes. There was no golden sand.

She looked over her shoulder at him. "Seriously? You're washing?"

He dropped the short hose and picked up the towel. "I'm not running around with crusty feet."

"This is a rescue, not a damned wake-up call."

He put his shoes and socks on. "These guys jacked me with all kinds of gear, reformatted my head, and beat the crap out of me. Just give me a minute."

"How about I leave you here?"

"Suits me." He crossed over to the table and bottles with labels covered in runes and symbols. A bottle on the floor had a label reading propranolol 10x120 mg, with the formula $C16H21NO2$ beneath it. Who would want to know that? Probably what these nutcases were using to keep themselves calm when all hell broke loose. Just what he needed. He swallowed one and stuffed the bottle in his pocket.

The snap and sizzling of a frenzied gunfight from somewhere

outside cut him short. The lights went out again, and everything shifted into a sharp focus. Magpie swung round into the room, grabbed his arm and pulled him back so he stumbled against the wall beside her.

"Getchurassdown," Pressed against the wall, she clipped her rifle shots to 'burst' and snapped a pair of slim, waspish goggles over her eyes, then edged forwards to peer around the door-frame. "Those terrorists are mad as cut snakes. We'll go on my signal. Wait for the all-clear." Magpie peered out through the door, aimed and fired three quick shots. Somewhere in the distance, voices cried out, and gunfire diminished.

The lights came back on, and she lifted her goggles, "Okay, let's move out."

He tore the list of names from the clipboard, stuffed it into his pocket, and then spotted a baseball cap. He picked it up and whacked it against his hand, waving away a tiny plume of dust before snapping it again and positioning it on his head.

A thunderous rumble behind the walls shook the entire cell and set off a wailing siren that became the backdrop to a calm female voice. "Pressure at twenty over critical. Emergency venting initiated. Please evacuate the area immediately."

"What the hell is that?" he said.

"Dharma, the supercomputer running this place." Magpie raised her voice over the avalanche of noise. "Do what the lady said, and let's go."

Chapter Two

"Stick by me, do exactly as I say and don't lose track of where I am."

"Or where my head is."

"What?"

"Nothing."

"You sure you're okay?"

"Just get me out of here."

"That's the plan." Magpie set off, and he followed, glad to be out of the small, musty cell. They were on one of over a dozen metal walkways stretching around and across a vast domed cavern. In the centre of the dome, broad pipes of transparent steel around six feet in diameter rose from the depths and towered into darkness. Each tube was filled with swirling dense gasses: red, green, and blue. The noise and blasts of fighting resonated around them. Two hundred yards away on the far side, crowds of people retreated in chaos along the walkways, firing wildly towards more organised pairs of soldiers.

Soldiers and terrorists struggled to hold their balance while running, using doorways, metal cabinets, empty munitions cases and crates for cover. Retreating terrorists hit by one of Magpie's soldiers shuddered and dropped to the ground, yellow wisps of smoke and grey vapours rising from motionless bodies. The riotous swarm of gunfire, shouting, and awful cries diffused with the smell of lemons and sulphur from the nano-steam rifles.

A hundred feet above them, surrounded by flashing red lights, giant shutters like camera iris' curled open and sucked grey mists into wide, dark tubes.

"Hey!" Magpie was already several yards ahead of him, "I said stay close."

He ran to keep up, the outfit under his clothes flexing, almost helping him run.

"What's your name, pal?"

"I don't know."

"What do you mean, you don't know? Try and think."

"With all this crap going on?"

"You really got no idea?"

"No, I can't remember a thing. You saw what those guys were doing to me."

The siren's wail died down enough for the noise of battle to take over again. "Okay." She tilted her head to the distant shooting. "This shit scaring you?"

"No."

She ignored the lie, "Just stick behind me."

"Where are you from, Magpie?"

"Queens, New York, why?"

"Your accent."

Magpie nodded, "Nothing like your weird accent."

"What's that supposed to mean?"

She looked over her shoulder and gave him a quick once over. "Mixed, like your damn head, English, Scottish and Afro-Caribbean, I'd say. "

"What's so weird about..."

"Hold it." A tunnel yawned away to their left. Magpie scanned the dark expanse and then examined the map that glowed green on her wristband. "Okay, this route's covered; we'll take the next. Stay close behind me. Things could get pretty nasty."

He ran alongside her. "You planning on killing people, too?"

"Too?" Magpie said, "You mean like those terrorists? Sure," She checked the chambers of her rifle, almost affectionately, "Before they kill me or someone else. I'm one of the good guys. I saved your skinny ass, remember?"

True, she had seen his skinny ass. But saved it? Too soon to say. At least his thinking was clearing up – almost. One of those vibes in his head had sharpened into fear, but it wasn't his. It was more like a distant call of someone else's fear, someone he knew. It was faint but very real. Where did his thoughts end, and outside stuff begin?

Magpie gave him a disdained shake of the head. "Keep an eye out for any guys with red headbands."

"Red headbands? Okay."

"Yep," she said, "some symbolic, self-sacrifice shit."

"And I thought I was nuts. Maybe if—"

A surge of shots and shouts interrupted them. "Save it," Magpie turned and jogged onwards. He followed, still haunted by that recurring sense of someone else's fear.

"Get over here," Magpie called from the entrance to a tunnel and took a quick look round the corner. Fat light bulbs glowed inside oblong mesh cages bolted to the wall. "This way." She strode along the paved floor and spoke into her mic without catching her breath. "Rescue nine heading south-west. The tunnels are laced with copper, Nu-iron, and steel-glass pipes running by heavy cables. It's got a little more light than the others." She stopped to wait, and when he came running round the corner, he almost knocked her over. She shook her head. "Quiet, there're hidden doorways and elevators all over the place."

She checked her time and location on the wristband, gave him a sideways nod, and set off in a jog. After about two hundred yards, they slowed to a steady walk, and she scanned the corridor.

"So what's going on, Magpie?"

"Your airship was hijacked. Over three hundred hostages captured by the Followers." Their voices and footsteps echoed around them.

"Followers?"

"Army of fanatics led by a madman," she paused, then added, "of course."

The tunnel curved round and down. "Easy, stay back," Magpie slowed her pace, and he slowed behind her. Reaching a T-junction, she crouched against a wall, gestured for him to do the same, and touched her earpiece. "Yeah, I copy. What's your twenty? Roger that." She looked him up and down. "How you doing?"

"Ache a bit, but alright. What now?"

"We'll wait here; we might be needed."

"Needed for what?"

"We'll see."

"So, what don't I remember?"

Magpie thought for a second. "The Big Freeze, twelve years ago, killed over three billion people."

"Billion?" his lower back ached, and he shifted to sit on the floor, resisting the temptation to scratch his ankles where the rope had torn at his skin. "How could I forget something like that?"

Magpie shrugged, peered down the three tunnels and checked her wristband.

"Did everything fall apart?"

"Almost."

"What do you mean?"

Magpie sighed. "Okay. History 101. Like I said, Big Freeze, billions dead. Here in America, Veterans stepped up to fill in. It's how the PI, the Peoples Infantry, got together." A row of lights blinked across her wristband. "Shh."

Heavy footsteps above them echoed and faded through the vents along the top of the walls.

"What about the Followers?"

"Hard-core believers willing to do anything for Plotinus and their cause."

"Plotty who?" he winced at the sound of gunfire off in the distance.

Magpie listened to the noise for several seconds, then said. "Plotinus brought his Followers here to Nevada a year ago. Around half a dozen of these domes are terrorist hives. Two thousand people followed him here." She shook her head. "Things were quiet until all this crap kicked off."

"I don't get it," he said, "why would all these people get together behind a psychopath?"

"Big Freeze, people stayed home, clanned up in Internet echo chambers. Plotinus got into their heads with his Big Plan. Said he could fix the weather, save the world."

"How?"

"Do you ever stop asking questions? How the hell should I know?" Magpie said. "He's a nutcase, telling a bunch of lies to feed his fat ego."

"But thousands of people believe him."

"Yeah, go figure."

"How, I mean, how's he doing this?"

"He calls it 'The Blessing', airborne drugs."

"You're kidding."

She gave him a sideways look, "It's powerful stuff. Your heads stay clear while you see angels and all kinds of weird spiritual shit. They think the drugs just show what's already there."

The Punk-angel; had those two moronic clowns wiped his memory and drugged him up so he'd be able to see? Punishing and purifying him. What's already there? That punk angel was so damn real; was she, he, it?

"What's up?" Magpie nudged him back, "You seen stuff too?"

"What? No. Where are we?"

Magpie lowered the rifle's scope she was peering through, "Hundreds of nukes were tested here in nineteen-something. Blowing a nuke underground leaves massive domes like these; they're everywhere." Her wristband lit up for a few seconds to display a line of numbers, then darkened.

He shook his head slowly, "You're telling me that we're in the middle of caves full of terrorists and hundreds of hostages, and out there, the world's one massive frozen disaster zone?"

"Pretty much." A momentary grief flashed across her face to be washed away by the wristband's green glow. The thin, flexible screen fizzled to reveal a map. "Cover your ears."

A short distance behind them, part of the wall exploded in a dull thump that echoed down the tunnel, followed by the clatter of stone falling over the rubble. In one swift movement, Magpie pointed her rifle at the dusty plume around a gaping hole in the wall.

"Thirty-eight feet away," he whispered.

"Quiet." They peered into the clearing smoke.

A terrorist stumbled out, quickly followed by a second terrorist who almost fell on the first. As they fumbled and pushed away from each other, a woman dressed in the same gear as Magpie leapt out after them and landed in a defensive combat pose on the uneven surface. She whacked one man's head with a graceful roundhouse kick, and he dropped instantly. Grabbing the other Follower, she spun him around and bounced his head off the opposite wall with a dull thud. The terrorist collapsed like a rag doll and slid down the rubble. A few stones followed him and settled beside his limp body.

Pistol in hand, the woman dropped to a crouch, swung left, right, and froze. Even from that distance, he spotted the slight twitch of the large gun as it pointed from Magpie to him. He shuddered and felt the outfit under his clothes rush and thicken across his chest.

In response to a trill whistle from Magpie, the woman slipped a pair of goggles over her eyes. She waved at Magpie and disappeared in the opposite direction, followed by two other women in the same gear leading a huddle of weary and frightened hostages.

"Friend of yours?"

"That's Raven and her team. They're into kung fu," Magpie whispered. "Now, keep quiet."

"Tell that to your ninja friend with the Desert Eagle and CL 20."

Magpie eyed him suspiciously. "You're pretty good with distances and weapons."

"Wish I knew how. Then again, can't miss the smell of CL or a big gun like that."

"She's from Texas. You could smell the explosive? Are you sure you don't remember who you are?"

"You mean which side I'm on? No." He paused. "They kept asking me who I was. Besides, what they were doing to me back there? I don't think we were friends."

"Maybe, or maybe you were from a different clan." She turned away and touched her mic. "Idris, Raven's opened the secondary escape route. Eve should be coming through with some hostages soon. I'm on track. I'll check second base, then head back." She checked the wristband. "Rescue five is Oscar Mike to the RV...Roger that. Magpie out." She turned to him, "Let's move."

They jogged down the tunnel, in and out of the pools of light cast from bulbs behind thick glass casings. The tunnel curved downwards and wound to the right.

"So, Magpie."

"What now?"

"What do twenty, Oscar Mike and RV mean?"

"Location, on the move, and rendezvous."

"Where are we going now?"

"Heading back to my team. We'll check one more compound, then up and out."

"How many are--"

"Hey! Enough with the pop quiz already. My name's not Google."

"Goo who?"

"Before your time."

"Is this part of your Peoples Infantry training?"

"What, rescuing hostages?"

"No, keeping a grumpy attitude for hours on end."

"Wise ass, huh?" Magpie held back a smile and shot him a sideways look. "Maybe I should have left you with your waterboarding friends back there."

"Oh, it wasn't that bad. I had a room, my own seat, stimulating conversation with people interested in what I had to say. More than what I'm...wow."

A shattered sphere of gold and silver metal shards floated at the top of the vast cavern they'd just entered. Pale shades of green, orange, and red clouds merged, curled and bloomed in the sphere's centre. Lines of slow lightning spiralled out of the metal fragments and snaked through the churning cloud. The sluggish pulse of fans hummed in the walls above them.

"What the hell is that?" Magpie murmured. "Damn, this wasn't on the map." She pulled a thin gauze mask from a small pack, which somehow stuck over her mouth and nose. "It could be hallucinogenic gas." She passed the pack to him. "Take one."

"No need; it's safe." A whisper passed through his thoughts. "It's Dharma, the AI computer. Fluid algorithms, the spiral sensor detects—"

She looked at him through narrowed eyes.

He pointed up, "Attenuated data-energy feedback streams--"

"Enough already."

"But there's light we don't see. I know something."

"Yeah, technobabble, that'll definitely get us out in one piece." She unclipped the safety on the rifle and raised it to peer through the scope into the swirling colours.

Again, he sensed the volatile steam in the priming chambers clamouring for release.

"Hang on," Magpie lowered the rifle and looked up into the cloud, "something's not right."

She could say that again. Invisible waves rippled through him and amped up his senses. Magpie's face never looked more alive. In a few fleeting seconds, he tracked every tiny movement and twitch of muscle in her features; they weren't so hard and fixed. There'd be a flash of a different emotion in her face or her eyes: sadness, grief, anger, attention. He could barely keep up and felt guilty about seeing what she hid.

"Magpie, I—"

"Shh." With a slight tug on his elbow, she stepped back into the tunnel and shot out the two lights. Darkness fell across the entrance, and they disappeared into the shadows. Magpie slipped the night-vision goggles down and tapped the 'adaptive' button to stop the glare when she looked out. She alternated between peering through the scope and looking up into the cloud while he stood beside her, lost in a dreamlike trance.

Overhead, the mists curled, blended, and parted, sending inaudible tones through his mind, a flow that echoed the mist's complex patterns. It was like a forgotten familiar tune. If only he had time to listen, to look at them for a while longer, he'd be able to figure out what it was saying, except -

Suzie! The name jumped into his mind. He felt her fear and anger stronger than before. He felt her twisting to escape her restraints, her defiance, emotions that rose like a current through a--

"Oh, shit!!"

"Will you shut up?" Magpie hissed from behind the mask, her eyes on the mist now punctured by thin beams of torchlight.

"Suzie," he whispered. And, before he could stop himself, he blurted out, "We've got to find Suzie."

Magpie shoved him, making him almost stumble sideways. "Keep it down. You'll get us killed."

Who was Suzie? His eyes scanned the ground, searching his head for anything else he could remember about her.

"Snap out of it," Magpie hissed, stony-faced. The nano-steams in the chambers under the barrel of her rifle turned a deep gold, fully primed.

Ropes fell from the ceiling, and three men rappelled down. Magpie followed them through the sight of her rifle and pulled the trigger. The gun made a muffled snap, and the first terrorist didn't even reach the walkway. He shuddered for several seconds and fell limp to swing on the rope. Magpie's next shot caught the second Follower as he hit the walkway. The man shook violently, staggering sideways, dropped over the walkway's edge, and disappeared. The third man landed on the central walkway, and the vast cavern swallowed the sound of his boots thumping on the metal. He unclipped the rope and swung his rifle around to take Magpie's third shot in the forehead. His head snapped back, his knees gave way, and he crumpled.

Magpie checked the wristband, removed her mask, and waited with the rifle aimed back into the mists. Then, with a slight swagger, she made her way to the corpse on the walkway, stopping to look back and check on Mr Memory. He wasn't going anywhere. He gaped, eyes sliding from the terrorist on the floor to the body slowly swaying on the rope. She followed his gaze. A thin red trail of blood snaked down from the blotch on the uniform and dripped onto the mesh walkway with a quiet plink, then disappeared into the black depths. Magpie stepped back, flicked the selector on her rifle, aimed at the hanging soldier, and shot the rope. The body missed the walkway by a few inches and dropped into the darkness. Magpie knelt beside the corpse on the walkway and went through the pockets. There wasn't much.

"Tracker," she threw a small box over the edge. "These smoke canisters will come in handy. No radio or any kind of comms." She stared down at the man's rifle and gave it a dismissive kick, then turned to walk back and stopped; Memory Guy had disappeared. Magpie peered down the tunnel. "Where are you?"

"Here." He stepped away from the wall.

"Where'd you go?"

"What do you mean?"

She shifted her gaze to the shadows, then back to him. "Never mind, come on." She looked up at the swirling cloud through the telescopic sight of her assault rifle, then lowered it. "People're waiting for us. Elevator at the far end. Nano AI computer, eh?" she said, strolling past him. "Least now we know you're a geek."

"You killed them."

"Yeah."

He didn't move, so she strode back, her steady pace resonating around the cavern. "Hey," she snapped, "You think I had a choice—that those guys would give us a choice?"

"You didn't have to kill them. You could have stunned them."

"Stun them," she murmured. "Yeah, sure, and give them a second chance sometime later. They didn't give my—" Lowering her brow, she pursed her lips and pushed back a raw memory. Magpie tilted the rifle to check the liquids under the barrel. "Like I said, I killed those terrorists because they would kill me and you. It's always us or them, always. Remember that, and you stand a better chance of not getting killed."

"Are they really that bad?"

Magpie responded with a single nod. "Get your game face on."

"Okay. No wait. Suzie, I'm not leaving without her."

"For crying out loud, Brainiac. I thought you had amnesia. Alright." She raised her hand and let it drop. "Who's this Suzie, your girlfriend?"

"Maybe. I don't know."

"You don't know?"

"No, I don't, okay?"

"So what are you saying?"

"All I know is…" His face scrunched in confusion.

"Come on, pal, clock's ticking. All you know is what?"

He blinked. "She's on level 23, south-east wing, the labs, room 7, she's not alone. I have to find…her." Suzie's fear washed from his mind, and he relaxed.

"What?" Magpie glanced over her shoulder and pushed him back into the dark tunnel where they wouldn't be seen. "Listen, pal, I don't know how you know this stuff or if it's just some crazy fantasy in your fuh…messed-up head, but we got a situation here, and my orders are to get you and whoever else is still alive, out of this corner of hell."

"Maybe this whole thing is a crazy fantasy. I don't care. Either way, it's my reality, and she's a part of it, and I'm going to save her."

"Save her?" A deep sadness flashed across her face. Her eyes echoed a grief he'd buried and forgotten long ago. They stared at each other for a few seconds, unable to untangle that one emotion they shared. A burst of gunfire in the distance brought back her stony expression, and they turned to face the echo and fade that followed.

Another burst of gunfire made Magpie take a step back. "Listen," she said, "five of the other hostages back there are already dead and not in a nice way. These Followers still have half the survivors from the airship. And they don't waste time when it comes to executing troublemakers. I'm not going rogue on some—"

"Fine," he snapped. "I'll go alone. I can feel her."

"You can what?"

"I…nothing. Look, forget about me, right? Go find the others; I don't care. Suzie's down there with... with some skinny professor guy, and I'm going to get her. I have to." He hesitated, lost in a strange sense of fear. "And she's scared, in real trouble, I know it."

"You don't even know your way-. Wait a sec, you said a skinny professor?"

He nodded.

"And you know this how?"

He shrugged, "I just do, and I'll save her, them, without you."

"Hold on," Magpie swore under her breath and then touched her earpiece. "Idris? Yeah, I'm in Halfbeak." She glanced up at him, irritated and suspicious. "I got a guy here who says there are hostages as far down as level 23, mentioned the professor. Copy that, but he's got his mind set on going down there without me if he has to. Should I leave him? I know she did, but we only got half her message about twenty-two down… Could be; hang on." Magpie turned to him. "What else do you know, how many?"

"Just Suzie, the skinny guy, the professor, and two terrorists. They want him to connect her to the supercomputer."

"Son of a bitch!" She touched her earpiece again. "Idris, the hostage I'm with has described what could be the prime asset…Yeah, the prof—says he's down there with a girl. Says Plotinus is using the prof to connect someone to Dharma." She paused and looked at him. "I don't think even he knows… Just the south side left… No survivors on the north…Roger that."

Magpie turned to him. "Okay, pal, we're gonna try and get some intel' to back up your story. It'll take a while. We'll wait here." The response didn't take long.

"Yeah, I copy," Magpie listened for several seconds, then looked at him suspiciously. "Roger that." She moved away from the wall.

"Okay, seems there's a lab on 23, one of two with a prototype neural interface helmet. If Plotinus was going to try that trick, it would be there. You and me are going to take a little detour down to 23. You better be right about this."

"I am," he said, glad he wasn't heading down there alone. "I just want to get Suzie out. That's it."

Magpie scanned his face. "Maybe you heard something when they were working you over back in the cell, and it's coming back."

"Maybe."

"Okay," She hesitated and then pulled out her pistol. "Think you can use one of these?"

He stared at the gun. "You want me to shoot people?"

"Not anybody, be choosy, just the ones who won't think twice about killing you or me. If we're going deeper into this hellhole, I don't want to be taking on these crazies alone. Us or them. Like I said, negotiation isn't an option. Well, you gonna take it or not?"

He took the gun.

"Right, simple rules; never point it at me or anything behind or beyond me if I'm in front of you. Hold it firm, and always aim at the chest. Less likely to miss that way."

It felt familiar like he knew how to handle it. It was warm from the holster tight against her upper thigh.

She poked him. "Hey, you got that?"

He weighed it up. "Yeah. Modded Glock S 20-C; single multi-feed, air-cooled chamber; thirty-second fuel-mix refill; super-concentrate fluids stored in the grip, enough for twenty fatal-charge shots or thirty non-fatal."

"How do you know that kind of stuff, detail?"

"No idea. The gun's heavy, the grip's full, and the chamber's loaded apart from two low-round shots you fired." He turned the gun slowly.

"Something bothering you?"

"Yeah, no, sorry, I can't do it." He held the gun out to her.

"Scares you, huh?" She took the gun and slipped it back in the holster.

"Only what I might do with it."

"Okay."

"Besides," he looked back to the body on the walkway, "what you did back there, it was... I don't know." he shook his head.

"It's what soldiers are trained to do."

"I couldn't do that, not the way you did."

"It's the only way."

"Not just that. Shooting, killing, I mean, so professional, fast, and accurate. You didn't think twice."

"Is that a compliment?"

"I'm not sure."

"Thanks. We'd better get moving."

They continued along the path around the grey-stone wall. Ahead of them, a large industrial elevator shaft stretched to disappear into the cloud's outer edge.

"These massive caves, it's not natural; they're so perfectly round."

"Like I said, underground nuclear test site. We're in Halfbeak, a biggie."

"Hang on." He rubbed his arm and raised his palm to the wall, "I can feel...some kind of wave."

Sliding his hand along the cold, rough grey surface, it felt like dipping into a soft, sizzling pattern. There was a click, and a part of the wall slid away to reveal a small elevator.

"You felt that?"

He nodded. "Maybe some kind of static."

"Or maybe you're not a stranger to this place."

"You think I might be a Follower?"

"You're the wrong kind of weird. Still." Magpie glanced at him, "You could have some kind of WiFi wrist implant that senses and controls these electronics. Guns could be a guy hobby thing."

"What about knowing a lot of stuff about this place?"

"No secrets. It's all on the web if you know where to look."

From behind the wall above the door, four muffled creaks and a series of short hisses ended with the six clanking snaps of the clamps holding the elevator being released. A whirring noise slid down the inside of the shaft.

"So what were they doing torturing me?"

Magpie shrugged. "Maybe you said the wrong thing, did something out of line. Some of these guys are pretty screwed up in a religious psychopath kinda way."

" Maybe I was one of the more sensible ones."

"I wouldn't bet on it." Magpie scanned the expanse of the surrounding dome, then lifted her chin to the open elevator door. "You first."

The dimly lit, green-walled elevator shook as he entered through the half-open door.

"Maybe you're...aw hell." She shoved him into the elevator as bullets splattered the wall outside, and the narrow elevator door began to close with a soft scrape.

"Crap." He jumped forward and started jabbing the 'open door' button, but it kept closing. He grabbed the door, but the damn thing still kept closing.

Magpie fired a short burst, and a voice in the distance screamed.

"Go!" she shouted and unclipped a grenade, then dived backwards out of view. The grenade rolled past the slim crack of the closing door and exploded with a blinding flash. He raised a hand over his eyes while outside, bullets crunched into the floor and wall through the billowing plumes of grey smoke.

"Magpie!" The door clunked shut, and the elevator dropped several feet and then stopped. He hit the wall, knocking the back of his head on the faded metal, then fell to the ground. The elevator started down again, and the subtle resonance of invisible waves around inside him faded away. The elevator lights blinked out, and it felt like he was sinking into deeper, darker spaces.

Chapter Three

His weird night vision kicked in. He got to his feet, reached up and tapped the light on the ceiling. The light flickered back on. The exchange of the vicious gunfight faded away above him; each burst tensing him up as the elevator crawled downwards. It had all happened so fast; one second, they were chatting; the next, she was on her own, facing off gunfire, and he was heading deeper into chaos, chasing strange notions. He tried not to think about who might be getting the bullets. Those last shots came from Magpie's N-Rec7. That had to be a good sign.

He leaned against the wall. How did he find this thing? Was Magpie right about the implant? The charge that had rippled up his arm felt so familiar. And those waves he kept tuning into and all that other emotional stuff he couldn't figure out was his or Suzie's. Then there was the professor, what he looked like, knowing about that Dharma connection on level 23.

Maybe none of this was real. Maybe the whole thing was a dream.

He touched the buttons, "How did I find you?" He half expected the small speaker beside the buttons to reply. He shook his head, "Get a grip, Cloud." Rule one: Stop talking to yourself.

Cloud? He pulled the sheet from his pocket and ran through the names and seat numbers list. Alister Cloud that must be him; no one else on the list had that surname. He checked the small mirror above the buttons and gave his reflection the thumbs up. Suzanne Emerson had the seat next to his. That must be Suzie. "At last," He murmured.

He scanned the other names. Nothing; he stuffed the sheet into his pocket.

The temperature dropped as the elevator descended, and his mind went back to what Magpie had told him about the Followers and the state of the world up there. Billions are dead, and people comforted by online religion and politics. Calling them echo chambers kind of made sense. No wonder that Plotinus guy managed to get all those people here and build an army. It sounded horrible. Were there any normal people out there? Focus. Just stick to the job and don't ask questions. Stay alive, find Suzie, and get out.

"This is taking ages. His breath formed small vapour clouds.

"Wish the damn thing would stop."

A soft rippling interrupted his shivering, and he fell against the wall, arms splayed out to keep his balance. "What the hell?" The outfit was oozing out into his clothes. Wide-eyed, he watched the grey gooey substance bleed through his sweatshirt and jeans and puff out. The shorts and t-shirt morphed through the fabric of his clothes to keep him warm.

Alister was still trying to get his head around this when the elevator jolted, dropped, and clanged to a stop at a slight angle, knocking him sideways. Then it started to move again, inching downward one crack and creak at a time, sometimes knocking and grinding against the shaft wall outside. Rubbing his shoulder, he stood up, reached out to the walls on either side and steadied himself. Then, the elevator scraped loudly against something metal outside that gave way.

"That didn't sound good."

A touch of the control panel made the elevator shudder to a halt. "Well, that was clever," he muttered. "What now?"

Lights flickered behind four of the pale-orange cracked glass numbers. He was on level twelve, eighteen, twenty-two, or thirty. The little italic numbers flashed 'me, me, me' for several seconds, and then all decided they were being honest and stayed on. A loud creak echoed up the shaft, and the elevator tilted and stopped. He reached to pull the door open when the light around him burst into a golden glow. "Not again, not now, please."

The haze cleared. Alister raised his hand to protect his eyes from the sunlight, staggered back, stumbled, and fell onto soft, golden sand. He was on a beach. Sunlight flashed on rolling waves that slid up the beach, spread along the sand, and then slid back to the sea. A tall, thin Asian man with sky-blue skin dressed in a long, flowing yellow-orange robe walked along the shore's edge. Beside him was a short, muscular grey demon with a strangely benign face.

"Let me get this straight," the demon said, "Everything is made of strings, and magicians focus on the ones inside them, change the vibe and bring weird stuff and energies in from other universes."

"Basically, yes."

The demon shook its head. "That's just crazy, Sid. How can giving attention to something you can't even see change reality?"

"The multiverse, Zen, a new one with every change. And what do you need to effect change?"

"Energy of some form." Zen said in a resigned tone, "This is the last time I'm coming on a 'walk to pass the time' with you."

"You did ask about how magic worked." Sid smiled, "Scientists fail to consider that giving someone or something your attention is to apply conscious energy."

"Consciousness is a kind of energy?"

"Precisely; by giving something your attention, you focus and direct a unique form of energy at it, thus influencing the subject of your attention. Experiments in quantum physics indicate this to be the case."

The demon lifted his head and let out a long, deep yawn, "So basically, me listening to you is a waste of energy then?" A short trident appeared in the demon's hand, and he scraped the prongs through the sand. Bubbles rose along the furrows to pop in the thin seawater wash.

Sid, the man in the robe, saw Alister and turned to the demon. "Do you know anything about this, Zen?"

"What the...."The demon took a step back in alarm when he saw Alister. Bat-like wings sprouted from his back, and two spiky horns appeared above each ear. "Oh yeah, I forgot to mention," The demon calmed down and shrugged. The horns and wings disappeared. "Raggy said he saw someone."

"Raguel?" Sid replied, "The angel?"

They knew about the angel; it had told them about him. Alister opened his mouth to speak, and a dozen questions jammed between his brain and mouth.

"Yeah, he said something about Ruya messing up and the nanoparticles ending in this one. Apparently, he was the first." The demon pointed at Alister.

Sid gave Zen a sideways look, "Messing up?"

"Well, that's not quite what Raggy said, but he was sure about the nanoparticles."

The demon's words scuttled through the solid tangle in Alister's mind and dug out a grain of truth. He had nanoparticles in him. He was sure of it. How did these creatures know? Hang on; all this was going on in his head, so of course they'd know.

The two creatures turned their backs to him and began to

argue in whispers, sometimes glancing over their shoulder at him. Ruya, Alister knew that name from somewhere. These guys seemed so real. No wonder Plotinus had such a hold on his Followers. What if Plotinus was…no, don't go there.

"Uh, excuse me," Alister raised his hand.

"Why are you even still here?" The demon flicked a grey wrist at him, "Get lost."

Alister fell against the elevator wall. "Wow," he lifted the baseball cap off his head and slid his hand over his cropped black hair. His crazy was really on fire. He rubbed his eyes hard with his forefinger and thumb. It all felt so real. He patted the walls of the elevator a couple of times. This was real; the only weird thing here was his shifting shorts and T-shirt and how half the stuff in his head got there. "I need a user guide."

The elevator squeaked to a halt, and the door cracked open an inch. Alister grabbed the edge of the door and helped it widen a couple of feet until it jammed. The elevator had got it wrong, and the outside floor was halfway up the door. A chill mist poured in and pooled around his ankles.

"My stop, I guess." A vast hall illuminated by long fluorescent lights spread along icy steel beams stretching through a silvery-grey fog. The space had a musty, metallic smell of grease and old engines. Turbines and machines the size of small two-up, two-down houses stood surrounded by a messy scattering of crates, barrels, trolleys, and forklifts. Their brown, blue, grey, and yellow colours glistening under a fine icy layer. Overhead, steel girders crisscrossed through a thick, cloudy haze. Tendrils of thick mist curled around long, heavy chains and broad metal pillars. Somewhere beyond the machinery, a group of men were talking and laughing.

The elevator door clunked shut behind him, and the noise resonated through the hall, silencing the voices.

"Brilliant."

Chapter Four

Alister dived and slid on his side past a long stack of chests and barrels to pass through a curtain of thick, misted plastic strips. He jumped to a crouch and peered out through the cracks. The ambling fall of boots, accompanied by two men arguing loudly and swearing about the cold, approached the elevator. The blurred shapes of two stocky men stepped into the bright patch made by the light over where the elevator door had disappeared shut. They were carrying weapons with the distinctive nano-steam glow of fusion rifles,

"Anything?" a distant voice said.

The short man gave the wall a once-over and shouted, "Nothing here, boss." The voices spread out and evaporated.

"Ibrahim, look at this." The other man pointed the muzzle of his rifle at the ground. From some distance behind them, the slow thumps and deep hiss of a piston machine coming to life punched echoes through the cold silence for several seconds, then died down in a long, metallic groan.

Ibrahim stepped up beside the other man, "Boss, Levi's found some kind of trail."

"You idiots," a voice boomed. "We've been dragging hostages around all day."

"C'mon, Levi," Ibrahim cleared his throat and spat. "I reckon Plotinus had been pressing wrong buttons again, trying to get through to that Dharma computer again, probably fired up some machine somewhere. I need a smoke. Want one?"

"That stinking leaf that passes for tobacco? Forget it."

They walked away, crudely teasing each other about their wives and sisters. The voices and footsteps faded, a door opened and closed, and there was silence.

Alister crept behind generators, machinery, large crates, barrels, and rows of long freight containers and arrived at an industrial elevator. It was little more than a large cage behind a metal gate on rollers. The shaft walls were made of some form of thick, reinforced glass. Behind it, glass, gold and brown pipes, hoses, tubes, wheels, and cogs stood silent and motionless. Veins of bruised and aged cables stretched and disappeared into a thick cluster of wheels and pistons surrounded by frost-encrusted pipes and support frames.

How do those things even make the lift work? There was the sound of vents opening, then the hiss and nano-steams, glowing with the colours of the rare elements they carried, flowed like spectral rainbows through the pipes, and the machine came to life, grinding the elevator upwards.

"Oh shit!"

A door crashed open against a wall, followed by stomping feet—three heavy guys, by the sound of it - heading his way. Shouting and heavy footsteps rumbled across the frost-encrusted expanse. Alister darted behind a large steam turbine.

"The elevator!" a voice snarled, and a deafening shot rang out like a lightning snap that spread into a short-lived echo.

"Jesus!" The shot sizzled past Alister and struck the steel-glass plates over the elevator's machinery.

"Metin, you fool," a voice shouted. "You want to get us all killed?" The rapid clomp of feet came closer.

The terrorists were almost upon him. The gunshot set his heart racing, and his breathing was trying to catch up fast. The shorts and T-shirt under his clothes swirled, and he almost jumped back in shock. The terrorists would see him in seconds. The rapid transformation of the outfit drove a surge through him that kicked his head into a zone of raw, reckless energy. Something seemed to be trying to calm him down, but it just made him madder.

"Yeah, go wild," someone said. It sounded like his voice.

***

He came to breathless and slouched on the floor against some cold beast of a turbine. He rested his head back on the frosted metal until the swirling, tangled chaos in his head settled. Shivers ran through him and shook out through his hands. Images flashed into his mind: bloodied expressions, the back of a fist crunching into the side of a face, grunts, a figure twisting away, a rifle flying through the air, a flash of floor, misty ceiling, faces grimaced in pain and choking for breath, confused fear, bursts of gunfire.

Burns pulsed across his chest, arms and back; his knuckles ached, and his elbow and shoulders were stiff and tired. He pulled out the small plastic bottle, now cracked down the side, and downed a propranolol+ capsule. After several minutes, his hands stopped shaking, and his breathing steadied. Just one tablet left, he shoved the little bottle back into his pocket.

He got to his feet and headed for the door and stairwell that would take him down to level 23. A man groaned into consciousness from the other side of the turbine. Alister went towards the sound and froze. The floor was covered in lines of blood splatter dotted through a mess of bullet casings, three assault rifles, two pistols, and a combat knife. He'd missed one helluva fight.

Two big men wearing red headbands lay slumped against a wall. The Arabic guy was still conscious, tilting onto the shoulder of a burly guy with long sidelocks and a beard. Opposite them, a third man, bald and clean-shaven, with tattoos visible around his neck and wrists, lay on the floor. Each had an emblem roughly sewn onto the shoulder of his combat jacket: a circle divided into six sections with symbols in each displaying a cross, a six-pointed star, a crescent moon and star, an intersecting S, and strange glyphs.

"Are you a Panther?" the Arab asked. Alister recognised Ibrahim's voice. "You look like a Panther. Please help us. We were attacked by someone all in black."

"A Panther? No. You three look like a bad joke that got into a fight."

"Our holy leader, Plotinus, the bearer of Sigillum Dei, he who—"

"I don't want to know." Holy leader, what a nut case. Alister removed a pack of hand-rolled cigarettes from Ibrahim's chest pocket and stuck one in the man's mouth.

"Thank you." The man smiled up at him, a globby red hole where a tooth used to be.

"What happened here?" Alister lit the cigarette using the lighter inside the box.

"One man, all in black." Ibrahim took the cigarette from his mouth and grimaced at the bloodstain on the filter. "Bulletproof body armour. He was a wild man, a demon."

A demon in black, that's all he needed. "At least he let us live," Alister turned to leave.

"Wait." Ibrahim tried to sit up, and his face twisted in pain.

"Don't think so," Alister said without looking back. "Enjoy the cigarette."

"Don't leave us. He might return."

"And that's why I'm not hanging around. Byeee." Whoever that black-clad guy was, Alister didn't want to say hi. If only Magpie were here.

Swing doors led into a dim, dusty stairwell, illuminated by a line of blinking lights curving round and downwards. The steps were strewn with spectacles, mobile phones, baseball caps, earrings, hair clips, hearing aids, shoes, broken heels, keys, and small toys. He passed several wide double doors labelled with large, painted numbers until he reached a door marked '023'. He pushed through into a clean, bright corridor and winced in pain. The lingering smell of lab disinfectant stabbed a memory and lit up flashes of a gloomy lab patched with pools of yellow light and foreign voices. He shook his head and focussed. The crackled hum of faulty air conditioning droned through the vents and pipes above him. Surgical equipment was scattered across the surface of chrome trolleys that had long since lost their sheen. On either side of him, doorways led into empty, shambolic operating theatres and laboratories.

Suzie was close; he could sense her. He strode towards the sound of frantic bustling from a room ahead on the left and stopped at the door. Inside, a figure lay on an operating table, the head and shoulders blocked by one of the terrorists. Clumps of red hair were scattered on the floor around the end of the table. The figure struggled against thick straps pulled tight over thighs, ankles, upper arms, and wrists, pressing into black jeans and a 49ers hoodie.

Two Followers in grey combat gear, assault rifles slung back over their shoulders, stood on either side of the table. The Follower blocking Alister's view of the victim fumbled with a helmet connected to wires while the other cautiously prodded at the wall of viewing plates, buttons, and dials. In the corner, a tall, thin, brown-haired man wearing wireframe spectacles stared fearfully at the figure on the table. Lights flashed, and needles bounced across the face of small dials.

The Follower holding the helmet stepped back. "There, it's on."

Alister couldn't make out the figure at first. Hundreds of fine wires connected the helmet to a large black box on a wall next to a table containing a small display plate with dials and a keyboard. A tingling thread of signals from that computer drew him in like a finely woven tune.

"Get it off," a woman cried.

"Suzie!" Alister whispered.

Suzie inched her head around, her eyes wide with terror. "Alister!" she screamed. "Look out!"

Alister twisted around and failed to dodge the sledgehammer of a fist that slammed into his shoulder and sent him crashing against the wall. Head spinning, he fell to the floor. A big hand clamped round his ankle, and a sharp yank swung him up and round. He flew for a second, then his head thumped against something metal, and he hit the ground. The corridor swirled into black, sending him into a sizzling dark space.

An explosion of motion gushed over him, and he instinctively took a deep breath, but there was no splash, just a distant shattering of glass followed by the clang of metal. His head felt like a crowded fish tank, millions of tiny flashes furiously slapping his brain cells about so he'd wake up.

It worked. He came to lying across a dented steel cabinet he'd knocked down. He'd been thrown through a window into the lab opposite. He rolled off onto the floor, and glass shards crackled under him. His arms and hands were black. It was his pants and T-shirt; this time, they'd gone all ninja through his clothes. This must be the armour that guy had been talking about. It felt like part of his body.

He wiped blood from his mouth with his hand and grimaced, fighting against the stabbing pain across his shoulder. A sharp clang filled the room, and he scrabbled to his feet. Shards of glass fell off him as he turned to the noise. The cabinet had fallen across the door, blocking it. The kicking on the metal door against the cabinet had it grating and scraping against the floor; then, the door flew off the hinges with a loud snap and crashed to the ground.

The man was big, seven feet of solid muscle covered in clinging black military flexi-armour. His red bandanna was wrapped around a big bald head."Who are you? Where's the boy?" The brute flexed his shoulders, which, like his knees and elbows, had reinforced joint protection

Alister raised a finger. "Gimme a sec'." Alister glanced at his reflection in the glass fragments on the cabinet beside the thug. So that's what he looked like, a solid shadow? Cool. "No boy here, mate."

"You dare interfere in the Master's work?"

"His work?" The outfit amplified Alister's anger into an electric rage that surged through him. "Oh man, I'll show you work."

This time, he didn't blank out. He managed to control it. He dived at the goliath, and the force of the leap carried him across the room so fast the terrorist blinked, his head snapping back in shock. With anger coursing through the outfit, Alister dug his hands into the thick muscle of the man's neck, leaned back and head-butted him, breaking the brute's nose before pounding his knuckles into the thug's face. Dazed, his nose broken, and his face covered in bruises, the giant stumbled back against the wall.

The man grabbed Alister's arm, and Alister levered his little finger back until it snapped. The terrorist cried out, let go, and staggered sideways to crash into the medicine cabinet, his finger sticking out at a gruesome angle.

Alister shot a fist through the reinforced glass of the cabinet and snatched a bottle. He smashed the top and threw the contents into the soldier's face. The man blinked and crumbled to the ground, unconscious.

"Thank you, isoflurane." Alister threw the bottle aside, his whole body shaking with the rush of adrenalin and whatever the suit was doing to his nervous system. Then he remembered, "Suzie!" He leapt through the window to land in the silent, empty hallway. The door into the operating theatre opposite was wide open. Suzie was gone.

Alister slammed his fist on the operating table. He was so close, so damned close. He fell onto a chair and leaned forward, resting his elbows on his knees. These guys weren't going to give up easily.

Chapter Five

The Followers.

Peter shifted his weight to his other foot. Several feet ahead of
him on a lower level, a line of men sat facing the array of
viewing plates and streaming images of hostages, tunnels,
warehouses, and laboratories. The wall behind the screens was a
single sheet of pristine, transparent steel-glass, exposing a
fraction of the technology powering the entire complex of
domes. Vibrant clusters of cogs, gears, levers and pistons, and a
criss-cross array of brass, Nu-iron, and steel-glass pipes carrying
various mixes of nano-steam. All dampened by the shadowy
glow from darklight strips around the frame's outer edge.

Anxious murmuring rippled along the long control desk
covered in dials, sliders, and small, oscillating equaliser screens.

Beside Peter, the bulky frame of Plotinus II filled a wide
armchair. Wisps of smoke swirled up from a large cigar while
his other hand held a pistol and tapped a slow beat against the
arm of the chair. This habit explained why Peter always stood to
the great leader's right.

Plotinus was using the pistol to widen a small tear in the
armrest and poke around the insides. He always smelt the same:
cigar smoke and perspiration mixed with the faint odour of
metallic hydraulics from the exoskeleton bodysuit laced over his
entire body. The exoskeleton woven into graphene fabric
gleamed around his neck and hands. Strands of metal muscle
and tendons worming through the fine mesh reflected the light
from the bank of viewing plates. Plotinus quietly snarled
incantations through gritted teeth, shifting in his seat and moving
his head in tiny erratic twitches that released thin, barely-audible
hisses from the micro-hydraulics.

"My dear Peter," Plotinus drawled breathlessly, whiny. "Find
out how well we are defending against the rescue. Forty percent
video coverage is unacceptable. And I still await news on the
progress made with the memory stick we retrieved from the
professor. Call a meeting with the Council of Faiths."

Warlords and maniacs, thought Peter. "Yes, Master." He
turned away, touching his earpiece to turn it on.

The men at the control desk whispered in short bursts while

staring at the wall of mostly blank, square plates. The five active plates displayed shots of soldiers, hostages imprisoned in various areas, and corridors and tunnels. The central viewing plate labelled 'Broadcast Feed' was larger than the rest.

"There," Plotinus said. "He falls through the glass into the operating room, and that's the last we see of him. Then that unbeliever dressed in black appears and defeats Yuri before he, too, disappears."

Peter touched the mic in his ear. "Master, Area 51 is being used as a transit point to transport hostages to Las Vegas."

"Excellent," Plotinus nodded. "Just as I expected. Order preparations to begin for phase two."

A voice crackled from a small speaker. "Master, the Peoples Infantry have rescued a hundred and fifty hostages, and twenty others also escaped. Five were sacrificed to allow us to move the others deeper into the sanctuary to give us more time to prepare. Thirty of our concealed Followers have reached the Peoples Infantry rescue point. They have been accepted as hostages."

"Good." Plotinus turned to Peter, "Is there not another neural helmet and active video feed in that sector?"

"Level 27, master," Peter replied, "the rainforest dome. It is the only other location."

"Ah yes, that's right. I want those poor unbelievers, the Scots girl, and the professor taken there." He wheezed, and a thin smile broke across his face. "May the blessed angel Anael grant that, unlike the others, she survives with her senses."

"Yes, Master,"

"As for that man," Plotinus addressed the men before him, "send the message. I want him captured. The world must see the consequences of resistance and rejection of the Teaching. His punishment must be severe and his death slow to draw out his sins so those who watch over us bless him with a reincarnation to a better life."

*****

"Where are you now, Suzie?" Alister rubbed his palms into his eyes, and flashes of a rainforest blinked across his vision. The sight melted and collapsed into a bright yellow hand-painted sign that read 'Garden of Eden'. Before, it had just been feeling;

this time, it was what she saw. How was this possible?

Lights and dials flashed across the panel on the wall behind him, and screens lit up with weaving green and yellow lines. The ache in his head became a steady pressure, and the dials bounced frantically into the red zone, and he heard that whispering again. "Dharma," he reached out. That's what Magpie had called the supercomputer running things down here; it was connected to this wall of computers. "Whoa!"

A sizzle coursed across his skin, making him shudder. His clothes were back to normal, and they felt lighter and cleaner. Then the aches crept back. That punk with wings wasn't doing much of a job if it was his guardian angel.

A radio crackled under the table. "We've lost the east side. The team's coming down the west stairwell."

"Not if I can help it." Wearily weaving through the wreckage, Alister stacked cabinets, canisters, and other furniture against the doors at the end of the hallway marked 'West Side' and then went back into the lab.

He lifted the helmet Suzie had been wearing. Clusters of hair-thin wires connected to a junction box sticking out between the array of screens and dials on the wall. His thumb touched the inside of the frame, and a loud hum filled the room. Sparks crackled off the wall and threw him backwards.

Head buzzing, he headed down the corridor, stumbling around cabinets and trolleys towards the end of the hallway and fell through the double doors just as an explosion boomed down from the opposite end of the corridor. "Woah!" Alister exclaimed. Looking around, he hauled a cabinet into the stairwell landing. Slamming the doors shut, he toppled the cabinet onto its side and wedged it between the door and the metal frame of the bannister with a few hefty kicks. The effort cleared his head, and he strode down four flights of stairs to the first landing and stopped.

His parents were dead, and he couldn't even remember them. He had a sister. All this crap going on, all this amnesia shit, got in the way of feeling something, missing them, being someone. The only real thing he felt connected to right now was Suzie. He followed the echo of his footsteps down into the flickering darkness, trying to remember more of his childhood. Something had happened to him.

The outfit morphed again, and he warmed up. Bulbs up and down the stairwell blinked on and off, giving the stairwell a strange strobe effect. Each landing on the stairs had doorways, each on different sides of the wall as he went down, leading off in any of four directions.

Above him, in the distance, echoed the shouts of Followers trying to smash through. He started opening doors so if the terrorists broke through, they couldn't tell which route he'd taken. A long tunnel at ground level led to a door where someone had sprayed 'Garden of Eden' in big fluorescent orange letters. Suzie was close; something inside told him she knew he was coming.

The old, black rubber seals at the base of the door had hardened over the years and scraped along the floor as Alister pushed them open to enter a short, semi-transparent tunnel. Vents at either end whirred with intermittent squeaks, barely circulating the stale air. Moisture trickled down the patchy exterior laced with knotted veins of clinging vines. Cocoons of various sizes and states of growth or decay hung along the vines, a few squirming with life inside. Fist-sized globs of webbing hung on the thicker vines.

Sensing Suzie's presence, he paused at the door leading out, then pushed through. The door opened with little effort, and, for an instant, he thought he was tripping out again.

Shimmering gold constellations of light scattered across a dense green canopy overhead let through a shower of needle-thin shards of light that sprinkled silver dots over the surrounding undergrowth, lighting up a thousand shades and shapes of green. The howls and cries of monkeys punctuated a cacophony of birdsong and a constant buzzing. Further in the rainforest, on either side of the path, wider beams of light sliced down and flickered across thick undergrowth where insects cut through the beams, releasing flashes of colour.

Through a clearing, up beyond it all, a silvery-yellow disc - the artificial sun - oozed across a thick nano-mesh sky rich with the subtle colours of daylight and patched with popcorn clouds. Like a slow heartbeat, the lazy pulse of fans soothed the strangeness of what he was seeing.

A mushy layer of leaves covered the path under his feet and spread over the border, running along either side. Leaves and rainforest litter swept in an arc across the floor. Over to his right, a vine became a snake and disappeared into the dense foliage. A branch snapped beyond the chaos of grasses, ferns and oversized leaves, and then a musky smell hit him and triggered a swell of fear, making his flesh crawl.

The undergrowth crackled behind him, and then something landed on the littered path with a heavy thump and let out a deep, slow growl. Alister didn't bother to look. He just ran. Behind him, the sound of pounding heavy feet was joined by more and turned into an avalanche. Fear surged through him, and the outfit spread, bunched and coiled around his legs and back, putting a leaping spring into each step. The noise gained on him, and the exit seemed miles away. A loud snarl sent another burst of adrenalin charging through him, and he threw himself forward, yanked hard on the door, and dived into another short tunnel. The door banged shut. He jumped away, fell and turned from the snarling and tearing of claws on metal beyond the polished steel door.

The door; Alister had no reflection, not even a fuzzy image; he was invisible. He stumbled back, fell against the damp wall and slid to the ground, his head spinning. The antiseptic smell from the labs beyond the inner door sparked a memory, and a wave of nausea flooded into him.

***

Alister sat up; he was visible again, the memory weighing heavy in his mind.

"Get off!" the shout interrupted his jangled thoughts. Alister jumped to his feet too fast and fell back against the wall. He took a few breaths and focussed on the door ahead, wishing he were still invisible. With a barely audible crackling, the Soft-Machine blended into the molecules of his clothes, and he disappeared— again – and again with that fabulous buzz.

Beyond the inner door, offices and laboratories, some with cages, lined a wide hallway. A motion-sensing CCTV camera in the centre of the ceiling whirred round to face him.

"Move it, doc. Strap the bitch and press the buttons already." A man's voice from a room at the far end.

"Please," a frightened voice replied, another man, "I need to measure her neural patterns, make the necessary adjustments, and calibrate the instruments attached to the helmet."

Alister strode down the hall, his anger bleeding into the Soft-Machine and turning him darker than black, a thing from which no light escaped. A terrorist rushed out and dropped to his knees with a horrified cry when he saw the human abyss heading for him. Alister grabbed the man and hurled him across the hall. The man smashed through a locked lab door and crumpled in an unconscious heap. A wild scream made Alister spin around to take a splatter of bullets against his chest. The outfit caught the shots, and he staggered back. From the outside, it seemed the bullets simply disappeared into him. Ignoring the burning across his chest, Alister twisted the rifle from the terrified man's hands and swung it into the side of his head. The man dropped to the ground.

Alister spun the rifle round and shot out the cameras. Sparks and shards of metal and glass spat out through the corridor. Eyes gleaming, he watched each spark glide across the air, leaving a glittering trail of photons. This was fantastic; he was light, slowed to matter. The brain-nanoparticle-outfit connection was just incredible. He was porous, consciousness swept along in the life-stream, saturated by a pulsing, living energy.

Those few seconds went on forever. The Soft-Machine receded back, revealing his regular clothes. Reality turned in on itself, and he was back to normal. So this was how it worked; the nanoparticles, driven by primitive survival instincts, somehow controlled the Soft-Machine when things got tough.

In the lab, the thin man he'd seen before, the guy with the glasses, froze and dropped a porcelain helmet. It swung on the wires and shattered on the wall of electronics.

"You the professor?" Alister asked, undoing the straps binding Suzie's feet.

The man nodded.

"I'm Alister." He made quick work of the straps on Suzie's wrists and across her waist.

The man glanced at Suzie, then back at him, "Alister Cloud?"

"Yeah, do I know you?"

"No, ah, no, we've never met as such. I'm Harold Lendon."

The blindfold came off Suzie to reveal a scraggy cut of red hair and beautiful blue-grey eyes. A faint scattering of freckles that perfectly complimented her red hair surrounded a cute, slightly upturned nose.

Alister helped her sit on the edge of the operating table, and her hand's touch sent a soft sizzle up his arm. Was she connected, too?

"Suzie?"

Suzie blinked, and a tangible emotion moved between them. She flung her arms around him. "Alister!" She kissed him hard. The warm, soft curves, moist pressure of her lips, and gentle caress aroused a similar response from him. They'd done this many times before. Emotions and memories swelled up and drowned his senses.

After some timeless period, she pulled away from him. "Alister, what's wrong?" She had an accent like his but stronger, like his father's. Glasgow, Dad was from Glasgow.

"My head's a bit of a mess," Alister said.

"It always is, but what's wrong?"

"I've got amnesia, didn't even know my real name at first. I remembered something, I…what is it, Professor?"

Lendon was staring at them. "Oh, um…" Flustered, Lendon fumbled with the zip of his black cardigan, clasped his hands together, and then shoved them into his pockets. "I, uh, know about your remarkable relationship."

"What do you mean?"

"Aye, well," Suzie said, "we've been through a fair bit." She prodded Alister in the chest with her finger. "What, can you no' remember anything?"

"Only bits and pieces. I remember being on a plane with you—not the airship before." He glanced at Lendon. That guy knew something.

"Thank God you're okay." She took his hand. "But you found me. I…I knew you were coming. How is that possible?"

"I kind of knew where you were."

"Remarkable," the professor repeated, gazing at Alister.

Both Suzie and Alister turned to him and said, "What?"

Lendon flushed. "Oh, nothing, just remarkable that you found us."

Alister eyed him. "Magpie, the soldier I was with, she said something about you being a prime asset. Why would she call you that?"

"I work for the Centauri Foundation. Raymond Ruya sent me

to—"

"Ruya?" A chill ran through Alister. The demon and Sid had mentioned him. There was other stuff; Ruya had talked with his dad. Things were starting to connect, and this professor guy knew more than he was letting on. Alister tried to dig out the fragments scattered through the clumpy mess of his head. "You said something about our relationship."

Lendon scrunched his face. "It's rather complicated." He looked around nervously. "Can we hurry up and go?"

Suzie spotted a mirror and ran her hands through the uneven mess the terrorists had made of her hair. "Lend me your cap, Al."

Distracted, Alister gave it to her without thinking.

"Al?" Suzie said.

"What? Right, this way." He led them down the corridor towards the rainforest. "There are four ventilation chutes that double as emergency exits to the surface," Alister said. You just strap in and--."

Suzie grabbed his arm, "Hang on, Al, I recognise that tone. What's the catch?"

"The catch? How'd you know...?"

She interrupted him with a smile and a slight tilt of the head. "I know you well enough to tell when you're hiding something."

No wonder he risked his life for her. "Okay," he sighed. "Thing is, there're some wild animals in there, and parts of the cage wall are broken."

"Wild animals?" Lendon said. "How many?"

"Six," Suzie said. "Ligers." She pointed to a faded poster pinned to the lab board. "'Staff notice: modified treatment regime to maintain the breeding capability of ligers.'" The text wrapped around images and printouts referring to six ligers. Scribbled on a scrap of paper beside it was a feeding schedule.

"Ligers?" Lendon said. "Is there another way out?"

Alister pointed to the steel door that led to the tunnel and rainforest. "We either knock out the ligers and go through the tubes or-" he hesitated, "No, there's no other way. The place is swarming with Followers."

"Oh," Lendon took a handkerchief from a pocket and fell onto a moulded plastic chair. "There must be another way, we should, we should.." He began cleaning his glasses and then wiped his forehead.

"We should go." Suzie helped the professor to his feet.

"The nearest tube's by the door."Alister said, "You can go first."

Suzie ripped a sheet of paper from the board. "It's a checklist of reminders. People haven't been using the tranquillizer rifles properly—which darts to use, part of the body to aim for."

"Excellent," Alister said. "Let's find them."

"The darts might be in a cooled compartment, like a fridge," Lendon added.

Alister found the storeroom and started to go through the boxes.

"Ally," Suzie called, "I've found the rifle and some empty darts."

Alister joined her in the laboratory. Lendon rummaged in a fridge, then turned around holding a wide plastic box divided into nine square sections like a tic-tac-toe grid.

"We have ketamine, Sucostrin, and Xylazine," he said, then his face dropped. "Five minutes before they take effect."

Suzie began to prepare the shots, "We better get a move on then, eh?"

"At least we've got those animals between the terrorists and us," Alister said

"What was that helmet all about, Prof?"

"Plotinus wanted a guinea pig, someone to connect to the Dharma supercomputer down here. I helped develop the prototype neural interface."

"The Followers have been here a year; why now?"

"I suspect he tried on other people and failed. The helmet must be carefully calibrated to the wearer's unique neural patterns. Plotinus didn't have me or my files." Lendon looked at Suzie. "I don't know why Miss Emerson was chosen."

"I wrecked a couple of his trucks trying to escape." Suzie grinned. "Plotinus wasn't too pleased about it."

"Wow," Alister said before he could stop himself.

"Aye, I'm tough." she winked at him, "Now let's get out of here."

***

Followers Surveillance Room

Standing beside his boss, Peter focussed on keeping his breathing steady. He almost jumped when Plotinus slammed his fist on the arm of the seat, cracking the thick wood frame under the padding.

"Why?" Plotinus roared, eyes full of tears. "Why do we suffer thus?" He took the fat cigar from his mouth and laid it carefully into the ashtray on the left arm of the seat, ensuring the inch of ash remained on the glowing tip. Peter gave him a neatly folded handkerchief, and Plotinus took it with a nod and wiped his eyes. Staring at the few screens still working, his face reddened.

"One of the last of our video feeds just went down. Why? Why? Do we not take to our tasks with a purity of heart and intention?" His voice rose to a screaming pitch. "Give me your attention."

Wheezing, face red with grief and rage, Plotinus undid the buttons of his combat jacket, revealing outlines of thick metal cables and plates running through the fabric of the exoskeleton. "There is one here who is weak in faith, a conduit for discordant karma. One who must shed the burden of sin and transition to learn life's lessons. A sad day." He wiped his eyes again.

Peter tensed up as Plotinus's emotions spiralled through sadness and anger. He knew what was coming. The six men at the control desk removed their headsets, stood silhouetted against the wall of screens and turned to face Plotinus. Peter shuddered when Plotinus slipped his hand under his jacket.

"Who is responsible for that video stream we lost?" Plotinus said. "Who?" The snick of the holster unclipping killed all sound in the room aside from the soft humming of the pipes and pistons.

Plotinus, a hand on his pistol, sat motionless as a judge, "Which of you dids't idle in his duties of worship, to be cursed by the dark hand of Kali?"

Peter ran through a mental calculation, his thumb touching each finger. It had been four days since Plotinus had seen anyone die, one day too long for the leader's liking. The faint background buzz from the six headphones on the editing desk seemed to echo the torment in Peter's mind, and his attention was drawn to Shakuni, who stood at the far left of the control desk. Peter took a short step sideways into the dark, then another. In the gloom ahead of him, silhouetted against the viewing plates, Shakuni reached back with a shaking hand, searching for the backrest of his seat.

Peter squinted at him and, tilting his head, strained to hear the cracked fragments of barely audible words from a throat choked with fear when a dull snap sounded beside him. Shakuni's head jolted up, his jaw dropped, and he fell back to slump heavily onto the seat, a gaping hole where his right eye had once been. Plotinus gazed at the suppressor on the end of the pistol for a few seconds before unscrewing it and slipping the weapon back into the holster.

Shakuni twitched then fell still, the smell of blood and urine spreading through the room and mixing with the faint citrus odour from the nano-steam. An ugly, fulfilled grin spread across Plotinus's face, and letting out a sigh, he turned to Peter.

"You are a medical student. What is your diagnosis, boy? Explain to me the cause of death," he said, rubbing his thumb and forefinger together like he'd popped a tasty morsel into his mouth.

"Point twenty-two," Peter croaked. Then he cleared his throat and started again. "Adapted point twenty-two bullet passed through into Shakuni's skull and ricocheted around the interior, decimating the brain before settling down."

Plotinus smiled and slid his tongue across his lips. "Good, that will suffice." Plotinus examined the cigar. "Record the sacred transition, and get someone to collect the shell of this poor soul." He dragged on the cigar, blew out, and waved his hand to clear the bloom of smoke. He gestured to the remaining Followers spread along the editing desk. "Return to your duties." He nodded. "Where are those jihadists and Sicarii, Peter?"

Peter stood motionless, staring at the ugly yawn frozen on Shakuni's face. "Finishing their morning prayers, Master," he heard himself say.

"Of course, their prayers." Plotinus checked his watch. "They'll finish soon. Send the jihadists to the Garden of Eden and the Sicarii to the other exit. One or the other should find those lost souls."

"Right away, master." Peter bowed, walked out and across the short hall into the bright, white-walled toilets and threw up in the nearest washbasin. Turning on the tap, he cupped his hands and splashed the icy water over his face before sinking to the floor.

Chapter Six

The wide steel-mesh walkway, sandwiched between the wall
and the fence, stretched around the rainforest perimeter. Alister
led the way while Professor Lendon edged behind him, stopping
when the walkway wobbled and let out loud creaks that sent
insects and birds into the air. Suzie encouraged him onwards.
Lendon grimaced with fear as he passed patches of fencing thick
with hollow brown cocoon husks that shook against the metal.
Fresh, fat cocoons twitched with life. Further along, vines, roots,
and branches had prised open holes in the wall large enough for
monkeys and animals to get through.

Suzie shook the top of her sweatshirt. "Talk about sticky."
There was a flash of fear behind the casual gesture. "You okay,
Professor?"

The professor wiped his sweaty forehead with a
handkerchief. "I think so."

Beyond several yards of the exposed walkway, the nearest
ventilation shaft, four feet wide and glowing yellow-green,
stretched up the side of the frame. Thin streams of condensation
ran down the outside, curling round green mould and clumpy
layers of fine webbing.

"Professor," Alister said, "there's your exit. Get into the
shaft, strap in and push the red emergency button. I'll watch out
for the ligers and Followers and come up as soon as you're both
out."

"No, come with us," Suzie said.

"Go on, I'll be right behind you."

Alister headed away from them in the opposite direction. He
banged and shook the mesh wall, attracting the attention of
several monkeys and sending birds scattering through the trees.
Fingers slotted through the mesh and the rifle slung over his
shoulder, Alister climbed a sloping part of the fence to where the
weight and growth of a thick vine had bent the mesh outwards to
make a large opening. He leaned forward, positioned the rifle
and scanned the rainforest floor below. A mother and two
adolescent ligers came into view. Alister shot the mother first.
She snarled and sat down, arousing the curiosity of the other
two. It took Alister less than a minute to take the younger pair
down. A rustle down to his right turned out to be two adult

ligers. They muscled through the undergrowth of thick green bushes and plants with an effortless elegance as if it were water. He quickly shot them, and the beasts yawned and reached around to the darts just out of reach on their shoulders.

"Got five," he called out. Alister flexed his fingers and straightened his back, rolling his shoulders. The other two ligers appeared just as a door slammed open, and the fence rattled and vibrated under a hail of bullets. A barrage of gunfire splattered into the branches and vines below him. Something down there gave way, and the mesh tilted further outwards. Alister pushed back and slid down as the clump of vines and mesh broke away and fell to crash into the forest below. Clouds of insects swarmed up around him, and the ligers disappeared. He hit the walkway with a loud clang and scrabbled over the shuddering mesh floor, hunched against bullets that crunched into the walls around him and spat out shards of concrete. The doors to the lab swung open, and three terrorists burst through and rushed up towards him.

"Crap."

A loud whoosh resonated upwards some distance behind him, and then Suzie cried out, "Alister, come on. Lendon's out."

"I'm fine, just go." He threw the rifle at the terrorists, then dived at them with such force they all crashed onto the floor in a sprawling heap. Yanking away an assault rifle, he slammed it into the face of one Follower and followed through with a sharp right swing into the side of the other's head, knocking them both out. A clumsy shove by the third Follower sent them both off balance, and they fell several feet through the gap in the walkway to hit the thick, soft ground with a dull thump. A muffled crack came from under the Follower at the same time as a cluster of growls resonated through the undergrowth. Alister jumped to his feet to see the man roll on his side. Hell, the guy was no older than him.

Still on the ground, the young man lifted his right hand away from his stomach, eyes fixed on the bloodied barrel of a pistol, then looked up at Alister with an expression of shock and fear. "I... I've shot myself." The gun fell from his hand, and he lost consciousness.

"Don't move."

Alister raised his hands and turned to face a terrorist gripping a grenade launcher attached to his assault rifle. The guy looked scared, too scared to pull the trigger.

Alister's stare shifted to the launcher, then to the terrorist's face. There's no way the Soft-Machine could stop a grenade. With an expression of guilt and mouthing an apology, the Follower raised the weapon and pointed it at Alister, wincing as he tightened his finger around the trigger.

A flash of yellow exploded out of the undergrowth, and the man flew sideways with a liger attached to him. The grenade shot out at an angle and blasted a hole in the walkway ahead of Suzie. Her scream was lost in the storm of birds screeching and flapping up through the canopy. Monkeys squealed and crashed through the trees in a blind panic. Over to his right, snarls and grunts burst from apes, their great muscular bodies barging up the artificial slopes, demolishing bushes and saplings as the beasts rushed from the destruction behind them. The liger had disappeared.

"I'm alright," Suzie called, her voice almost crowded out by the animal cries and creaking and groaning metal walkway that now hung away from the wall, lolling under the weight of a large fragment of hanging mesh frame. "The shaft is cracked. I can make it to the second one. Hurry up, Alister."

Suzie manoeuvred along the shredded fence and walkway, little more than a blur behind clouds of smoke and insects disturbed by the blast.

"Suzie, there's another few minutes before the tranq's kick in. Be careful."

Alister turned towards the lab entrance and froze. A liger stood between him and the door, a tranquillizer dart hanging from its shoulder.

Alister stretched his arms out to protect himself, but they weren't there; he was invisible again. Moving forward slowly and twitching its head, the creature sniffed the air, searching for his smell. Alister backed away, looking for an escape route, and the liger followed slowly, sniffing the air.

Then Alister spotted the tree, vines curling up the trunk. He jumped and started climbing. Below him, the liger snarled and returned to the terrorist and buried its teeth in the armour of the man's chest. It struggled to drag him off into the undergrowth, scraping a shallow path through the leaves and foliage, the heels of the man's boots cutting a line into the soft ground. The liger stumbled, dropped the Follower and let out a yawning roar, then thumped beside its prey. The man groaned and staggered to his feet. Almost falling over the unconscious beast, he cried and ran back towards the labs.

Another long burst of gunfire sent high-velocity bullets crunching into the shaft ahead of Alister. Jagged cracks webbed out, merged, and shattered the column. Table-sized shards smashed through the green, spraying foliage, birds, and insects. Suzie was barely visible, crawling away into the forest on her hands and knees.

"Keep going, Suze!" Two more Followers barged in through the doors. "Don't wait," he called. "I'll be fine." Hopefully, that sounded more convincing to her than it did to him.

He caught his breath when the terrorists stopped and peered up the tree where he clung to the vines, still invisible. The taller terrorist nudged the other and started to walk along the path, firing wildly in his direction. Bullets exploded, sliced and shredded through the branches and leaves around him. Over his left, Suzie had reached the next shaft along and stood by it, looking around.

"Go!" Alister shouted. "Now."

Suzie stepped into the shaft and swiftly strapped herself in.

Assaulted by a hail of bullets, Alister didn't see her fly up and out. One shot smashed against the vine he was gripping and sizzled into the trunk. The vine ripped away, and Alister fell. Reaching out, he managed to grab a branch. Pain shot up his arms and back as it took his weight. His fingers started slipping, and the Soft-Machine swarmed past his wrist. The thing was going to form a glove and grip the branch. Then some other notion appeared in his head, 'Let's make this interesting,' he thought and let go.

"I said what?" He said, shocked by his decision even as he kicked away from the tree and fell onto the terrorists. The burly one with the beard swung out impulsively, and Alister barely missed the man's arm. The other terrorist, a slightly smaller, younger guy, screamed and jumped back, arms over his face, when Alister appeared a few feet from them.

He snatched up the heavy fusion rifle, the shoulder rest warmed by the broiling nano-steam underneath, and stepped back, letting the two soldiers get to their feet. Neither of them had reacted to the whoosh of Suzie's escape. He was alone again, fighting some weird impulse to take these guys on hand-to-hand.

"Lose your weapons," he said in between deep breaths, "and get out."

The shorter man nodded and immediately dropped his pistol. "Come on, Uncle Mo," he said, looking nervously up at the man beside him.

Mo's face twisted into an ugly sneer. "You always were a coward, Nehir." Mo unclipped a delayed blast grenade from his belt. He pulled the ring that released the primer into the main liquid chamber, holding it nonchalantly in front of him as the whistle from the tiny vents in the old grenade became louder, and an acrid smell filled the air.

"You crazy..." Alister fired, and the force of the blast tore an ugly hole deep into Mo's upper arm and knocked him back, releasing a spray of blood. The grenade flew into the undergrowth. Mo howled and dropped to his knee, his free hand barely stopping the blood gushing from his shoulder.

Hands raised and wide-eyed, Nehir looked pleadingly at Alister, then his expression turned to horror. A liger had appeared out of the undergrowth ahead of them, mouth open, lips drawn back, revealing a curve of gleaming fangs. A slow growl rolled out of its jaws. Nehir screamed again, and the liger pounced.

Alister shoved Nehir aside, and they both fell to the ground, the liger diving over them to land and spin around, snarling. Alister yanked Nehir to his feet and pushed him towards the door. Nehir hesitated for a second, then bolted. Alister disappeared just as the second explosion from the grenade sent the liger into the undergrowth.

Alister found the young Follower leaning against the wall, breathing fast in the safety of the tunnel leading to the lab. Compared to the long unkempt beards and messy hair of the other Followers, Nehir was immaculately groomed, with a spiky black haircut poking over the bandanna and a neatly-cut, jazzy beard.

"You could have killed us," Nehir said. He removed the red bandanna from his head. "Killed Mo, but you shot his arm instead and saved my life."

"Yeah," Alister said, looking over his shoulder, wondering about the liger he hadn't shot.

"Do you think - he's dead?" the young man asked, afraid of the answer he might get.

"Who, Mo?"

Nehir nodded.

"Why should you care? He was going to kill us all." He cracked the door open and looked through. Just rainforest.

"I know," Nehir said. "But he really is my uncle, a cruel man, a psychopath, just uses people, doesn't care about anybody. He attacked a girl and wanted to cut her foot off because she had a tattoo on her ankle. I think he may have once killed someone. He even—"

"Alright, I get it."

"Sorry, It's just – I didn't think we'd find you and that jungle place. I'd heard about it but never- I've never been so scared. I've never held a gun before, I'm a cook, I-"

"Hey, calm down."

"Sorry, yes. Thank you. For saving me." Nehir seemed not to hear. "I was really scared out there; that was terrifying." He looked over Alister's shoulder to the door.

"Not much of a terrorist, are you?"

"Terrorist," Nehir repeated as if it were a foreign word. "My name is Nehir." He offered his hand.

Alister gave him a wary look and shook his hand; they were clean and manicured. Nails clipped short. The guy probably was a cook.

"You should get back to your people."

"No. No, I can't do this any more. Take me with you."

"What?"

"I never wanted to come here. Dad and his brother, my Uncle Mo, said they would kill me if I didn't join. Dad became even more fanatical after Mum died. I thought coming here might help him. I was wrong. I just—"

"Mate, it's okay!" Alister stopped him.

"Oh, sorry. Take me with you, please."

"Seriously?"

The young man nodded with an expression of pleading desperation.

Alister thought for a moment. "Come on then, just keep up."

"Oh, thank you, thank you so much."

"Alright." Alister grabbed the door handle. "We have to run, head in that direction. Ready?"

At the end of the short tunnel, another door slammed open beyond the doors into the lab. There were footsteps, one person's, and a wheezy voice. "Brothers, wait."

Nehir's eyes widened in fear.

"Stay behind me," Alister said.

Nehir nodded. Alister felt sorry for the poor guy, but just for a moment. There was one more liger out there, fully conscious. He shoved the door open, and they shot away from the path and into the undergrowth towards the last remaining vent. A few seconds later, someone else came through the door behind them. There was a pause; then shots whistled and splattered through the undergrowth. Nehir fell to a crouch. Slapping a hand over his mouth, he stifled a scream and began to spin around in one direction, then another, not knowing where to run. Alister grabbed his arm and pointed.

"Over there. Get in the vent and strap in. You know your way around up there, on the surface?"

Nehir nodded, and Alister pushed him forward, "Run, go!" he said. "Help Suzie and the professor get to safety."

"Yes, yes, I promise." Nehir dashed the last few yards towards the shaft, jumped in, fumbled into the harness and slapped the escape button.

A Follower, some old boy, strode out of the undergrowth towards Alister. He had a long, sad face, an even longer grey beard with silver streaks, and brown tobacco stains around his mouth. The old boy probably got left behind by the others. His drained expression was creased by years of grief. His deep-set, tired eyes flashed with momentary bursts of unnatural rage that cracked his features. The fight with his personal demons was spilling out and picking on anyone mad enough to care or get close to him.

"I will kill you," he wheezed, "like I killed those…unbelievers and the…monstrous, unnatural beast."

He must have shot the last of the ligers with his wild firing. Alister shook his head and scrunched his face at the man's twisted, bitter words. There was a movement to the old man's right, and Alister stepped back towards the shaft entrance and disappeared while the man fearfully darted his head around, trying to place the growling sound now coming from the growth.

"I will find you," the man wheezed, "and I will kill you."

Alister stepped into the shaft, wrapped his arms around the shoulder straps and elbowed the escape button. The shunt upwards knocked the wind out of him, and he sucked in a deep gulp of warm air. He caught a glimpse of the small circle of cold sky, and then a powerful blast shook through the tube and ripped it away from the wall. Alister was halfway up when the tube tilted and ground along the metal grill of the walkway. The noise resonated through the tube and sent deep, scraping creaks booming over the canopy. A long scar spread and cracked the shaft wide open, and Alister dropped, thumping against the sides of the clear plastic-steel. He fell through a gaping fissure and smashed into branches. His body twisted and bent as he fell through clumps of green and brown, and the Soft-Machine blended into the fabric of his clothes, swelling into a hard, foamy pad to protect him.

The forest responded to the explosion and noise of plastic-steel tubing demolishing branches with a cacophony of howls and squawking. Alister hit the ground unconscious.

***

That same angel, Raguel, was speaking. "We live inside you all. Within your quietest thoughts. A world behind forgotten dreams and all the realms unseen. Yet nought you see is real."

***

The entrance to the rainforest opened, and footsteps moved along the path. A patch of air morphed in a shattering of light, like glass breaking, then three black men shimmered into view to stand motionless as their camo-outfits settled into a patchwork of green and brown shades.

"I'll take the path. Ben, take three. Steve, you're on the nine. Move out."

"Roger that, boss." Steve nodded, and both men checked their weapons.

"Will you look at this place, Ben? It's a damn wreck; hope the kid's alive."

"I said we should have left sooner."

"I didn't expect such a large group to be patrolling that tunnel."

"The terrorists use it as a shortcut."

"You were the damn fool standing by the door when it opened."

"You never said anything about a hidden door."

"I didn't know it was there."

"Let's just find this Alister fella and get him topside ASAP."

Steve called out, "Hey, debris knocked out a Follower, an old timer."

"Leave him," came the reply. "I've found the guy we're looking for."

Chapter Seven

Suzie found the professor huddled and shivering in a corner in the second of the small emergency exit blocks. They sat and waited several minutes for Alister. She jumped up when the whoosh of the vent sounded in the other room and rushed out to see Nehir stumble out.

"Who are you?" she said.

"Nehir." he panted, "Alister helped me escape. You are Suzie, yes?"

Suzie nodded, confused. "How do you... Where's Alister?"

Nehir stood up, "More Followers came. He told me to help you."

"Why?" Suzie took a step back. You're a Follower."

"No, no, no, I was forced here by my dad and my mad uncle. I'm a cook; really, I am. Look." Nehir fumbled in the long side pocket of his combat trousers and brought out a white chef's cap. He put it on and delicately adjusted it. "There, see? I have a photograph, too," he went through his pockets.

"Okay, okay. I get it." Suzie eyed him warily. "Do you know your way around this area?"

Nehir went to the door and cracked it open. A cold breeze swirled snow off the ground and into the room. Nehir stepped out and returned several seconds later. "We're on the edge of the forest. I can see the airship. We don't want to go there. We, I mean the Followers, dropped mines on the way back with the hostages. I think the rescue centre is the other way beyond the forest; that's what I heard. I don't think Followers are patrolling it. They were all called back when the rescue began."

"We'll wait for Alister," Suzie said. "He shouldn't be--."

An explosion bloomed up from the vent exit, followed by a crash and shattering of wood and plastic. Frozen to the spot, Suzie gaped at the tube exit. She stepped forward and stopped when the pressure suddenly dropped, and the tube exit cracked at the base, sunk several inches and tilted to one side.

"That was the last one." Suzie threw her hand to her mouth.

"Do, do you think he was in there?" Nehir said.

Suzie responded with a slow nod, and Nehir gasped.

"I think he's alright," Suzie said, perplexed by her response and certainty.

Nehir gave her a strange look. "I hope so."

Suzie's attention remained fixed on the tube. "We have to help him. We can't leave him down there."

"How? There's no way down from here."

"Wait, you have a radio."

"Yes, but it's a Followers frequency."

"Just hand it over."

Pressing buttons, Suzie accessed the settings menu. "Hell. Battery's almost flat on this thing."

"What are you doing?" Nehir said.

"Sending a message to the P.I.," She spoke into the radio. "This is Suzie. Alister is in the Rainforest cavern. Send help."

A crackly voice replied, "Suzie, this is Eliot. We've been monitoring the Followers who went after you. Don't worry, we'll find-" The radio fell silent.

"That's it, battery's dead."

Lendon came in, "Is Alister -" He took one look at Nehir and stepped back. "What's going on?"

"It's okay, Professor. Alister sent him to find us, help us. He knows his way around."

"Where is he?"

Suzie pointed. "Down there. The tube…" She hesitated. "It broke. He fell and got knocked out. He's not injured. The Panthers got my message."

Nehir cried out when the door swung open to let in a sharp gust of chilling air. "Oh," he said with a sheepish smile, "I didn't close it properly."

"Aye, well, we should get going," Suzie returned the radio. "Batteries dead. Let's shoot the craw. Which way, Nehir?"

"What about Alister?" Nehir said.

Suzie looked at the professor; "I think he's okay. Besides, there's no way down from here."

"We might be able to send another message," Nehir said. "There's a path leading out to an old radio lookout post. I think there's a road not far from there."

"How far away?" Suzie asked.

Nehir shrugged. "Half an hour, maybe?"

"A mile or mile and a half then," Suzie said. "The sooner we find help for Alister, the better." She took Alister's baseball cap from a pocket and headed for the door.

"Wait," Nehir said. He used a branch to wipe away snow from the door to reveal thick, dark-brown wood panels and then did the same to the roof line.

"What are you doing?" Suzie said.

"So I can look back and see which direction we should go in, for a while anyway."

They trudged for an hour through the thinned-out, snow-swept forest. Most of the trees had been felled over the years, and none had grown back. "It's like being in a drawing," Nehir said, "done with a fine-tipped pen. Everything is so sharp, so still."

"When was the last time you came out?" Suzie said.

Nehir thought for a while. "A few months since I was last up here."

The professor struggled to keep up. Arms wrapped around his chest and hands tucked under his armpits, he walked rapidly behind them, sometimes breaking into a slight jog when the path was clear.

Suzie stopped at the top of an incline, "Let's wait for the Professor."

"Okay," Nehir panted small clouds of vapour into the air.

"It is quiet," Suzie said, "Like we're the only ones alive out here."

Nehir shuddered.

"What is it?"

"The Followers come out here sometimes to have their visions."

"Do they really see angels and genies and stuff?"

"Oh yes, definitely, they really believe it. That they see what's already there, just hidden."

"Have you ever seen anything?"

Nehir shook his head. "I'm not allowed."

The professor arrived breathless and bent forward, leaning on his knees, "How much farther?"

"The old security hut with a radio is just over the next hill," Nehir said.

Lendon straightened up, "Thank God."

***

Suzie pushed at the door, then kicked it, "Damn thing's locked."

Lendon's face dropped, "We'll have to carry on to the road."

Nehir looked around, "I'll look for a stone or something to break the lock," and wandered off only to run back. "The roof," he panted. "There's a hole on this side. We didn't see it coming up from behind."

Suzie walked back, looking up, "You're skinny, Nehir. We'll give you a boost."

Suzie and Lendon clasped hands, and Nehir stepped up and clambered in through the small hole.

"There's a missile here, gone right into the ground. Looks like it's been here for years...I've found an axe."

It took several blows before the door swung open. Suzie and Lendon entered a snow-dusted room and edged around the half-buried missile. Beyond that, an old radio sat on a bench at the other end of the room. Wiping the dust from the chair, Suzie fell into the seat facing the radio and swept some breadcrumbs away from the space in front of it. "Looks like it was used not long ago." She flicked the function switch, and the radio hummed to life. The light behind the REC-TRANS FREQUENCY channel dial came on, and the speaker buzzed and faded.

"Is that good?" Lendon asked behind her,

"Not sure." Suzie tried PRESET, and the radio crackled momentarily, then fell silent again. "Damn!" She slammed her palm onto the box and then looked around the room. "There might be a spare battery around here. Help me find it. I'll look for a toolkit, screwdriver, or knife."

"The only place where anything could be is in one of those two boxes," Lendon pointed a shivering finger to a large box.

Suzie took the small axe Nehir had used and smashed at the padlock on the box.

"What about my radio?" Nehir said.

"Let's have a look. Here, you have a go at the lock with the axe."

Nehir handed over the radio and took the axe. "What's in there?"

"Something useful, I hope. Go on, get to it," Suzie said, examining the radio.

Nehir fumbled in his pockets and produced a Swiss army

knife. "Might this help?" He gazed at it affectionately.

"Excellent," Suzie said. "Hand it over then."

Nehir raised it slowly towards Suzie. "My father gave it to me when I was twelve, on my birthday, before the Big Freeze."

"Don't worry. I'll be careful with it," Suzie said.

Nehir smashed at the lock while Suzie unbolted the back off the radio and removed the battery.

The rusty padlock fell off with a clang, "Done it," Nehir lifted a box out of the chest. "Is this any help?"

"Tch," Suzie said. "That old battery is useless in that state. Is there anything else?"

"Some box with a winding handle."

"Let's have a look."

Nehir struggled to lift and place the rigid plastic box on the table. One side had a simple curved gauge behind a small glass screen with a row of lights on top. Suzie opened a small door opposite the handle and pulled out two wires. "Wind-up battery; we're in luck."

"How do you know so much about radios?" Nehir asked.

"I always used to take things apart with my Uncle Stuart. Here, hold this circuit board so the wires don't come off this section here."

"You…Stuart?" Nehir stared at her. "Are you Suzie Emerson?"

Suzie peered back. "How did you work that out?"

"Stuart Emerson does all the hacking for the PI. I guessed he'd be here. I've heard about the two of you; you were both wanted for hacking for years until you saved all those lives in Toronto. They say your intuition as a hacker is almost magical."

"Ach, it's nothing. Now, help me lift out these three sections. Hold onto the board, and I'll take out these two."

"Yes. You were on the airship?"

"Aye, on our way to New York for Al's birthday to visit his big sister and her husband. We'd planned to do some Centauri volunteer work on the Newtown Creek recovery project."

Ten minutes later, Nehir's radio was rigged to the working remains of the larger radio. She connected the wires from the charger. "Prof, we'll need you. It'll take a while for enough charge to build up and get the radio going. Nehir's arm will fall off before we're ready to broadcast. Okay, Nehir, get winding."

Suzie spent another ten minutes adapting the frequency tuner while Lendon and Nehir took turns to wind the generator. Finally, the gauge started bouncing on the middle line.

"Okay, let's try talking to someone and see what we get."

A touch on her arm stopped her.

"Miss Emerson," Lendon looked worried.

"What is it, Professor?"

"If you get through to our rescuers, I'd like you to pass on a message in case we, uh…" He hesitated. "It's rather important they know."

"Know what? Can it not wait?" Suzie asked, still working on Nehir's radio and the exposed interior of the field radio.

"The Followers have the LS codes."

"What?"

"The security codes for encrypted LS files."

"What are you talking about?"

"Please, just send the message."

The radio crackled into life, and a garble of voices fell out of the speaker.

"What? Hold on. Mayday, mayday, this is Suzie Emerson. Do you read me?" she said, staring at Lendon.

"Suzie Emerson?" a voice asked. "This is Snow Patrol. We read you. Stay on this frequency, and we'll have your coordinates in a Mike."

"I have Professor Lendon with me." She paused and looked at Nehir in his uniform. "One other. The prof said the Followers have the LS security code."

Lendon nodded and mimed the words as she spoke, then breathed a sigh of relief.

"Say again?"

Lendon leaned forward. "LS code. Lima Sierra," he repeated slowly. "The Followers have the code. Tell General Cape immediately. Please."

"Okay, Prof. Miss Emerson, we have your position." The voice began to fade. "…You safe?"

Suzie leaned away from the microphone. "That's it. Now we wait and hope they get to us first."

Chapter Eight

A sharp wind lifted and swirled snow off a bleak white landscape. Off in the distance, a forest had been roughly dusted along the horizon. Plumes of dark grey smoke, pale-blushed by a rising red sun, rose above the ghostly, ashen trees.

A solitary truck rumbled along the muddy road that stretched through the desolate plain. The mud-covered brass and steel-glass pipes along the side panels curled down and merged into exhaust fins that belched citrus fumes to splatter in the swirling wake. The truck bumped along the uneven road, loosening the weaker clips so the canvas flapped wildly over the metal frame. Inside, four soldiers sat on benches, gripping straps to keep their balance. Each looked the same in shades of pale grey, lightly armoured combat gear and ski masks, leaving only their eyes visible through crystal-clear goggles. Aside from slight variations in height and weight, there was no way to distinguish them.

Beyond the forest and snow-swept plain ahead of them, the rapid and sporadic snap and rattle of gunfire filled the air along with the booms and dull thuds of explosions.

The driver tightened his grip on the steering wheel.

"Watch it, Jim." said the soldier beside the driver, "Incoming."

A whoosh, quickly followed by an explosion, sent the truck swerving off the road.

The four soldiers in the back swore and cursed at the driver, their curses forming short-lived vapour in the air in front of them.

"Well, you should have booked business class," Jim shouted back and yanked on the steering wheel. The truck turned and crunched through a small mound of snow back onto the road and into another explosive spray of mud and smoke.

"Think they've tagged us, boss."

"Pull over," the officer beside him said. Tearing open the canvas flap, he shouted into the back, "Everybody out! Now."

It took a mere few seconds for the truck to empty, and the soldiers scattered left and right to either side of the road, disappearing into the forest.

"Head for the target. Split by the numbers, eleven and one

o'clock."

The soldiers broke into two groups of three and ran into the forest, dodging around the trees when the truck exploded out from the road to splatter in a wide circle around a six-foot-deep crater. The orange and green particles from the nano-steam fuel cells swarmed furiously through the air, seeking unity. Within seconds, the particles merged into two balls of thick mist, then collided to spiral and swallow into each other. The turbulent ball spun upwards into the sky and bloomed into a thin, whistling cloud before disappearing in a sizzling arc of white flame.

"Damn," Jim said, "I spent four hours harmonising the resonance conductors last night." He spat on the ground, "And I'd optimised the spectrum mix."

"We got more you can play with back at base," the officer said and nodded to a man with a pizza-box-sized radio on his back. "Get that steam linked to the armyweb, Tangles."

"Yes, sir," Tangles replied. Half the radio was a fresh supply of rare element-mesh soaking in quantum-entangled steam. A wire trailed up to an egg-shaped earpiece with a graphene mic over the linkman's right ear.

"Polar Bear, Polar Bear, this is Snow Patrol. We're two klicks from the target's twenty, continuing on foot…No, no casualties…Roger that." He nodded over to the officer, who tapped his earpiece.

"This is Smoke, Captain Arjun... loud and clear," Smoke said. "How many? Well, it was never going to be a walk in the park… No, there's no time. We'll handle this ourselves. Just send an APC pick-up… Copy that."

Tangles crouched with his back to a tree. "Flash, sir," he said. "I'm picking up a local low-frequency call cutting in on the team line. It's Suzie. She has the professor and one other. They've made it to the old outpost bunker—that's a klick from our position. She's saying something about a key, LS key, a message for the general."

"Good girl," Smoke said. "Tell her we're on our way and to stay put. We'll get there before the terrorists. Call base, give them the heads-up with our new target, and ask them to send the reserve to back up team two and continue to target. As for the key, pass it up the line."

"Copy that, sir," Tangles repeated the messages, pausing

between each, then nodded to Smoke.

"Well," Jim said, "I'd like to know how Lendon and a couple of kids got out of a hole in the middle of nowhere and hacked a terrorist line."

"The girl's a situationist, niece of Stuart Emerson."

"Emerson? The old geek who hacked the Follower's network and video feeds for us?"

"Yep. Okay, men, we're Oscar Mike." Smoke stood up, "Chris, take point. Stan, fire up your detector. The rest of you fall in a single line. Ben, Tangles, you're on our six."

Chunks of the winter forest broke away from the background to take the shape of six soldiers, and they began to snake forward.

Chris ran forward in short bursts, stopping to peer through binoculars. The fourth time he stopped, he spoke into his microphone. His voice crisp in Smoke's earpiece. "Tango at one, sir."

"How many?"

"He's alone, sir. Probably a scout."

"Take him out."

When the figure in the distance stood up again, there was a tiny, faint burst of pink above its head, and the figure fell to the ground.

"Alpha Mike Foxtrot, pal," Chris said. "Tango down."

Stan's voice came over the headphones. "Sir, I'm picking up IED and landmine signals on the mine screen. This is gonna slow us down."

Smoke adjusted his goggles, and the feed from the camera on Stan's helmet appeared in the top right of his vision. Fuzzy yellow dots on Stan's handheld scanning device marked the presence of subsurface anti-personnel mines and improvised explosive devices.

"I'll adjust the resonance detector; that should sharpen the signature vibration of the mines."

"Okay, people, move on Stan's lead," Smoke said.

The patrol weaved slowly through the minefield while gunfire continued to cut out of the distance. Once through, the soldiers spread out and scurried forward again to stop at the edge of a clearing. Stan gave the all-clear.

Smoke responded with a thumbs-up and spoke into the mic.

"Tango's just beyond the clearing. Dawn Patrol is holding off the main terrorist search party about half a klick to our right. With me, Jim., we'll circle west to the rear of their position. The rest of you stay here and, on my mark, draw fire."

On Smoke's signal, soldiers appeared like grey ghosts, barely visible against the pale, shadow-speckled forest background. They swept through the silent white to circle around and flank the enemy position. On Smoke's second signal, the suppressed popping of gunfire crackled across the cluster of trees, and in the distance, mounds of snow-laden branches collapsed onto the terrorists taking cover behind fallen logs. A large group of Followers exposed their positions as an irregular line of dark smudges darting across the white landscape cracked by skeletons of trees.

"Are they crazy?"

"Shut up and open fire."

Gunfire crackled through the silent forest and stopped on Smoke's signal, and the soldiers shuffled to their next position. After moving just a few feet, an RPG thumped into the bushes around fifty yards ahead. The soldiers dropped to the ground and covered their ears. A second later, a cone and dome of earth, snow, and yellow and orange smoke bloomed. No one moved.

"Jim," Smoke murmured, "make use of that thermal scope, will ya?"

"Told you it was worth paying for, chief."

Another grenade exploded behind them. Jim peered through his scope and turned a dial on the side.

"What the hell you playing at, soldier? Put your damn toy to use before this turns into a bag of dicks."

"Copy that, chief." Jim pulled out his thermal, optical sight, clipped and locked it into place in front of the existing sight, and with his breath settling, he pressed and held the power button for a couple of seconds until it was ready to go.

Following Jim's gaze, Smoke watched the wind scoop thin snow curls off branches and up from the ground, tossing soft sprays left to right in the light breeze. Jim would deal with the minuscule push of the breeze on the bullet, as he would the tug of gravity and resistance of friction as the shot surged through the air. Jim could have been a statue or a guy frozen to death peering down the scope. Then his finger moved and pulled the trigger.

Over 800 yards away, visible only to Jim, an electric blue-white shard of light, surrounded by a tiny puff of red, bloomed from a Follower's head. The terrorist collapsed to the ground, firing the launcher. A pale-yellow vapour trail rose into the air, drizzled back down to its source, and exploded. Smoke and Jim ignored the cries that reached them a few seconds later. Jim had already adjusted his aim. He waited a little under a minute and fired again. Another tiny electrical burst and puff of red were followed by several soldiers breaking cover and running, some towards Smoke's team and some towards Dawn Patrol. They didn't get far, and the area soon fell silent.

"Any more of them?"

"No signs, sir," Jim said, examining the cylindrical, steel-glass nano-steam chambers under the barrel. "Just the hostages."

"Outstanding," Smoke stood up. "Let's bag our prizes."

The six soldiers trotted towards the bunker where Suzie, Nehir, and the professor sheltered. Passing the terrorists' position, Smoke slowed. "Keith," he called out, "we have injured people here. Call in the medics when transmission's back up."

"Yes, sir," Keith replied. "Do you want me to provide treatment?"

"Not yet. See how our hostages are first, then come back for these guys."

"Smoke?" a voice called.

"Well, if it ain't Suzie Emerson," Smoke replied. "How you doing, kid?"

"I'm good," Suzie pointed to the bunker. "Professor Lendon needs some help though."

Smoke nodded to Keith, who ran past them towards Nehir and the professor.

Suzie looked around. "Alister's not out yet?"

Smoke shook his head. "We got your first message. The Panthers are looking for him; they'll be in touch. Let's get you back to base." Smoke tapped his earpiece. "General, we have the three hostages and are heading to the pick…Copy that. Let's go, kid, we don't have much time."

He turned to his soldiers. "There's another enemy troop bearing down. Move out; there's no reason to engage. They can take care of their own injured here. Ben."

"Chief?"

"Give Keith a hand with the prof. That little guy just ain't cutting it."

Freed from carrying the professor, Nehir hurried over to join Suzie. "Is there any news on our friend?"

"Smoke says he's not out," Suzie said, distracted by something to her right.

"Smoke?" Nehir stared up at him, shivering, having given the prof his jacket.

"That's me." Smoke pulled a thermal sheet from a pack on his belt and gave it to Nehir, who unrolled it and threw it over his shoulders.

"In my country, we say you have a lion's voice."

A grin crossed Smoke's face. "Lion's voice, huh?"

"Yes. When I was a child, I remember—"

Suzie jabbed him in the back. Nehir turned to her, and she shook her head.

"What do you mean in your country?" Suzie said. "You sound like a Londoner."

"Stories we used to hear when we were children, me, my brother and sister."

"They back down there?"

"No, my brother is in the Royal Marines, and my sister is in London with her family."

"Suzie," Smoke said, "just got word the Panthers have found Alister. They're taking him back to base now. He said something about Plotinus planning an all-out attack on the rescue base. General Cape has been notified. We'd better get back before it all kicks off."

Chapter Nine

Groom Lake had changed little since the Freeze. The satellite pictures from old maps hung in frames around the walls were still pretty accurate: barracks, single- and two-storey buildings, offices, the unusually long airstrips, and half a dozen old aircraft hangars where Gold Hawk airships were now parked. Their blue and gold fusion tanks, visible through their stripped-down wasp wings, slowly turned and stirred the fuel, filling the hangars with an eerie glow and rhythmic hum.

Alister dreamed he was holding Suzie's hand. Her face was white, lifeless. Someone was speaking, "Nanoparticles at thirty percent saturation. The poison has been neutralised." There was a noise. They were in a jet plane. He woke and sat up when someone came into the room, and for a moment, he thought he was still on the plane.

"What's going on? Where am I?"

"Groom Lake medical unit. I'm Doctor Wong."

"How did I get here?"

"The Panthers found you and brought you here."

"What about Suzie and the others?"

"All here. They're fine. Get dressed. You're good to go. The bruising over your upper body might hurt for a few days. Don't worry about any visions you might have been having. The Followers have been releasing the hallucinogens everywhere lately."

Alister blinked and wiped a hand over his head, "Why would they do that."

"Convert them, cause confusion maybe, I don't know. Almost all the hostages have been seeing supernatural creatures."

"Thanks," Alister said, "Good to know I'm not losing my mind."

The doctor smiled, "I hear that a lot. Your girlfriend's waiting for you at reception."

"Thanks, doc." Girlfriend? The doc' didn't know the half of it. Thoughts started to rush through his mind. Suzie had the particles in her too. Did she know? What did Ruya call it? Neural Wi-Fi. If there was such a thing as nanoborg'd, he'd be a prime candidate.

Passing an intensive care room, a flash of memory came back. Standing at the foot of a hospital bed, where a frail man looking old before his time, tubes coming from his arms, bald head covered by a mesh neural-scan cap connected to a monitor. Dad. A hollow bloomed in his gut. He remembered the expression on his father's face of someone knowing he was about to die and hoping he'd done all he could for his son, already missing him. The memory of wanting to pull his father from the bed and take him home where he could get better.

"Alister?" Suzie came round the corner and found him leaning against the wall. "What happened?"

"I had a flashback of when I was a kid, seeing my dad in a hospital bed—I think he was dying." He took a couple of breaths. "I'm alright now."

"You sure?"

"Yeah."

"Your dad died when you were around eight," Suzie hooked her arm around his.

"I wish I could remember him."

"I'm sure it'll come back in time," Suzie squeezed his arm. "Can you remember anything else?"

"Ruya's name keeps turning up in my flashbacks, and the creatures I saw mentioned him, too."

"What?" Suzie leaned back and stared at him. "They actually spoke to you?"

"Well," Alister paused, confused by Suzie's shocked expression, "yeah. Don't they all?" he asked, his voice slowing. "When others see them?"

"God, no!" Suzie's eyes widened. "What did they say?"

"All kinds of crazy stuff. I think it was all stuff from the back of my head. They mentioned Ruya, nanoparticles, and lots of quantum physics gabble. Pretty trippy."

"Could be parts of your memory coming back," Suzie said. "Ruya was funding work on nanoparticles; your parents and sister worked on the projects."

"It felt pretty real, though. This your room?"

Suzie nodded.

"Bed's a single."

"Oh, we've managed before." She clicked the lock.
***

By late evening, two perimeter defence rings had been set up two miles and a mile from the airbase, and the last of the troops, tanks, and cannons disappeared into the misty distance.

Alister sat beside Suzie at a table in the mottled grey hardside marquee mess hall surrounded by groups of older hostages of all ages finishing their meals. Most now relaxed with a hot drink or played cards, murmuring. Some of them wore bandages, and many were in army fatigues. Rumours of the Followers' plan had spread throughout the base, and an uneasy tension drifted around the hall despite the announcement that hostages would be flown out first thing in the morning.

Alister had chosen a seat beside one of the many filters in the hall, breathing in the refreshingly cool air. People around the filters seemed more relaxed. The filter was a steel-glass device about as tall as a chair, a couple of feet wide and nine inches deep. Inside, brass pipes, cogs, wheels, pistons, and fish-scaled Nu-iron tubes surrounded by a thick gel.

Alister spoke in whispers. "I remember bits and pieces. Dad talking to Raymond Ruya about nanoparticles and neural Wi-Fi. I think Dad injected me with something to do with getting nanoparticles into my system."

"Nanoparticles…the type your sister was working on before she disappeared?"

Alister nodded. "That's why she disappeared, to protect me, gave the impression she destroyed them all. My dad…we…we both thought she'd died."

"But she was with Graham all the time."

Another name that Suzie had mentioned last night was Graham, his sister's NSA minder who married her. Was he going to piece his life together like this, from fragments?

"I reckon it's how I picked up all that info about where things were in the caverns and how I found you."

"But I could sense you too," Suzie said, a puzzled expression on her face.

Alister broke the silence that followed. "There's something I should tell you."

"You're not going to get all soppy, are you?"

"No." Alister smiled, "I think you have some particles in you, too."

Suzie shook her head. "I've never been to your parents' laboratory or met your dad."

"I think I transferred them to you somehow."

"Somehow?" She nudged him and smiled cheekily.

"No, not like that. You're not worried?"

"Are you kidding? I should thank you. That explains why I'm so good at hacking networks and computers." She sipped hot chocolate, "I wonder when the transfer happened. I got good at hacking long before we...hooked up."

"I remember us being on a plane somewhere with your uncle Stuart and a few things about my dad and big sister."

"The plane!" Suzie's eyes lit up. "Yes. When you were holding my hand after I passed out from the poison. Of course, you must have sent nanoparticles into me to save me. It was after that the hacking got real easy." She leaned into him.

"We should keep it secret." Alister paused, then said, "Though I feel Lendon knows about us. Remember how he was back down in the lab the first time we were together?"

Suzie nodded. "Don't worry, I won't say a word. This is amazing, though. I wish I could tell Stuart."

"I'd like to know what this Ruya guy has to do with it. If he's Lendon's boss, I bet he knows more than anyone about what's going on."

Suzie adjusted her baseball cap, which she still wore over her hair, now cut short to remove the mess made by the terrorists.

"Can I have my cap back?"

"No," she threw him a smile. "Ruya, eh?"

"I bet he's a big part of whatever happened to my family."

Suzie took his hand. "Once we get to your sister's in New York, we'll start putting things together again."

"Yeah," Alister put his hand on hers, its soft warmth reminding him of the comfort they'd shared. "What happened to Nehir?"

"More troops arrived a couple of hours ago. His brother's here, vouched for him. The general has him filling in the team leaders and Stuart about the Follower set-up."

"General? Stuart?"

"Cape? You met him a few months ago."

Alister shook his head.

"Cape leads the Peoples Infantry. My uncle Stuart heads up

the hackers. We're working together on the rescue."

"We?"

Suzie smiled, "Is this your way of saying you want to kiss me again so you can remember more?"

"Do I need an excuse?"

"Peoples Infantry, Stuart Emerson, Situationists? My Uncle Stuart, a hacker, helps the PI hack gang networks and sabotage raids. Hacked the Follower perimeter security. It's how Magpie and her lot got in."

"Oh."

"Yes, oh indeed. Nehir's probably boring the pants off them with more detail than they need. That man can talk the hind legs off a donkey."

"You're not kidding."

Suzie looked up over Alister's shoulder. "Talk of the devil."

He followed her gaze and spotted Nehir weaving around the tables towards them with a small tray of food and a big smile on his face. Striding towards them, Nehir bumped one of the air filters and quickly reached out to steady it, apologising to the surrounding people.

"What are those things?" Alister said.

"Air purifiers. Protect against those nano-chemicals and hallucinogenics the terrorists use," Suzie said. "Stop those visions people keep having."

"Yeah, the terrorists did inject me with all types of stuff."

"Oh, the injections, aye," Suzie said. "That'd trip you out for sure."

Nehir fell into the seat opposite Alister. "Look at this," he beamed. "I'm out. It's wonderful. And I met my brother. I'm so glad he's here. I feel so much better; I'd forgotten what happiness felt like. It's like a dark cloud has cleared from my mind. Back with normal people." He looked around. "Almost anyway. My life can begin again, I…"

"Nehir, calm down," Suzie said. "How did you get on with the briefing?"

"They asked so many questions. General Cape is such a nice man. Your uncle Stuart was there. He is a quiet man. And I couldn't understand some of what he was saying. His accent is so much stronger than yours. Alister, it's so good to see you again. How are you? I'm so glad you escaped."

"I'm okay." Gaps and dark spaces still spread like fissures across his memories, stranding him far away from them, anchored only by what he felt for Suzie.

Suzie put her arm around Alister's waist, giving him a hug. "Hey, you alright?"

"Yeah, this amnesia thing—I think I'm getting used to it, then it hits me out of nowhere. We were talking about the hallucinations. Suzie was going to tell me what she'd seen."

"Wulvers and a kelpie," Suzie said.

"What?" Nehir turned to Alister, who shook his head and shrugged.

"A wolver is a man with a wolf's head. They're friendly, leave food for poor people." Suzie shifted in her seat, "The kelpie, though, was amazing, like a clear ice statue of a horse come to life. It would catch the light as it moved, and rainbow flashes would glint inside its crystal, watery body."

"Brilliant. I only saw some punk angel, a grumpy demon, and some Indian guy."

Suzie let out a short laugh and said. "The sooner we are out of here, the better."

Alister nodded. "Being somewhere warm with decent food would make a big difference."

"Aye, and normal people and not a place full of squaddies and Veterans."

Alister looked around, "I wonder if all these people have seen stuff. What about you, Nehir? You were with the Followers for months."

"I never saw anything."

"Really?" Suzie said. "You must be one of the few people not to have seen anything."

"I think it's because I have something called hepatolenticular degeneration."

"Hepa, what?" Alister asked.

"Wilson's Disease, I can't eliminate copper from my system. I have a treatment implant in my chest just below my armpit. Feel." He raised his arm and pointed to a spot.

Alister carefully moved his finger over the sweatshirt and the oval bump under Nehir's skin. "Well, that's creepy."

"People have all kinds of drug implants. Not like mine, though. Mine actually produces the treatment from my own cells. Never needs to be refilled or anything."

Opposite Suzie at the table behind Nehir, one of the hostages, a short man, unusually clean-shaven for a hostage and dressed in ill-fitting clothes, stared at Suzie for a few seconds before quickly looking back down at his food.

"Oh, I forgot to say, I had to tell you," Nehir continued. "No more airships are flying out tonight. We're going to Vegas first, then to New York."

"Why can't we fly straight from here?" Alister said.

"Not enough fuel stored here for the airships to fly back with," Nehir took a mouthful of food. "It was such a relief to hear you got out, Alister," he continued. "You were lucky to be rescued by those Panthers. Man, those guys look scary. They must work out every day."

"Probably," Suzie smiled and looked out the window, "It's hard to imagine an army of Followers gathering a few miles away."

Alister glanced down at the filter. People were only mildly stressed at the fact an army of terrorists was getting ready to attack. What else were those filters releasing into the air?

It seemed the whole idea of thinking straight was just a fantasy. Invisible things were controlling his entire life; things people like Graham, his sister, and even Lendon knew more about than he did: the nanoparticles, the demons and angels saying he'd be needed for something, and this Ruya guy everyone kept mentioning. The guy had told his dad someone else was meant to get these particles; the creatures on the beach said the same thing. Was something bigger going on, something his dad had dragged him into by accident long ago?

"Al?" Suzie put her hand on his. "You were miles away."

"What? I was wondering if I'd ever figure out what happened to me."

***

Eight billion miles from Earth, the Wrychun probe, like a gigantic serpent the length of a football pitch, stretched and curled through the heliopause into the Termination Shock, the outer shell of the solar system where the Sun's solar winds collide with particles swarming through the spaces between stars, slowing and heating under pressure.

Quantum resonance filaments spread across the scales covering the probe, captured waves of dark energy and channelled the particles down thick black fuel veins into the spinal drive.

Blinded by the cosmic turbulence, the probe shifted its head side to side, the honeycomb array of sensors failing to detect the life signs from what appeared to be the corroded, meteor-mottled debris of a slow, tumbling space cruiser.

The twisted, jangled mess of wreckage instinctively curved away from the snake's detection range. Deep inside the bricolage space cruiser, behind layers of invisible shielding that rippled around the hull, a pea-sized red light blinked on the central console of the bridge.

In a small cabin, the soft voice of the Prajnid sensor on the shelf penetrated Foss's dream and woke him, as it did Keasha, curled up beside him.

"Proximity alert, Foss," the Prajnid said. "You should check it out; it may be serious."

"I'll go," Foss said.

"Mm," Keasha mumbled, "damned Prajnid."

Foss yawned and stretched. He swiped back the strands of his long black hair caught in the stubble across his face and peered at the little Prajnid light.

"Red?"

He scratched the side of his jaw and put on a jacket and trousers, the baggy clothes covered in pockets, small straps, and hooks. He shuffled into the bridge and checked the instruments, swearing under his breath at a static blue light on the screen.

"No wonder I'm cold." He slid his hands along the dial. Nothing happened, so he crawled under the console. Pulling a small spanner from his back pocket, he flicked on the built-in illuminator and prised apart a pair of soft metal pipes to rub away some dirt with a misty cloth. He let the cloth float in the low gravity while he tightened a nut and adjusted the release on a small piston. Getting to his feet, he turned a dial, and the bridge immediately warmed. Foss swept up the misty cloth and slipped the spanner through, so it gleamed.

In the cabin, Keasha dozed under the blanket, a sweeping flow of brush-stroke curves and shades outlining her slender figure. The egg-shaped Prajnid glowed softly on the bedside shelf, flashing a red alert dot that circled slowly around the top, reacting to a few of the neutrinos emitted from the Wrychun probe.

Foss slid a button up a screen to zoom in on the probe; shades of red, green, and blue bloomed and spread across its oily rainbow-black scales. "Unbelievable," he murmured. He turned and threw the tiny spanner, the size of his little finger, towards Keasha. The spanner spun lazily through the air in a smooth arc and bounced gently on her shoulder. "Keasha, wake up. I've got an ancient Wrychun probe on the screen."

Keasha woke up, sensing the gravitational conditions and, from his voice, Foss's location and position. How the spanner touched her instantly revealed a wealth of knowledge, including the size, weight, velocity and angle of approach, force and duration of impact, and angle of departure.

"That's nice," she mumbled. Eyes still shut, she raised a lazy hand and caught the spanner. She curled it through her fingers and flicked it back along the exact same route. Then, she turned to face the wall, pulling the blanket over her shoulder, leaving her slender face and the small scar above her left cheek visible. "We're on holiday, remember?"

"This one's still fully functional." Foss watched the spanner glide back and caught it. Her elegance seemed to infect everything she touched. "It could be heading for a blue-green planet," he said. "Third rock from the Sun."

"Blue-green?" Keasha groaned, "Why is there so much life in the universe?" She sat up and ran a hand over her cropped scalp, and the soft points of her ears twitched. "My head is killing me."

"I'm not surprised. I threw a lot of bottles into the recycler last night. Get over here. This time, I'm the one that needs you."

"Very funny," Keasha slipped her arms and head through a long pale-blue T-shirt. "Turn the heating up, love."

"Just did."

The blanket over her shoulders stretched and undulated like a cape in her wake as she glided across the bridge. Starved of gravity, her T-shirt clung to the front of her body as she moved; it slowly slipped along her thighs, stomach, and breasts, failing to catch in the curves. She grabbed the end of the T-shirt and pulled it down while, with a simple lift from her toes, she rose into the air and glided sideways to settle in the seat beside Foss.

He glanced over. "Hello, gorgeous."

She gave him a wink, leaned on the console, took a deep breath, rubbed her eyes, turned up the gravity, and relaxed back into her chair. "That's better. Now, let's have a look at this thing." She scanned the display, tapping buttons and sliding dials around the control screen. "Wrychuns," she grumbled, "forever hunting down magical talismans, wanting to colonise every universe out there."

"What do you think?" Foss asked.

"That we shouldn't have parked here to top up the fuel cells and gone straight to Orryn for our honeymoon. This'll only take a minute." Keasha's fingers danced across the screen. "Why don't you get me a drink while I'm doing this?"

"For you, anything." Foss leaned over and kissed her cheek. "Orryn will still be there whenever we arrive."

Keasha smiled and shot him a sideways glance before fixing her eyes on the patterns weaving around the large, transparent display hanging on the wall. Several strings of numbers scrolled across the bottom of a star chart, and with a nod, Keasha pressed a green dot on the console to load up the space-time point where the String-Condensate Anomaly opened up inside the black hole.

"When you load up the fast-forward algorithm to see if any talisman-making chunks came this way," Foss called from the galley, "remember to factor in the dark energy variable."

"Smart arse."

Keasha adjusted some variables and sat back while the formula elaborated across the screen. The thought of the Anomaly made her shudder, "Imagine Wrychuns colonizing entire galaxies in other universes." She pulled the blanket around her shoulders and turned her attention to the screen. Soft waves of colour speckled with probability sparks merged, dissolved, and then merged again to form relative certainties.

When Foss returned with two mugs of hot Sura, he found Keasha leaning on her elbow and biting her thumbnail. He put one cup down and saw the expression on her face. "That doesn't look good."

"You're not wrong." Keasha nodded. "Pretty big elements crashed into this habitable planet around 65 million years ago."

"Habitable that long?" Foss turned to his screen. "Prajnid, what information do you have on the third planet from the Sun of this Solar System?"

"Please wait," the computer replied. "Earth currently experiencing an Ice Age that began eleven Earth years ago. Population four point three billion."

"What about Vaaleans, Prajnid?" Keasha said.

"Vaaleans came through the micro-portals and spread planet-wide 65 million years ago. Believed by local inhabitants to be religious or fictional creatures created by imagination, supernatural forces or divine intervention."

"Great," Keasha leaned back, pulled the blanket around her, and reached for the mug.

Lines dotted with blue and yellow spots swirled across a grid covered in symbols, then settled into an undulating circle. Foss tapped on the screen. "Based on its current trajectory and factoring in the gravitational force of the outer planets, the probe might get close enough to detect the talisman elements."

"I'll wait until the probe's a safe distance away, then set a missile on it," Keasha said. "Solve all our problems."

She punched some numbers into the missile system and leaned back," There you go, all done."

"Here's some good news," Foss said, "There's a contact there, some guy called Raymond Ruya from Carounia."

"Raymond Ruya?" Keasha looked across to Foss' screen. "I remember when he was a kid back on Carounia. He must have evacuated here during the Wrychun invasion."

"Wonder why he didn't go home?" Foss clicked on the name, and another window bloomed onto the screen. "Seems he's built a Kyros Supercomputer, a marine model. Calls it Janus."

Keasha's eyes widened. "Wow, a marine ecosystem supercomputer. I'd love to dive into that. We should call in."

Foss imagined her deep diving into the clear azure waters of the Janus supercomputer. Swimming amongst the schools of glimmering marine algorithms through clouds of rainbow-coloured jellyfish data clusters as their long pink tendrils gathered redundant nano-processor zooplankton. Would the thin beams of gold and blue laser light scanning patterns in the multiplicity of waves and undulations in everything that moved find her as beautiful and graceful?

Keasha dropped the blanket over the chair. "I'm off to have a shower. Coming?"

Foss couldn't help but stare at her slender, muscular body, toned and perfected since childhood in the Warrior Sanctum. He jumped to his feet. "For you, anything."

"I know."

Chapter Ten

Grey-blue streaks of pre-dawn lingered in the cragged distance, haunting the horizon. Amorphous shades pinked, thinned, and surrendered to the morning's hazy glow, releasing a cold light to stretch across the barren white landscape. Shadows oozed and sank away from the airbase, exposing the tops of defence and transmission towers to an orange-red glow. The gloomy, bronzed bodies of motionless Gold Hawk airships rested like giant sleeping insects in the yellow-ringed landing bay. Four waspish solar wings folded along either side of each airship, covering the broad, scaled steel-glass pipes and oval orbs of steam beneath. Maintenance crews emerged from workshops, buttoning up yellow and black overalls, putting on helmets, and checking tool belts. Exchanging tired, coarse words, they formed into small groups and approached the airships before breaking off towards different parts, some going inside, others to the wings and engine panels. Baseball-sized spotlights along the big yellow X of the landing bay lit with dull clangs while a softer light illuminated the steel-glass bellies and Nu-Iron and brass pipes beneath the airships. Thin lines of Veterans emerged to move between the buildings and munitions boxes stacked in short rows.

Magpie sat by the window in a small office, cleaning her assault rifle and chatting with Suzie, who stood beside her, looking out across the dawn and floodlit airfield. The door opened, and Alister and Nehir came in, each carrying a hot drink in a plastic cup. Nehir, as usual, was in a chatty mood.

"I bet your sister was pleased to hear from you," Nehir said.

"It felt strange talking to her. I started to remember stuff, but it was a really poor connection," Alister replied. "I barely managed to say 'hi, I'm okay' before all this crackling made it impossible to talk. I could hardly make out what she was saying, and then we were cut off. At least she knows I'm alright. And like I said, she'd be happy for you to stay with us for as long as you like."

Alister and Suzie exchanged a quick smile, which did not go unnoticed by Magpie. She nudged Suzie and whispered something that had them both speaking quietly.

Nehir gave him a sideways look. "What time did you get

back last night?"

Alister shrugged. "Late. Me and Suzie talked for hours," he said, then quickly added, "How did you get on?"

"I had a long talk with my brother. I, too, could only make one call, so I called my sister. She was pleased to hear I was okay and said she'd let our brother know. I spoke to my nieces, too. They are such lovely kids. My dad would have…" Nehir fell silent and shook his head. When he spoke again, his voice was quieter. "He'd changed so much after mum died—so unhappy, always angry with everyone."

Alister pulled two chairs out from under a table and sat down. Nehir took the hint and sat beside him. He put the hot chocolate down and continued holding it, staring into the brown liquid.

Alister reached out and put his hand on Nehir's arm. "It's out of your hands, Nehir. You tried for a whole year, and it didn't work out. I'm sorry."

Nehir shook his head. "I didn't have to leave, but you were right. Staying with Dad wasn't changing anything. The only thing that changed was my worrying about him more each day. Maybe if I was more of a man in his eyes."

"You were the only one in the family to try, Nehir," Suzie said from across the room. "You put him first. You stayed."

"I did. I tried really hard. But the Followers, all that loud preaching and prayers and chanting and reading." He shook his head and fell into another silence.

"But you're out," Alister said. "You can start over."

Nehir took a deep breath and managed to smile. "Yes, with some good friends." He looked over to Suzie. "Are you going to try contacting family again, Suzie? How many sisters do you have? Three?"

"There's three of us altogether," Suzie responded. "Hopefully, I'll be able to speak with them when the link is back up. Can't call anywhere outside the US yet. I can't wait to speak to my ma. You'll be alright, Nehir. We'll help, won't we, Ally?"

Alister blew across the top of his drink and nodded. Nehir smiled and took a big gulp of hot chocolate. Alister leaned back, yawned, and stretched his arms out. "Dunno about you," he said, "only four hours sleep, then the whole base wakes up. What's going on out there, Suze?"

A broad smile crossed Suzie's face.

"What?"

"You just called me 'Suze'. That's the old you; you're remembering."

"Did I?" Alister's eyes scanned the matt-grey table top as if the answer had been written there. "I never noticed."

"To answer your question, Romeo," Magpie said, "heavy weapons have been positioned around the entire area. Once the rest of the Hawks arrive with the last hostages, they'll plan the trip to Vegas, and I'll join my squad. We're waiting for more P. I and camo-suits to turn up."

"Aren't you worried about the Followers?" Alister said.

"People are on watch and patrolling the perimeter. Can't see through their jammers, and visibility is poor for both sides. We're waiting for scouts to come back with intel on their numbers and munitions. They'll have to switch the jammers off to start communicating themselves. The Panthers are doing what they can to make life difficult for the Followers. So for now, we sit tight and wait."

A deep humming outside grew louder, and Magpie clipped a strap on the reassembled N-Rec7, slung it over her shoulder, and crossed to the window. "That'll be the Gold Hawk bringing in the last hostages. Let's hit the mess hall now before it crowds out."

The Gold Hawk glided over the buildings, the sunlight reflecting washed-out rainbow shades through its translucent wings.

"Don't you think it's strange?" Alister asked. "They could have put up one helluva fight at the domes."

"Yeah, well, those last ones are lucky," Magpie replied. "The bulk of the Follower army coming to surround the base and nearby fortress made it easier to get the hostages out."

***

Rows of metal tables and chairs stretched under the glow of long fluorescent lights in the busy mess hall. Tired hostages, regular soldiers, and Peoples' Infantry Veterans stood guard by the doors. In the far corner, Magpie sat beside Suzie, leaning back and listening to Nehir, who had cheered up and now chatted animatedly.

"So I put some liquorice and other spices in their curry that had them stopping every half hour to use the toilet. They took turns; one crouched behind a rock, and the other watched for wild animals or demons."

"They think those things are real. Nutcases."

Alister glanced at her and said nothing.

"But wild animals?" Magpie said, smiling. "There's hardly any left."

"That's not what I told them," Nehir said. "Teach them for forbidding cable TV back home. I had to go to a friend's to watch TV with his family, and they were hooked on the most awful reality shows. So humiliating. I didn't know what was worse. Anyway, I said the meat was off, so they began to shout at the man who bought the lab-lamb."

Magpie grimaced. "Those protein-tank meats taste awful."

A long, broken row of hunched and tired figures shuffled into the mess hall; some wearing their own clothes, others dressed in army fatigues. The line spread outside and past the window, blocking the view of the airstrip and Gold Hawks beyond. The murmuring took a lighter tone as the hostages moved closer to the serving counter and trays of steaming food. More catering staff appeared behind the counter and began to serve the newly arrived hostages.

"Okay, guys," Magpie said, "let's get back to the briefing room; looks like they'll need all the tables for those folk."

Outside, the new arrivals huddled in small groups while soldiers patrolled the airfield. Alister and the group stopped when a loud boom resonated across the base, and a small plume of smoke rose up into the sky several hundred yards away from the airfield. Around them, soldiers glanced up and instinctively raised their weapons while hostages anxiously clung together, gazing towards the tower of smoke that leaned and frayed in the wind. Then, a deep hum rolled across the base, followed by two Gold Hawks rising low and gracefully over the protective shelter of the hills, their wings reflecting and refracting the warm glow of dawn and releasing thin trails of watery blue n-steam.

"Something's not right," Alister said.

"You're not kidd—"

A pulsing blare of sirens drowned out Magpie's words. The noise punched across the base as another explosion, this time closer, sent people cowering to the ground. Screams and cries erupted around them while the final Gold Hawk tilted towards the landing bay overhead.

The sirens faded into the chilling wind, and a voice announced, "All personnel report to designated command zones. Any unaccompanied civilians, please follow the yellow lines to shelters." Soldiers and Peoples Infantry were already on their feet; they shouted instructions and hurried hostages towards shelters while smaller explosions blasted the airfield's perimeter.

"Follow me," Magpie commanded. She ran up to Alister, who was staring across the airfield and grabbed his arm.

"There's a pattern," he murmured.

"Aw hell," Magpie said, sensing he was having another insight from who knows where and how. "Wait there," she called to Suzie and Nehir, crouched by a landing light a few yards away. Magpie and Alister stood motionless amid the pandemonium, scanning the airfield and buildings and absorbing every detail: the number and location of soldiers; hostages; whether they were men, women, or children; the speed and direction of their movement; the delay rate and fall pattern of explosions; the safest areas.

Three explosions isolated the third Gold Hawk, forcing hostages and soldiers in all but one direction. The fall of missiles along one side of the airfield was less random, driving people away from a small, single-storey building built against a ridge at the far end of the base past the vehicle pound.

"We're being forced away from over there," Alister shouted, pointing to the building.

Magpie peered towards it. "What the…? That's heavy shelling you're looking through."

"There's a pattern. Magpie, the bombs are moving everybody away from that building. I can get us through. Come on."

"Stop," Magpie shouted, and all four waited beside a group of stragglers held out of the way by soldiers. Three house-sized cannons rumbled past, fat caterpillar wheels grinding across the tarmac. The shunt and hiss of massive pistons driven by nano-gasses threw bursts of warm, citric air as the monstrous vehicles curved away and round to pass a nearby Gold Hawk, where the last of the hostages had clustered beside a soldier.

"My God," Nehir shouted. "What were they?"

"NLOS, non-line-of-sight cannons," Magpie said. "XXL size by the looks of it."

Nehir shifted his gaze from the cannons to stare at the hostages and soldiers gathering under the chopper's wings. He raised his hand to point and was about to say something when Magpie's stern voice snapped through the noise. "Follow Alister," she said, and the four of them raced across the tarmac, zigzagging through the streaming crowds and into a barren field of small craters and smouldering rubble. Shock waves from explosions around the perimeter sent bursts through the surrounding air, putting everything out of focus. Heading for the building was like running across the surface of a giant drum. They moved towards the low grey building in a stop-start rush through the maze of craters, explosions, and small plumes, veering around the water tower that creaked and groaned in vibrations.

Alister slapped his hand on the lock, and the particles swarmed through it. There was a click, and the door swung open. Magpie stared at Alister, slammed the door shut, and scanned the room. Benches ran along two walls, and two tables with hard plasteel tops and sturdy steel legs sat in the middle of the room. They looked capable of holding some heavy gear. Half a dozen chairs surrounded the tables. In one corner stood a pipe-fed water cooler. Old computer cables along the wall suggested that the room used to be an office or monitoring station.

"Get away from the windows and door," Magpie said. "Nehir, Al, help me shift these tables and build a shelter." As they pushed tables together and tipped three over to put a wall against the side facing the windows, she asked, "Nehir, what the hell were you doing out there?"

Nehir spoke in short bursts, stopping to catch his breath. "Those hostages…in the last Gold Hawk…back there—I recognised them, they're Followers, elite guards."

Alister crossed the room to the door at the far end, where the building leaned against the hillside. It had a keypad system with a palm recognition handle under a retinal scan camera. "There's something down there." He turned to help Nehir upturn a table against the window but ended up leaning over it. "I don't feel too good."

"Don't you dare pass out, Al. Any idea what's with the level

9 door into the side of a mountain? And you need to explain your trick with the lock."

Alister collapsed to his knees, then fell sideways.

"Shit," Magpie said. "Suzie, see to your man. Nehir, you're with me. Grab the other end of this table."

Suzie knelt beside Alister. "Just rest a while. Do you want some water?"

"Nah," Alister mumbled, his head lolling forwards.

"Followers," Nehir said.

"What are you saying, Nehir?" Magpie asked.

Alister sat up, and his head slumped against the wall. "That's why they took away my—everybody's—ID," he said with his head tilted back. "So the Followers could steal their identities and get here into Area 51. Plotinus planned the whole thing so hostages would be brought here first." He slid sideways to lie on the bench, and his head thumped against the top.

Magpie looked from Alister to the solid door with the maximum-security locks.

"You've really landed us in it now," she touched her earpiece. "Can anybody copy? This is Magpie, I'm in the… Shit, it's chaos out there."

"Ally," Suzie said. "Ally, what's wrong?"

"Dunno," Alister managed to say. A weightless wave pushed through him, washing away his thoughts and leaving a sensation of flying upwards. Then, briefly, there was nothing but a radiant white glow.

Chapter Eleven

The beach again. The roll of a glittering azure sea, the splash of waves and hiss of seawater retreating across warm silvery-gold sand, soft blue sky. Ahead of him, Raguel, the leather-clad angel he'd seen earlier, stood beside the same pale red-grey demon. The two creatures gazed at an enormous galleon sailing slowly along the horizon. Towering, dusty grey sails filled by a rolling wind laced with ribbons of oily smoke that seemed to have a serpentine life of its own, slithering in the wind as the monstrosity swept along the horizon, leaving a swirling, grim, murky haze in its wake.

"It seems you were right, after all, Raggy. The Nightmares are gathering again, rising from beyond the nine realms." The demon tutted, "If they've got it right, then we really are fuh...well, well, look who's here."

Raguel looked over his shoulder, spread his wings, and lifted a few feet into the air, turning to face Alister.

"What?" was all Alister could manage, unable to choose which question to ask from the multitude swirling through his mind.

The demon lowered his head and shook it. "I tell ya, Ruya really has screwed things up, Raggy."

"Is this real?" Alister said, "What's going on?"

"He doesn't even know the basics?" the demon said, exasperated. "Can you believe this guy?" He stabbed his trident into the sand. "Raggy, do you really think this, this..." He threw his hand in the air. "This excuse for a human has a hope in hell of getting it right? We can't help him stop the Lightning Seed. He's barely ready."

"Lightning Seed?" Alister asked. Was this the LS Suzie had mentioned?

"The Lightning Seed," Raguel said, "is an ancient device that can open a planet-sized portal to another universe – perhaps destroy both in the process. "

"How do you know all this?"

"Jump to the end, Raggy," Zen said impatiently, "We know how to disable it without the tech."

"What? How?"

"Haven't you heard?" Zen said, "We're spooky, get around,

have connections. Which also means we learn stuff, can work together on all kinds of quantum levels. We're legion."

"So you can stop it from going off?"

"Yes," Raguel said, "But we need a human outside, on your side, to make the connection. It's why Ruya..."

"Wanted to find the Lightning Seed." Zen quickly interrupted. "To keep it safe."

"Okay," Alister said, "so what are the nightmares?"

"The Nightmares. They have manipulated the dreams of tyrants for centuries. Now they speak to Plotinus."

"No, this really is crazy. Are you guys for real?"

"Of course, more real than you realize," Raguel said.

"So," Alister said, "do you live in some other dimension or realm?"

"Dimensions!" The demon turned to the angel, "I told you, Raguel, he really has no idea."

"Let me explain," Raguel said, "There are nine realms spread across an infinity of universes. But your tiny galactic clustery here has a layer of every one of the nine realms. There's no other place like it anywhere."

"Yeah," the demon interrupted. "And that makes it ultra powerful and ultra bloody fragile, too. It's why there's so much weird stuff everywhere and why we don't go anywhere else. Don't gawp at me like that."

"No, this is some drugged-up trip," Alister said. "You're not real, you can't be. Just a mash-up of stuff I've heard, forgotten, and made up."

The demon waved his hand dismissively. "Yeah, you wish."

"No, I'm not getting into this. This is just a dream, just a dream."

"Repeating it won't make us go away, y'know." Zen shook his head. "If it weren't for us turning up back in the day, you'd all be bleedin' reptiles, and you wouldn't even be dreaming." Zen turned to Raguel, "This clown is Ruya's solution?" He shook his head. "Ruya should just call Sam and be done with it."

"The mechanic?" Raguel shook his head, "the anarchist?"

"Anarcho-syndicalist."Zen said, "Or Val if she doesn't already have a finger in this pie. Maybe she--."

Raguel dismissed Zen's irritation and answered Alister. "You are on the shores of the collective unconscious, where.."

***

Water splashed over his face, and he came round, looking up at Suzie kneeling beside him, holding an empty cup. The explosions had stopped.

"What happened, Al?" Suzie said, helping him to the bench.

"Not sure. What's going on?"

"Magpie's taken Nehir to General Wakefield. She'll be back with support. I said I'd stay with you until she returns."

"Thanks."

"How are you?"

"Apart from getting knocked out in a white light, fine," he said. "Lightning Seed, that's what the terrorists are after here." There was other stuff buried too deep to remember.

"The Lightning Seed?" Suzie said.

"Yes, it will—"

Machine-gun fire peppered the door with holes, sending a strange ripple through Alister's head. Adrenalin kicked in, and the nanoparticles responded instantly. In less than a second, the Soft-Machine coiled around his limbs, ready to protect him from gunfire and accelerate his movements. His consciousness danced wildly like a juggler catching tenpins coming at him from all directions; then everything fell into place perfectly. By the time the door had smashed open, he'd spun round and saw three figures through the window by the door, like a 3D image. In front was a terrorist, his foot almost back on the ground after kicking the door open. Two more terrorists followed. Suzie stood frozen in fear beside Alister.

Every single thing around him was a bubble of possibility. He stood in a vast foam of possibilities, where anything could happen. Burst a bubble at the right point, and all the other bubbles will follow. He was the perfect point of conscious choice and decided to burst the terrorists' bubble.

He kicked a table onto its side and pulled Suzie to the ground behind it, then dived over, rolled onto his feet, swerved, and yanked the machine gun from the first man coming through the door, knocking him down. He thumped the base of the man's skull with his rifle, and the man keeled over, unconscious. Before the man even hit the ground, Alister gripped the door frame and swung through to connect the sole of his foot with the face of the man about to enter, knocking him into the yard. He crouched, pulled a pistol from the man's holster, and shot a third terrorist struggling with the clip of his assault rifle. Reality reeled back to normal speed.

"Suzie?"

Suzie stood up from behind the table when he called her name. She stretched her arms out to him. "Thank God."

He smiled and raised his hand towards hers. "Well, that wasn't so—" There was a loud snap, and his back arched like he'd been punched, then Alister jolted forward and hit the floor.

"Ally!" Suzie screamed.

The second terrorist, his face bloodied, stepped over Alister and staggered into the room. With his free hand pressed against his face, he approached Suzie and raised his assault rifle. He shoved the muzzle into her stomach. "The Lord moves in mysterious ways and has blessed me with the honour of punishing a pagan whore."

She recognised him as the man staring at her back in the rescue tent the previous evening.

The man ignored Suzie's defiant glare, grabbed her shoulder, spun her round, and punched the back of her head so she stumbled forward against the door. With the muzzle brake pressed into the back of her neck, he pulled her wrist down and pressed his body hard onto her, pushing her flat against the door.

"Enjoying yourself?" she said.

"I've had better." He forced her hand onto the door handle. "Keep it there," he snarled.

"But it's lock—"

"Shall I kill you now? I said hold it, you filthy whore."

Suzie grasped the handle, and cold metal wrapped around her wrist with a click. Face pressed against the door, she strained her eyes to see an explosive cord wrapped around her wrist with the other end tangled around the door handle. The fuse oil was already oozing through the cord's inner explosive ring.

"Move, and I'll blow your brains out." The smell of his blood and pungent breath was warm on her face. The pressure against her neck and back of her body lifted, leaving a painful, dirty echo on her flesh. His boots clumped away, and she looked over her shoulder to see the bloodied face at the opposite end of the room, the rifle still pointed at her. The man wiped his face with his sleeve and flicked the safety catch on the right of the gun. Alister lay motionless on the floor. Tears rolled down her face.

The terrorist spat a globule of blood, shifted the strap of the assault rifle, and raised it, aiming at Suzie's head. He shifted his shoulder and prepared to fire. Suzie closed her eyes and heard a thump and something hitting a wall. She opened her eyes slowly to see Alister at the broken window, squinting into the thin, cold wind sweeping across the tarmac and blowing against his face. The terrorist lay in a heap against the wall.

"Ally?" She looked down at the explosive around her hand and then back to him with tears in her eyes.

Before Suzie could shout a warning, he moved across the room in a blur and grabbed the cord. The explosive fell to the ground with a light ping, and the lock connection burned into him, making him grimace in pain. "Run! Duck!" He grabbed her to him, wrapped his arms around her and dived back over the upturned table. Seconds later, the cord exploded, and the door bent outwards and blasted from the wall, shunting the table against them.

Ears ringing, they stood up in the wind-torn smoke rising from the debris, and Suzie flung her arms around him. "My God, I thought you were dead," she said through the tears. "I thought you were dead. He shot you in the back."

"Did he? I never..."

Suzie hugged him, kissed his face, and then his mouth. She pulled away when Magpie and Raven appeared with another soldier. Aside from Raven, they were dressed in grey, lightly armoured urban combat gear. Raven wore a darker grey outfit and balanced a heavier assault rifle on her shoulder. They stepped over the bodies and entered the room. Ignoring Alister and Suzie, Raven hooked her boot under the shoulder of a Follower and kicked him over onto his back. She swung the rifle down and poked him hard with the muzzle, leaving dark stains on the unconscious man's jacket from the brake.

"Save the celebrations, you two," Magpie said. "What happened here? Where are the guys who took these three out?"

"It was Ally," Suzie wiped her hand across her eyes and hooked her arm around his.

"Yeah?" Raven poured herself some water without taking her eyes off Alister.

"On your own?" Magpie said. "What, Karate, Ju Jitsu?" She and Raven were now both staring at him.

"Kenpo, I think," he said.

"Okay." Magpie nodded slowly, looking around. "Either of you injured?"

Suzie shook her head. "I'm okay, but Alister was—"

"I'm fine." Alister winced.

"But I heard—you fell," Suzie said. "Ally, what...?" She recognised the faint expression of 'I'll tell you later' on his face.

"Forget it," Magpie said.

"Is this the guy, ma'am?" Raven asked, eyeing Alister.

Magpie nodded. "Raven, Crow, meet Alister and Suzie. They're..." She paused and gave Suzie a quick smile, "close."

"Hi," Alister said, rubbing his eyes. He gave Suzie a quizzical look, and she squeezed his hand.

Crow replied with a barely noticeable upward nod. Raven's cold stare didn't waver.

"Ally," Suzie said when he picked up an assault rifle, "what are you doing?"

"He was going to kill you, Suzie," Alister turned the rifle in his hands.

"Drop the weapon, pal," Raven said.

Alister ignored her. "We're miles away from their madhouse, and they drop bombs on ordinary people waiting to go home. They'll never stop." He shook his head. "Magpie, I've changed my mind about guns."

Magpie responded with a simple nod.

"Boss," Raven said, "with all respect, you sure about this?"

"Alister," Suzie grabbed his arm, "don't. What are you doing?"

"Protecting us, protecting everyone worth caring about." He picked up a belt and pushed an extra-large cartridge into the slot under the barrel.

"Ally, this isn't you, don't do this."

They stared at each other, and Alister shook his head. "I'm sorry, Suzie, I can't let them... I'm not going to let this happen again."

"No," Raven said. "This is our work. You put that gun down right now. You don't know what you're doing."

"He can handle his gear," Magpie said, "Tell this soldier

what you got there, Al."

"N-Rec7 Mx50," Alister said, "latest model. Fires 40cv high-density shots, ultra-compression fifty-round cartridge. This one's fitted with a volt-suppressor fire at thirty-six hundred feet per second. The one I didn't pick up is the old M16A4."

"Alright, smart-ass," Raven said, tapping her gun. "What's this?"

"Heckler and Koch N-S3," Alister said without looking at Raven's weapon twice. He continued to examine the N-Rec7 in his hands while describing what Raven held. "Twenty-inch assault rifle with a thirty-six-round magazine. Looks like you sometimes use a well-worn, seventy-two-round low-profile drum on it. You've six 50cv shots left, by the way. Are we done?"

"No," Suzie said, and Magpie reached over and touched her arm. Suzie pulled away and glared at her.

"Suzie," Magpie said, "we don't go looking for trouble. Our job is to protect people, not kill them, not unless we or the people we are protecting are at immediate risk."

"Magpie," Alister said, "can I have a minute with Suzie?"

"Make it quick. Crow, Raven, you're with me."

Suzie grabbed his hands when they were alone. "Alister, please don't do this."

"Suzie, I'm doing this because I care about you. These Followers have to be stopped. I'll be fine. I have this outfit, the Soft-Machine; it morphs into my clothes. It changes to protect me, becomes bulletproof, and even turns me invisible. It works on its own, really fast."

"The Soft-Machine is real?" Suzie leaned back and looked at him. "The nanoparticles give you a connection and a way to control it. Is that how you didn't get shot?"

Alister nodded.

"Where did you find it? How did you…?"

"Time's up," Magpie said. "The Followers have split into groups. One has made it down there." She nodded to the blown-out door. "Half our troops are holding back the assault. Smoke is trying to get plans of the area down there so we can block them off and—" An explosion sent a bloom of warm air bursting into the room from the hole where the door used to be. Magpie glanced an order to Raven, who ran to the door, pressed against the wall, and then peered around before slowly descending the steps.

"Can't remember," Alister whispered.

Raven returned several seconds later. "All clear. Some of our people are on the lower levels of another cavern."

"What happened to that door?" Magpie asked.

"The terrorists rigged it," Suzie said, "with me stuck on it. Alister freed me before it blew."

Raven was about to speak, but Magpie raised her hand, and the room fell silent. "Say again?" She put her hand to her ear and lowered her head. "Roger that."

"Crow, cuff these guys and call in a collection. Then, get Suzie to the transit hangar. The rest of the squad are on their way. Go back the way you came, and you should be okay."

"Copy that, ma'am," Crow nodded.

"Magpie," Alister said, "the Followers are after the Lightning Seed, a WMD, down there."

"Okay, Al, follow orders."

Crow stood up, spoke into her earpiece, and headed for the door. "Stay behind me, Suzie." Suzie gave Alister one last hug and a long kiss, then fell in with Crow. A Jeep and a small van pulled up outside. Three soldiers emerged and entered the room's wreckage to drag the Followers out. Suzie and Crow went past them and climbed into the Jeep.

Alister watched it drive off, then turned to face the doorway that led down into the darkness and the Lightning Seed, the stuff of nightmares, angels, and demons.

Chapter Twelve

"WMD, eh?" Raven said.

"The Lightning Seed," Alister said. "It's some kind of alien bomb."

"You know a lot for a guy with amnesia," Raven said.

Magpie shot her a look. "Al, has this anything to do with the briefing cancelled because of this damned attack?"

Alister shrugged. "Maybe."

Raven swore, grabbed his collar, spun him around and slammed him against the wall. She snapped out her pistol and stabbed the muzzle into his neck.

Alister's shock dissolved into that familiar, delicious, reckless buzz of energy, and he fought against the impulse to go with it.

"Why don't I just shoot you now?" Raven snarled, yanking her shoulder out of Magpie's grasp.

"Dare you to try," he muttered under his breath.

"Who the hell are you working for?"

"Raven, stand down," Magpie said.

"How does he know all this stuff, boss? He's triple-A with guns, takes out three armed terrorists barehanded, disarmed an explosive, probably survived being shot, knows his way around Halfbeak and this place, too. Led you here knows all about the Lightning Seed—or whatever the damn thing is. The hell he doesn't remember anything. How do we know he's not one of them?"

He moved his head ever so slightly to see her from the corner of his eye, and the muzzle scratched his skin.

"I said stand down, soldier!" Magpie said. "He's clean."

Clean as a whistle.

"Amnesia, my ass. He's a sleeper, another damned spy playing us along until the time is right. Why else would he end up here and want to go down there with us?"

Alister looked up. She could have a point, but she'd be wrong.

"Back off, Raven," Magpie repeated. "That's an order."

Raven glared at him, then poked him hard with her assault rifle, "I'm onto you, punk," she whispered and went to turn away.

That was a mistake.

There was a flash of movement. Either he spun around real fast, or the room did. Raven's face appeared in front of him for an instant. She grabbed his arm. Magpie came into focus, then flew across the room. Raven again, her face in pain, a rifle spinning away from him, darkness.

***

Alister awoke, leaning against the wall. Magpie was across the room, getting to her feet. Raven was slumped face down over the table, her rifle snapped off its strap and lying some distance from her.

"Magpie, what happened?"

"Damned if I know, it was all too fast." Magpie picked up her rifle. "You cut some kind of move using Raven's reaction as a counterbalance and threw me back against the wall when I tried to get between you."

"Sorry," Alister said. "Something happens when I'm in danger. Is she okay?"

Magpie crossed over to Raven and checked her wrist monitor, "She'll live." She turned Raven round. "Here, give me a hand to get her to that chair."

Raven slumped on the chair. "Sorry, Raven," Alister fitted a working strap onto her rifle and put it on her lap. Raven looked from the gun to Alister and rubbed the bruise on her chin. There was an awkward silence.

"I'll get you a drink." Alister crossed over to the water cooler. Filling a cup for himself, he downed the last propranolol and took the other filled cup to Raven.

Raven glanced at Magpie, then downed the water and wiped her mouth. "You're damn fast. I'll give you that." She crushed the empty cup and tossed it into the bin. "Your face went all weird."

"I lose control and black out. It's happened before, down in Halfbeak, three big guys, all pretty badly beaten up. I didn't think it was me..." He trailed off.

"Trust me, it was you." Raven got to her feet and dusted her shoulder.

Alister noticed for the first time the marine insignia she

wore, an anchor with a long knife as a shank, the crown and arm along the bottom forming the base of an egg.

"We've wasted enough time as it is. Let's check this out," Magpie said. "Raven, you're on six. I'll take point. Al, stay here. You've collapsed once and went all ninja on us. I can't risk you down there."

Magpie shot her hand up, and they fell silent. Footsteps were heading along a metal mesh surface towards the steps beyond the door. She gestured, and the three pressed against the wall on either side of the door.

Two Followers rushed up the stairs to be met with several blows that disarmed them and left them unconscious.

"The Seed's gone," Alister said.

"Right." Magpie knelt and began to go through the Follower's pockets. "Raven, frisk that one. Al, watch the door."

A memory stick lay on the first step beyond the door, and Alister picked it up. Didn't the prof say they'd taken it from him?

"They're scientific tools." He touched the bright burgundy surface, and a tingling flowed up his arm and rippled through his head. Hundreds of images and pages of text streamed through his mind. A few kept recurring: the Lightning Seed, Wrychuns, and Carounia. He staggered back, missing Magpie, and fell to sit at a table.

"You okay?" Magpie asked. "Whatchya got there?"

"The professor's memory stick." Alister took a sharp intake of breath.

A buzzing filled his head and faded away, leaving more stuff behind.

"What?" Magpie said.

Alister opened his eyes and stared at her; no time had passed. "Uh, nothing. We should get this to your boss."

How was that possible? The creatures in his head were right about what the Lightning Seed could do, how old it was. It was all real. Those angels, demons, and the Nightmares.

***

Around a hundred weary soldiers sat waiting in the dull, washed-out briefing room. Veterans' Peoples Infantry under General Cape and soldiers from the New National Army under General Wakefield. Tired faces, dressed in outfits grimy with dust and moisture, they reclined or leaned forward on plastic chairs barely big enough to seat the larger guys. Several sitting to the front along the wall had fresh bandages and plasters on their faces and around their heads. Unlike the younger soldiers, the People's Infantry Veterans were all in their forties and fifties. The men and women chatted and occasionally checked the screens. Water dripped from their uniforms to form thin streams and damp patches that crisscrossed the floor. A faint humidity in the air mingled with the odour of sweat and stale gunfight residue.

Wearing a long, fur-lined grey coat, Alister sat on one of the metal fold-out chairs along the back. Over to his left, two soldiers flanked a set of double doors. Along the wall to his right, a heater droned under one of the windows that stretched the room's length. Outside, a swirling wind scooped snow into the air and threw it around stationary Gold Hawks. In the distant corner of the airfield, prisoners bustled inside a crowded caged enclosure, waiting to be processed. Beside the enclosure were rows of medical tents set up to treat the casualties from both sides. Army soldiers patrolled a secondary inner perimeter fence, and more gun turrets had been placed along one side of the airfield.

"Are you saying the Lightning Seed is over six thousand years old?" General Wakefield sounded sceptical.

"Far older," Lendon said. "Initial analysis of trace particles on its surface indicate the device had been buried in sediments laid beneath the ocean floor millions, not thousands, of years old."

A murmuring rippled through the room. Wakefield stood up, and the room fell silent. "We'll need to know more before we can start speculating about alien weapon technology." He scanned the room. "I need not remind you all that this is a top-secret installation. Forget about how old this thing is; our job is to stop it from detonating. Professor."

"Thank you," Lendon continued. "The memory stick recorded what we believe are the tones to detonate the device. Before anyone asks, sensors attached to the seed detected a long repeating cycle of faint, inaudible sounds and corresponding clicks from within the device. We determined that the first three quarters described the standard model of particle physics. My team began to fill in the gaps where sounds seemed to be missing, and the first few notes triggered an unrecognisable radiation pulse, which destroyed all the electronics in the laboratory and generated a brief lightning storm. From what I overheard during captivity, Plotinus has experts who decrypted the full sequence that will activate the Seed."

Lendon stopped and took a sip of water. "The full sequence lasts two minutes. Once the Seed is fully activated, so to speak, we believe it will generate a pulse of unknown particles."

"Do we know what kind of damage this Lightning Seed can do?" someone asked.

"We have a pretty good guess," Wakefield said. "Lendon decrypted only ten per cent of the missing sequence. We calculate that if fully sequenced, the seed would generate a storm with several thousand lightning strikes varying between fifteen hundred and three hundred thousand amps."

"And," the professor added, "we have no idea how the release of a magnitude of unknown particles would have. The full sequence release might shift energy levels to generate particles beyond those we know of, with effects we cannot predict."

"So this lightning storm," someone else asked. "Is that a lot?"

"Deadly. Based on their calculations, the lightning storm generated is less than one-half of one per cent of what the Lightning Seed is capable of."

Wakefield and Cape exchanged glances.

Lendon continued. "The superheated air temperature in the air around a lightning strike can range from eight thousand to thirty thousand degrees Celsius, more than five times the surface temperature of the sun. Not to mention gamma-ray bursts that would be visible from space."

"And I didn't bring my sun cream," a voice in the room said, raising a murmur of laughter.

Lendon paused to look at Cape. Cape gave him a nod, and Lendon continued. "Plotinus may want to destroy a city, but there's no telling what kind of radiation might be released or how far the storm will spread if not controlled. The Seed can generate a lightning storm and reaction that could go global and destroy every living thing on the planet."

A tide of murmurs and swearing rippled around the room.

"With all comms down and no way of getting the message out," Cape said, "We are the only people with eyes on the target and a chance to stop it."

"My people are going after Red convoy," Wakefield said. "Commander Cape will oversee a squad that will track and intercept Blue convoy at the first safe opportunity."

Cape turned to Smoke. "Blue convoy will have to refuel somewhere between location one and two, here and here." He pointed to a map.

"Yes, sir," Smoke said.

The viewing-plate display crackled for several seconds and went blank. Wakefield ignored it and stood up. "That is all, gentlemen. Your group leaders will brief you on the details."

Commander Cape scanned the soldiers, "All remaining troops have been deployed to defend our position here. As some of you may know, the Panthers and Samurai, who occupy their own domes in the complex, have been more than helpful with the rescue. They contacted us before comms went down. Their last message reported they were now controlling the areas where most hostages were being held. It looks like the advantage and endgame is ours."

A cry of 'Oorah!' sounded across the room.

"Let's get to it, people," Cape said.

There was a shuffling and scraping of seats as the other soldiers moved around and left the room. Alister zigzagged through the mess of chairs and patches of water towards Magpie, who was speaking with Cape.

"Where's Suzie?"

"With Nehir and a small group of hostages in the comms block on the far side of the base," Magpie said. "If it weren't for the dead air, they'd be talking to family. Give me a minute here, and I'll take you over."

Through the window, two rows of Peoples Infantry and US soldiers headed towards a line of Jeeps and APCs. They checked their kits and weapons and then boarded the vehicles. The engines hissed and rumbled into life, and the vehicles sped out of the base to split into two pairs at a fork in the road.

"Yes, sir, I'll get on to it straight away," Magpie said behind him. "C'mon, Al." She crossed over to him. "Let's go meet your girl and new best friend."

They were halfway across the tarmac when a beam of light rose from the roof of the building, followed by a blinding flash. The comms block pulsed, then disappeared in a pillar of smoke, followed by an eruption of flames that ripped through the mushrooming plume.

The shock wave sent Alister and Magpie staggering back, arms raised to cover their faces. Then they watched in horror as the flames and smoke froze for a second before being sucked down into a swirling vortex to smash into the remains of the building. A second thunderous shock wave knocked them to the ground. Crouched on the cold, wet tarmac, they instinctively turned away from the explosion.

Alister didn't react to the rush of the Soft-Machine over his body, protecting him from the searing heatwave that washed over him. Ears ringing from the explosions and shift in air pressure, he stood up to face the roar and burning remains scattered across the crater where the building where Suzie had been.

Chapter Thirteen

A storm of stone and metal crashed down ahead of him. Chunks of blazing masonry hit the tarmac with monstrous thumps and melted the surface. Smaller debris exploded on impact, spraying fireballs into the air.

Alister felt like his insides had been gouged out. When the destruction settled, the remains of the Comm's building, a few broken walls and a metal staircase, stood in a shallow crater. Debris, some still flecked with flames, lay scattered in a rough circle across a landscape of scars and smaller holes. Thin trails and scraggy lines of smoke drifted over the ruins and dissolved into plumes of light mist.

Magpie appeared beside him.

"What's happening?" he said flatly, his face blank.

"Alister," Magpie said, coughing. "I'm so sorry."

Her voice was a whisper lost in the wail and roar of the fire engines and ambulances speeding past them. Two more thunderous booms threw up a spray of debris and flames from the distant rubble. Seconds later, stones crunched into the ground ahead and splattered onto the emergency and rescue vehicles. The black pit inside him swallowed up the noise.

Magpie ducked again, then straightened up and grabbed his arm. "Al!" she shouted. "We have to get away from here."

She led him away, and the mask around his mouth receded. Dazed, he followed her through the soft shower of ash and snow, past soldiers and hostages huddled in groups, all staring with the same cloudy expressions of fear and confusion.

Then, a thought, a knowing, bled up through the grief. Suzie was there again in his mind, like before. He could sense her, almost feel her, reaching out to him like the gentle edge of dawn lingering on the horizon of his dulled mind. The gut-wrenching helplessness and grief drained away, and Alister fell to his knees. The powerful sense of Suzie overwhelmed him so much that they seemed to be one person, one frighteningly elegant, intimate weave of vulnerability.

Her hands were bound tight, and she sat squeezed against someone else on a narrow bench in the back of a moving vehicle. It stank of perspiration, copper, and mud. A rattle of metal surrounded them, and the rumble and squelch of the wheels hurtling along a muddy road. Bursts of hail occasionally splattered on the outside of the truck, drowning out the surrounding noises.

"He'll come for us, Nehir, don't worry," Suzie whispered. A hard palm struck her face and cut the connection.

"Easy, Al," Magpie said and sat him down on the steps leading into the barracks. "Stop here for a minute until your head clears."

"Did you just slap me?"

"What? No."

"They're alive."

"No, Al, you saw the blast."

"I was with her."

"Alister, get a grip."

Alister looked up to the sky and took a deep breath. "She's alive, Magpie."

"Crissake, Al."

"No, she's in a truck with Nehir and the Lightning Seed." He scrabbled around in the echoes of Suzie's thoughts. "A few of the others...who went to make calls from the comms building...they were Followers. Vegas, they're going to Las Vegas."

Magpie straightened up and looked over to the fire trucks, ambulances, and groups of soldiers clustered around the crater. Bomb disposal guys in protective gear made their way around the small fires and plumes of smoke rising from the ruins and fallout.

"Just wait a sec," Magpie said.

"No, there's no time." He moved to get up, and Magpie pushed him back down.

"Al, will you just shut up and let me think? I'm trying to help you here." She stared back at the bomb site and sighed. "Okay, come with me."

***

Magpie spoke with the soldier in the sentry box at the entrance to the vehicle pound and came back to Alister.

"We did a count. All the vehicles are accounted for, including the four the terrorists stole and the one destroyed in the blast."

"It wasn't."

"What? Alister, get back here, dammit."

Alister hurried across the site, through the fire hoses, and around trucks to a dirt track exposed from under the snow by heat from the explosion. A path led up the hill and into the snow again ahead of him.

Sid, the Indian guy, appeared beside him.

"You can feel her?"

"She's alive," Alister nodded. "Sometimes I get these thoughts or a picture of what she sees."

"You believe these feelings to be real?"

"I know they are."

"Good."

"What do you mean?"

"Love, grief, compassion, all emotions are real, a form of energy."

"What are you talking about?"

"It astonishes me that a person senses another's emotional disposition in everyday life—a warmth, a threat, a fear, loss, loneliness, anger, love. They talk about the mood of a crowd or the atmosphere in a room or hall." Sid shook his head. "Emotions are as real as the unseen radio and cosmic rays around us. Be sensitive to your gut feelings. Trust your emotions."

"Trust my emotions? My head's a mess, even without the amnesia and nanoparticles tuning me into all kinds of stuff I've no way of knowing."

"Yet you are capable of discerning what you feel from what you know or are told. You should value that skill."

"What are you talking about? Everybody can."

"Not so, the Followers, like so many seekers of one apparent truth or another, are lost in the worship of words; their faith, corrupted version of old knowledge from dead books."

"The Followers kill because of emotions."

"The Followers kill because they choose to be driven by anger, betrayal, and a perverse sense of injustice. They kill because their emotions are moulded and shaped by strange beliefs and corrupted loyalties." Sid looked off into the distance. "Your nanoparticle connection with Suzie has within it an understanding of something more profound, an emotional intimacy, a quality valued by those around you."

A cold breeze swept down the hill, and Sid was gone.

"Hey," Magpie headed past the barriers and wrecked fence on the far side to stand beside Alister and a broken set of tracks, partially blown away and buried under the debris. "You were right," she said. "These are tracks under the debris, Oryx APC, heading out. Let's get back to General Cape."

"Magpie?"

"Well, you look like a weight's been lifted from your shoulders. What's up?"

"Can you tell what people are feeling?"

"Oh, gimme a break!"

Cape's bare office had just a desk and a wall covered in old paper maps. Alister sat by Magpie, tapping his foot restlessly. Cape put down the report a soldier had just handed him.

"Thank you," Cape said to the soldier. "Carry on with the investigation."

The veteran saluted and left the room. Cape turned to Alister and Magpie. "We think they may have used something as simple as a laser pen to guide the missile to the comms building," he said. "Now..." He turned to the map on the wall.

"Yes, they could be heading for Las Vegas. That would fit in with the other possible destinations. But the Followers we questioned only talked about San Francisco and Los Angeles, and we don't know how old those tracks are. Even if terrorists took the truck as a decoy, it does not mean your friends are alive. Alister, I'm very sorry about Suzie and Nehir, but you may well have to accept they are gone."

Alister shook his head. "They're alive."

"I know you want to believe that, Alister. It must be tough for you. I'm sticking with the intel that says the Lightning Seed is in one of the two vehicles we have targeted and that the comms explosion left no survivors. The Followers lost a lot of people getting those two trucks out."

"They're going to Vegas. You have to do something."

"They're a quarter of a million families in Vegas, Alister, many of them families of Followers in the domes. I can't see how Plotinus would want to destroy it. And neither General Wakefield nor I have the resources for a third team. As I said, we're out of touch with any support, including all the troops still in Halfbeak chasing down Followers and securing the other caverns. We're fighting blind. And with all airships grounded, we're stuck here with hostages and prisoners to care for. There's a fortress blocking the only traversable route between here and Vegas, and I need all the troops I have to deal with things here and prepare for another possible assault."

"I'll go, sir, and take him with me."

Cape turned to Magpie. "Reason?"

"What if he's right, sir? We only need to tail the truck. We'll alert our troops in Vegas when we get there. Al's been right before. Back in Halfbeak, he knew his way around, found a secret lift, and knew where Suzie and the prof were. He could well be right on this one, too, sir. He'd be an asset. He knows more about weapons than I do; plus, he's damn good at CQC."

Cape scratched his cheek and shuffled through sheets of notes. "And the fortress between Las Vegas and us?"

"Just two of us could get through with diversionary tactics, sir. If this weather keeps up, it could be an advantage. The Followers are just a gang, not soldiers trained in combat and defence."

"Hm, it's a risk that might work."

"Sir, if that Seed is heading for Vegas, it's one we have to take. We need to go after it, warn people."

"True. Very well. Alister, are you sure you want to do this?"

"Yes, sir. I know Suzie's alive and with the Lightning Seed."

"Is there any way to convince you not to go?"

"No, sir. I'll find a way and go on my own if I have to."

"I guessed as much." Cape examined a map on the wall, then sat down and picked up a tablet. He scrolled the screen, read through a lengthy document, and then looked up. "Magpie, get your gear and give Alister a primary and secondary, too. Take one of the Jeeps and a radio kit and go after the third truck. Keep your distance and keep the radio on; transmit your coordinates as soon as the wireless is back up, then wait for support. Under no circumstances do you engage. Any excessive physical movement of the Seed produces severe weather patterns. If they have it and it goes off-road, you'll know about it. When you get to Vegas, contact Colonel Rogers, the PI there. If you are right and the Seed is there, Rogers will take over and be in charge."

"Yes, sir," Magpie said.

"Dismissed, soldier," Cape said. "Alister, wait a while. I'd like a word."

Magpie saluted and left, giving Alister a tap on the shoulder as she passed him.

"The orders go for you too, Alister," Cape said. "Do not engage, and follow Magpie's orders at all times. One other thing—I got a call from Raymond Ruya when we rescued you."

Alister said nothing, waiting for Cape to continue.

"He said your intuition and instincts have an uncanny knack for being correct. It seemed he knew more than he was willing to tell me. Do you know what he meant?"

"Yes," Alister said, "I think it has something to do with nanoparticles in my brain and nervous system."

Cape nodded thoughtfully. "Neural Wi-Fi. Your sister was working on it some years ago."

" I keep hearing this Ruya guy's name."

"His Centauri Foundation is global. Your parents and sister worked in his labs, and he funds the P. I and a lot of development work around the world."

"I had a flashback of my dad and Ruya talking. And I heard those things, creatures, talking about him."

"Maybe you need a bit more time to sort out your memories and hallucinations, get your head straightened out."

"I guess so."

"Son, going after that truck is a big risk and may not end the way you want. However it works out, stick with what Magpie says. She may seem cold-hearted and blunt sometimes, but the things she's seen and been through." Cape paused, choosing his words carefully, "she's a survivor, and it would be wise to respect that."

"Yes, sir."

Cape nodded. "Godspeed. You be careful."

"Yes, sir, I will."

Alister found Magpie checking her gear in the prep room down the hall. A small trolley beside the table was laden with bottles of water, dried food, ammunition magazines, night-vision goggles, a flash-light and spade, sleeping bags, as well as a proteus versipack, a fuel canister, and an emergency med kit.

"Y'alright, Al?"

"Yes. Thanks for backing me up in there, Magpie."

"You haven't been wrong so far," she said. "You still have

no idea how you're doing this?"

"I think I got some kind of connection."

Magpie continued loading the gear onto the trolley. "You were butt naked when I found you, and I didn't see any wireless augmentation on you. If you have a connection, it's under your skin somewhere. I was involved in a Lycus mess back in Toronto. There was a Suzie involved there."

"You've met Suzie before?"

"Came across her," she paused. "A lot's happened since then." She fell into a grim silence.

"What?"

"Nothing, you don't wanna know."

"And I thought I was the one with secrets."

"Just drop it, okay?"

Alister shrugged and examined a pile of clothes. Magpie had found some thermal-breathe winter combat gear for him: grey canvas trousers, a thin sweatshirt with a hood, a grey camo jacket, socks, gloves, a ski mask, a belt, and boots. He picked up the trousers, stared at them, threw them down on the table and turned to face Magpie.

"I can't figure you out, Magpie. You came across a real hard-nosed grumpy bitch back in that Halfpeak…"

"Halfbeak," Magpie said under her breath.

"Yeah, whatever," Alister continued. "You've seen me naked, didn't know me from Adam, but trusted me with all this stuff I've been spouting with no idea how I know it. You back me up in front of Raven and Cape, and now you're ready to go after a truckload of armed nutcases because of what I believe. But you get uptight when I ask what's on your mind for a change." He stopped and took a breath. "What is it with you?"

Magpie shook her head. "That's my business."

"Not when we got a way to go, and you plan to carry on poking me with the sharp end of whatever it is that's pissing you off. At least tell me what it is."

"Okay," Magpie lowered a scope she was examining and turned it in her hands as if the memory was written around the surface. "There was a major operation in Chicago last month. I lost my sister when the Old Lemont Road Bridge went down. That's it, my sister died. I was there."

"Oh."

"Yeah."

"Was she a soldier as well?"

Magpie nodded and turned to the shelves of weapons.

Alister picked up the trousers. They looked new. He raised the leg and saw the finest thin fibres around the foot. The kneepads were new, with the old adhesive mark visible around one edge. What had happened to the guy who had last worn them? Somebody's brother, dad, boyfriend. He glanced back up at Magpie, who examined two pistols, one in each hand. She put one on the trolley and the other back on the shelf.

Alister removed his outer clothes and placed them in an empty clothesbox. Ignoring the Soft-Machine's grey shorts and T-shirt, he slipped the trousers and sweatshirt on as they loosened around his body. Then, he sat on the chair to put on the boots and socks. "What happened?"

"We received intel the Red Flag gang were going to mount a major assault on the Hindu temple the night after Maha Shivratri."

"A what ratri?"

"A Hindu festival. There was lots of food there to end the fasting. We pushed the Red Flag back across the bridge, but it started to weaken with all the shelling and gunfire, and both sides started pulling back. Smoke and a couple of guys got pinned down. It looked like the bridge ahead of us, where the Red Flag were, would crumble first." She paused. "But it didn't. They'd somehow got their hands on mortars, and the entire section behind us just disappeared."

Magpie took in a deep breath and let out a long sigh. "Pauline was behind us. I didn't get to her in time. I could have saved her; I heard her scream just before she fell. Smoke was under fire, but he shouted 'go', and I turned and ran. I saw her in the water, being carried away. I called, but she didn't grab any debris. The fall must have knocked her out. She sank, and I dived in after her, but it was too late. So, now you know."

"I'm sorry, Magpie."

"Yeah, I get a lot of that. Let's haul this load out to the Jeep."

"You can't just say that like it explains everything."

"What's there to explain? Shit happens. All the time. I thought you'd have noticed by now. Take a look around, even the weather is all screwed. There's no plan, there's no order. So yeah, shit happens, and sometimes it's real bad. Fact is there's nothing we can do about it but stick to whatever job we have and make sure it works. Nothing else makes sense."

It wasn't worth arguing with her. That steady flow of grief under pressure was ideal fuel for any kind of anger; it just needed someone to add a spark. He strapped on the belt, picked up his pistol, checked and clipped in the cartridge, then snapped two other cartridges into the brass containments on his belt.

"Do you think we'll need this?" he asked, holding up the ornate shoulder cannon with the tangle of brass and Nu-iron tubes and convergent primers behind the dual layers of steel-glass.

Magpie lowered her rifle. "Hell yeah; take it all. It's us against a dozen drugged-out gun-crazy goons; we'll need all the firepower we can carry. Load up."

"But Cape said—"

"Yeah, I know what he said, but my gut says different. Once we're outta here, there's no coming back for more if things go south. Come on, the sooner we get going, the better. The terrorists have a couple of hours on us."

They climbed into the Jeep, and Magpie punched the fusion switch, checked the auto-flow release and vent regulator, and then shoved the Jeep into gear.

"Why are you looking at me like that?" Alister asked.

She smiled and released the clutch. "Oh, nothing, just reminding myself."

The n-steam stormed through the pipes to merge at the crossover and explode in the engine's six fusion chambers.

"Of what?"

"Not to piss you off and end up getting what you gave to Raven. Buckle up." She laughed out. "Hell, just like the movies, we're gonna get the girl and save the world."

The Jeep surged forward into the night with a smooth, whispering howl.

Magpie punched a button, and a fog crossed through the windscreen. When it cleared, the scene outside glowed an eerie green, the buildings and landscape etched in silvery grey beneath a smouldering full moon. Out on the horizon, clusters of jagged white lightning shards cracked and flashed through dark clouds, revealing a raging sky's bunched contours and shadows.

"Looks like we're in for nasty weather," Alister said.

"Bad moon rising."

"What?"

"Nothing, just an old song. The Lightning Seed—Lendon said moving it around makes it do that."

The Jeep turned off-road with a bump, bounced a hundred yards, then turned onto a smooth surface. Steering with one hand, Magpie curved towards the bare hills in the distance. The APC was nowhere to be seen.

"Why are we going off-road?"

"The APC they took has defence mechanisms. The Followers may have deployed Mini-mines, VHTs—very high-temperature incendiaries. We're on a covert road. This whole area is laced with them to allow increased military manoeuvres and tactical options. The Veterans Memorial Highway is dangerous at the best of times. We'll have to steer clear of it."

"No wonder the ride's only a bit rougher than that road. Whoa!"

A demon, about four feet tall, darted onto the road. Seeing the Jeep, it threw its hands up in fear. Bat-like wings sprouted from the creature's back, and, mouthing a scream, it flew into the air, arching several feet to drop to the ground and disappear. The shock hit Alister like a punch in the chest; he gasped and gaped at the bare landscape.

"What the hell is that?" Magpie stomped on the brakes and jabbed a button under a small viewing plate just below the dashboard's centre. The screen came to life. She pressed the rewind button for several seconds. The viewing plate showed nothing but snow-dusted night filtered into a dull green. "I don't get it."

"Where is it?" Alister asked and rewound through more green and grey wasteland.

"You're wasting time, Al," Magpie flicked off the playback. "Let's go." Shunting the Jeep into gear, she drove with her hands tight on the steering wheel and a steely look in her eye. "Probably a wild animal. Settlers around here have dogs. Some of them have gone feral." She looked away from him, but Alister registered the flashes of fear, disbelief, and confusion.

"You saw it too, didn't you, that...that demon?"

"Not sure what I saw," Magpie stamped on the accelerator.

"We got a job to do. Let's stick to the plan and not get into any crazy guessing."

***

Magpie stopped around ten yards from the brow of Pilgrim's Hill. "Come on." They walked through the light drizzle thrown about by a busy wind and crept up to crouch behind a cluster of large boulders resting on the hilltop. The plain stretched ahead, scarred by a sprawling Follower settlement blocking their route.

"Indian Springs," Magpie took out a pair of small binoculars, looked through them, and then passed them to Alister. "We go through there."

A fortress wall of freight containers topped with turrets, watchtowers, and spotlights broke the wall's smooth line. Portakabins dotted the land beyond up to a metal fence. Images flashed up from his memory.

"Portakabins. I went to one in London. I mean a community of those mobile units. People had converted them into kitchens, living rooms, bedrooms, even a kindergarten."

Magpie nodded. "Europe was lucky. A lot more people survived there than here in the States. We have around one aeroplane flight arriving at Logan from Europe a week."

"Where?"

"Logan International Airport, Boston. We've switched to nano-steam airships here in the US. You were on one flying from Logan to New York when it was hijacked."

"That's right, I remember. There were four guys on the airship. They... wait, what? You said we go through there?" He looked through the binoculars again. "You're kidding me?"

Behind the entire length of the Fortress and portakabins stretched a swath of frozen no man's land around fifty yards deep. A wire mesh fence around twelve or thirteen feet high ran on either side of the wasteland. Beyond the barren area, a broken constellation of lights from caravans, tents, trailers, old aeroplanes, portakabins, and shacks crowded the plain and curved up the hillsides. Makeshift street lights marked roads crisscrossed between.

The reason why they couldn't go around was spread on either side of the settlement—steel-glass turbine towers a hundred feet tall rose up out of a thick forest of razor wire like the frozen, twisted innards of a metal beast. Wheels and pistons pumped and churned yellow-green n-steam through pipes and filters, casting an eerie glow over the glimmering, deadly wires.

Magpie took the binoculars, "we'll have to go through that to keep up with them. Going around will set us back around four, maybe five hours—if we're lucky. Probably longer. But we get through that fence into the buffer zone, and we'll have a safe route across."

"If we're lucky."

"That buffer zone separates the Followers' fortress and camp from the settlement on the far side, a neutral place where families and relatives of Followers live. The PI and army helped them start the community before Plotinus's cult arrived with his drugs and radicalised them."

"That community is a mile-deep maze of carnage just waiting to happen."

"No, we get through the fortress, then drive along the buffer zone around the community, close to their side of the zone. They won't fire at us there." Magpie lowered the binoculars and wiped the rain off the Nu-iron body and fine brass frames. "It's a straight road to the gates and the fence, and then the perimeter road curves around the community." She scanned the single road that wound down towards the enormous doors and through the fortress settlement. "About half a mile deep. We get across the fortress and into the buffer zone. We're through the worst."

"And the fortress?" He didn't like where Magpie was going with her plan. "You're really saying we go straight through?"

"Yup."After several seconds of looking through the binoculars, she cleaned them again and put them away. "We'll have to make sure their attention is somewhere else while we're in there. We'll sneak in, plant flash-bangs, then go through while they deal with the explosions."

"You make it sound easy. Didn't you see those snipers on the watchtowers?"

Magpie nodded, "Outfits say Red Flag, hard-core. We'll light them up with the Hydra. Once they're down, there'll be way too much going on for anyone to notice a plain old Jeep driving through."

He stared at her.

"It'll work, Al."

"No, it won't. All hell will break loose."

"Okay then, fifty-fifty."

"Brilliant, thanks. I feel better already."

"Knew you'd come round."

"Funny."

Back down the hill, swirls of smoke slid around the Jeep.

"What's with those lines of smoke swirling around the Jeep?"

"Huh?" Magpie looked around. "What smoke?"

"Not again!" Alister groaned. The smoke solidified into human forms—slender genies with short, curling hairs of flame over their bodies and bald heads and short, flaming beards on their chins. The three creatures stopped and returned Alister's shocked gaze. The taller, thin one pointed at Alister and looked from him to Magpie. "Trust her, tell her." He punched the shoulders of the others on either side of him, and they disappeared.

Magpie gritted her teeth. "Maybe the Followers who stole the APCs spiked the other vehicles. Smuggling drugs in is easier than explosives. Let's go."

"Yeah." Alister stood up, eyes fixed on the Jeep, dark, silent, and alone, exposed to the elements, buffeted by the wet, cold wind. Thin veins of rain drizzling over the body gleamed in the moonlight.

"Let's hope this tripping out passes quick. We need to keep our eye on the ball." Magpie gave him a wary look. "Al?"

Alister stood motionless, staring at the Jeep.

"Hey, Al, get your game face on. Forget about those spooks, we got real crap to deal with. You ready for this?"

"I should tell you a few things."

"Save it. We got a job to do."

"You have to know."

Magpie sighed deeply. "Make it quick."

"Okay. When I was a kid, my dad injected me with something, and then I absorbed nanoparticles from a beaker in the lab where my parents and sister worked. I have…" He thought for a second. "Neural Wi-Fi in me, and I got some into Suzie, too. That's how we're connected."

Magpie was silent momentarily, then said, "I'll be damned. But the comms are down. How did you know she was alive?"

"Some kind of quantum-entanglement thing with the

nanoparticles we share."

"Huh. No kidding?"

"You know what that means?"

"Sure, you split a particle, and the parts still act as if they're connected, no matter how far apart they are."

After another silence, Magpie said, "Well, least we know we're on the right track and not on a wild goose chase."

"Thanks, Magpie."

"No worries." She filled two backpacks with flash bangs and dropped one in his lap. "Right, back to work. Remember, plant the flash-bangs away from our route. We want those guys running in the opposite direction. You sure you're ready for this?"

"Yeah, my head's a lot clearer."

"Give me your hand," she snapped a dull blue plastic strap about three inches wide to his wrist. It unfurled, revealing a small flap and a flexible touch screen that rolled out along the back of his hand and came to life. Buttons lit up on the strap.

"That map of the fortress is pre-installed. Touch your twenty when you're..."

"My what?"

"Your location, when you get into in position, and it will track you on the map as you move around. It has motion and electromagnetic sensors. It'll pick up and map the electrical system of cables running through buildings to extrapolate their size and structure by calculating the residual discharge and background radiation. It'll recharge at the same time."

Alister examined the band. "You're a bit of a geek, aren't you?"

"Yeah, I like to know how shit works, comes in useful. It's a Centauri prototype. They're working on some kind of absorbent-gel computer that'll rest just under the epidermis."

"Wow," Alister said, examining the small screen on the back of his hand.

"Yeah. C'mon, let's go light up their lies, I mean lives."

Chapter Fourteen

So it is written, so it shall be done, so it shall be known for all time that what we do, we do for the sake of all mankind. Those of the city should not fear but rejoice, for the multitudinous light and radiance that descend from the heavens will transport all who are touched in both body and soul to Heaven. It is with joy that I will present myself within the heart of the Great Sacrificial Blessing and ascend with my Followers and kin to meet the Creator to sit by his side, and on Earth, all shall be forgiven, and spring will return once more.
The Book of Plotinus, Chapter One, verse 14

Plotinus, dressed in a pair of baggy white shorts and a broad, loose-fitting sweatshirt, reclined sideways on a large black leather sofa, his feet resting on one of four dark-blue cushions scattered with gold stars and other celestial bodies—comets, ringed planets, and galaxies.

Behind him, a wide doorway led into a study with bookcase chests containing the works of John Dee and his followers and commentators. Before him, in the centre of the room, flames from a fire burning in a shallow metal bowl cast orange and red ripples across cold metal walls. Overhead, copper pipes of different lengths hung from the ceiling, swaying gently in the warm air from the fire bowl, absorbing the fumes and whispering in eerie, random, hollow tones.

"Thoughts of Plotinus, enter date here. The preparations are near completion. The Followers have never been better prepared, and I am humbled by their devotional services and sacrifices to the furtherance of delivering the Divine Estate to this mortal realm. The guidance of the shadows that speak to me in my waking and my dreams have all borne fruit and are a testament to my vision's truth. The existence and presence of the Seed and other celestial devices left on this world have been revealed to me. I have one regret."

He sighed deeply and looked over to a photograph of a young girl sitting at a table eating blueberries, a big grin on her face. Blinking back the tears, he continued. "My beloved daughter continues to struggle and resist the medication, but truth always prevails, and she serves the mysterious will of the

Lord despite the pain it brings upon her. One day, she will be free of the gracious burden, and her rewards will be greater than any man, greater than even mine.

"Few are the rewards of the humble renunciate," he said, "but it is not rewards of this world that we seek." Tapping his toes on the far arm of the sofa, he lifted a lazy hand. He pushed aside one of the long strands of matted hair that lay in clumps over his back and shoulders, humming to himself while musing over the tubes hanging from the ceiling, which produced its own particular sound. Every half minute or so, he'd twitch when the exoskeleton realigned and calibrated itself as it recharged through a thin cable connected to the charger on the floor beside him.

The orange charge light switched to an electric blue with a ping. Plotinus grunted and sat up. He kicked the charger aside, triggering automated wheels that, guided by the charger's sensors, carried it to the docking bay against the wall. Flexing his fingers, he stood up. The data lens on his right eye flashed '100% charge'. He twitched his eye muscle, switching the infra-red scope on and off, and raised the system-status viewing plate with his eyebrow. He scrolled through by looking up and down and selected 'semi-predictive mode'.

He moved across the room with the swift grace of an athlete a third of his actual weight and, within a few seconds, stood at the balcony overlooking the vast, empty military assault course below him. Usually, the entire arena would be awash with groups of soldiers laden with full backpacks and weapons, running, climbing, and crawling their way around from one end of the course to the other.

The doorbell chimed.

"Enter."

Peter came in, bowed, and waited for permission to speak, which Plotinus granted with a nod.

"The Seed of Redemption is in the hands of the righteous, Master. Three convoys are now en route to their destinations."

Plotinus's data lens detected the slight temperature shift in Peter's face when he stopped speaking. "What is it, boy?"

"I've been told," Peter paused to remember the exact words, "The main compound perimeter has been breached."

"As I expected. Make preparations for my departure."

"Yes, Master," Peter spoke to a runner outside and returned. Plotinus looked at him with a slight tilt of the head.

"What else, Peter? I sense a disturbance."

"Master, a messenger from the settlement has arrived. The true carriers of the Seed are being followed." Peter made a slight gesture with his hand and glanced back to the door.

Plotinus flicked his eyebrows to acknowledge the man behind the door and, with a slight shake of the head, indicated he was not interested in speaking with him.

"Who, who dares to even consider interfering?"

"It is the one who saved the Emerson girl, Master. He and a woman—"

"What? The fools know not what they are doing." Plotinus's voice rose as he strode across the floor and tore the door off the frame. "The dark guardian, it has to be!" Smashing the door to the ground, he stormed into the bedroom.

"The Panthers, Master, they found him and took him to a Peoples Infantry search party."

"Send the horsemen after him and the woman with him," he shouted, demolishing his room as he dressed. "I want the horsemen fully prepared to ride in twenty minutes. Did you hear me?" he screamed. "The horsemen, twenty minutes. The Revelation is upon us. Nothing must stand in the path of our glorious perfection, our reward of radiant elevation to Truth. God is just, and we are his true and final messengers. Go, go."

***

Peter hurried towards the hangar where Plotinus's armour-plated Winnebago towable was parked. Ash and embers drifted through fading wafts of warm air, carrying the stench of burnt rubber, diesel, and flesh. He curved his arms over his head, then headed down the wet road that a hundred Red Flag mercenaries had trampled not five minutes ago. He sighed with relief when he turned down onto a sloping white road and into a welcome, cold, fresh breeze.

He punched the keypad by the tall metal roller door at the hangar. Gears creaked and strained, and the doors shuddered into motion. The wheels on the right slipped, clunked, and snapped, failing to get a grip while the left side began to rise smoothly, forcing the shutter to open at an angle.

"No, no, please don't jam on me now."

Peter dived under the shutter into the garage, slipping on the icy surface before he could reach the lever that operated the chain on the left side.

A deep laugh from a dark corner of the hangar was followed by the appearance of Yuri Stalin. The facial injuries from his last encounter with Alister hidden under swirls of black nano-skin tattoos.

Peter pointed a shaking hand at the lever. Yuri grabbed the bottom edge of the shutter with one hand and turned the lever with the other like he was whisking an egg. The left side caught up with the right, and the shutter rolled up to clang loudly into the broad metal catch.

Yuri, his entire body covered in his scaled 'Strife' armour, towered over him. He hauled Peter up, then leaned back to examine him. "Are you hurt?" His deep voice resonated through the spacious garage. "I have a well-stocked first-aid kit in the Nissan."

"No, I'm alright. Thanks, Yuri."

Yuri nodded. "As you wish, young man. Where is our venerable leader?"

A quiet, raspy, hissing voice said, "Here he comes now." Jesus-Ernesto, the knife-thrower, dressed in a long, thin white nano-thermal cape, his pale face fixed in a sneer, perched atop a stack of two freight containers. His head twitched, and the silvery beads on the end of his white goatee flicked about while his eyes darted around. Peter had seen this before. Jesus-Ernesto eyed possible vantage points from where to throw his blades and calculated range and distance.

Plotinus strode past them to a gleaming gold truck that stretched thirty feet long and stood thirteen and a half feet high. "Where is Famine?"

"By the diagnostic console," Jesus-Ernesto gestured.

Peter could see nothing at first, then with a fluttering and cascade of hisses, the darkness took shape like thousands of leaves turning in the light. A loud roar echoed around the garage, and then Famine—Omar—appeared on his oversized quad-bike.

"My cloaking device," he pronounced loudly. "My glorious,

Lycus cloaking device. Isn't it fabulous?"

Peter smiled. Omar was the constant spoilt child—and a complete psychopath. He now spent the wealth his family had made from oil and wine before the Freeze on stealth and weapons, always keen to show the world his new toys. He was obviously proud of this one, and Peter couldn't help but reflect Omar's infectious smile back at him.

Jesus-Ernesto appeared beside Omar, and together, they admired the new vehicle.

Plotinus grunted indifferently. "And Death?"

The hangar fell silent but for the hollow echo from the rumble of old generators in the far corner releasing a faint odour of diesel. Rows of yellow fluorescent lights glowed dully in the half-light high above them. Omar, Jesus-Ernesto, and Yuri stood motionless, looking around, glancing at each other to check if they had seen anything, sharing quick expressions instead of words.

Seated on his black-leafed quad-bike, surrounded by his weapons, Omar visibly shuddered and finally broke the silence. His voice was a croaky whisper that barely escaped through the fear that gripped his throat. "Saying her name is an invocation. Master, you don't know about the change?"

Peter stared at Omar, perplexed at what had so frightened the man who relished being Famine, the rider of the black horse. Death was pretty awesome already; what had she gone and done now?

"Fool." Plotinus scowled at Omar, but only for an instant. A shadow swept past him, and a grey pallor washed over his face. His eyes widened and froze, then he staggered back drunkenly, mouth moving like a fish out of water. The exoskeleton that gave him so much power and grace hissed and whined noisily under his clothes, hundreds of tiny gyroscopes and hydraulics adjusting pressure and tension to keep him on his feet. After several yards of spasmodic, mechanical motion, the fail-safe kicked in and barely managed to sink him slowly to the ground, where he squirmed like a slug on salt, moaning like a helpless child.

"Please," his pleading drawl begged, "give me back." His voice crawled through a gargle from his throat, and saliva leaked from the edges of his mouth. Face twisted in an ugly, crumpled mush of grief and fear, he mouthed silent pleas between gasping sobs while his body quivered.

Death had arrived, and Peter looked around for her. At first, he got the impression that Yuri was the least concerned. He wouldn't be scared, Strife, the seven-foot-ten, solid-muscle cage fighter. Yuri leaned against his blood-red, pimped-out 4x4. He seemed to be yawning. The pop of a fluorescent tube transformed the scene. It burst into full radiance and revealed Yuri, mouth agape and his face cast in fear as if he had something caught in his throat. Yuri cried out, "No, it was not me. I did not call, I did not call. Justice, I claim…" The Russian sucked a slow rasping intake of breath and fell to his knees so heavily that Peter winced at the noise that echoed through the hangar.

The giant buried his face in his hands and cried helplessly. "There is nothing, nothing." Yuri tilted sideways to the floor and curled up like an embryo. Shudders rattled his breathing and escaped through the fingers of the fat hands covering his tear-soaked face, and his voice faded to a moan.

Jesus-Ernesto, Righteousness, the white horseman, walked slowly backwards. At five feet tall, he was the smallest of the four. The knife thrower tugged nervously at his stringy white hair while twirling a long blade between the grey-gloved fingers of the other hand. He peered around. "I swear, bitch, try that trick on me, and I'll put this blade through your eye."

A sharp buzz swarmed through the hangar. Jesus-Ernesto threw back the cape draped over his shoulder, revealing the armbands of silver and black shuriken needles and a knife belt around his waist. All in white, except for his nano-steel gloves. Dull grey eyes frozen in fear peered from behind spectacles that seemed to balance magically on his sharp nose.

A tall sway of dark smoke appeared out of the shadows, bowed and slithered towards him. When the misty edges curled around his ankles, he stepped back and screamed, "No, no!"

Another force, this time from behind him, yanked the Mexican so hard he flew back and slid several feet along the floor. An expression of terror and confusion froze on his face. His head darted left to right as he scuttled away, pulling himself backwards on his elbows and kicking at the ground with his heels, his features twisted and neck strained so tight that the tendons stuck out like taut ropes. Then his elbows gave way, and he hit the ground with a thump, lying on his back and raising thin white arms over his head. A long wail rose from his throat and sank into a pitiful weeping.

"I am going, please, not me. Please, pleeease."

Peter was sure he heard a sweet, faint laugh. Jesus-Eernesto's breathing became a succession of gasps like each could be his last, the difference between life and death. Then he drew a rasping deep breath and began sobbing.

Peter and Omar stared at each other. Something less than a shadow, a hollow vapour, a cold, empty space, rose up to form above Omar, and Peter's jaw slowly dropped. But the voice came from behind him, not Omar.

"Gently, Peter." The warm whisper caressed his cheek. Something about the tone, a fragrance, a strange essence. He couldn't help but take a deep breath, and the smell, a mood passed into him and awakened a yearning that filled his heart.

"Let it go, Peter."

"Yes." In less than a breath, his thoughts faded into a distant hum. Whatever he had, or was, dissolved away. Choices, music, food, books, clothes, stuff; even memories, worries, and dreams— they were all coming to rest, fading away, ending. All just meaningless stuff that, in time, would decay into dust, like his body. But for now, this abandoned Peter remained with nothing to cling to, nothing to cling with. Everything meant nothing. Someone was crying.

***

Peter awoke to Plotinus kicking him in the thigh. He sat up and rubbed his forehead, full of sadness and a lingering dread, mourning his life.

Omar, Jesus-Ernesto, and Yuri busied themselves in silence,

"Get up," Plotinus said as if nothing had taken place. "We leave in ten minutes." He glided across the hangar to disappear into the rear of his red and gold Winnebago trailer.

Hazy and grief-stricken, Peter slowly got to his feet. Busily examining his quad-bike, Omar passed a graphene plate over the electronics and ran diagnostic tests.

"What happened to us, Omar?" Peter said. "Where is she, the fourth horseman?"

"Calls herself Shiva now," Omar whispered, not looking up.

"Plotinus's little secret. Bitch mixed up a brew of hallucinogens and nano-toxins; it messes with needs, hopes, attachments, self-awareness, and all that shit. Take that away, and you steal anyone's reason to live. A big enough dose and the brain freaks out at the emptiness; it shuts down, and you die."

"It was horrible," Peter mumbled. He slid his hand along the fine, scaly frame of the quad-bike. Omar was the only one of the four to play his part, not for money, but because he enjoyed the hunt and kill with his weaponry.

"She was toying with you, kid," Omar said, "you were lucky." He closely examined each weapon, peering at various parts before snapping them back into place and checking their grips.

"What about you?" Peter said.

"One is always left to bear witness. Watching you all go through it and thinking you will be next. Scares the shit out of you."

"Do you think she knows how it makes you feel?"

Omar shrugged. "Who cares?" He cleared his throat and spat on the ground, "We have to go kill some teenager. What a joke." He climbed into the seat and roared out into the snowy wasteland.

Peter crossed to the Honda CR-X4, hauled out his travel bag, and carried it to the truck. Valkyrie, Plotinus's daughter, was sitting in the passenger seat of the driver's cabin.

"Oh, Valkyrie. Hello. I wasn't expecting you."

Slim, with piercing eyes, full lips, and a beautiful face right down to a softly pointed chin, Val was dressed in the same clothes she always wore: loose-fitting black jeans, military boots, and a thick black hoodie over a thermal T-shirt. Her long black hair hung around her shoulders as she looked across the white landscape. Her small case and backpack sat on the seat between them.

"He's ready. Let's go," she said.

Peter didn't understand. Val was always so blunt with him, with everyone. Plotinus, her father, never spoke of her. She spent most of her time in the kitchen or her own place. He had no idea what she got up to. There was only a four-year difference between them; she was twenty-five, and he was twenty-one. He'd once played with the idea of asking her out, but her indifference to conversation quickly put him off.

Jesus-Ernesto's Terrafugia N-X9, the rotors folded back, and its stubby wings curled out, shot past overhead while Yuri's Nissan sped past them up the road. Omar had already disappeared. Peter followed behind the Nissan past charred skeletons and wreckage of vehicles that had been pushed to the side of the road. The Nissan accelerated away, trailing a swirling spray of snow, and Peter flicked on the wipers until it disappeared.

Valkyrie touched the radio button controlling the link to the truck's rear. "Is that switched off?"

Peter glanced down and nodded.

"This is the worst he's been, sending the entire Red Flag Army out with faulty gear just to create a firewall so he could get away. He knew the Panthers had mines everywhere, and fighting alone wouldn't keep the marines and Peoples Infantry out."

Peter said nothing. Talk like that could get even her killed. They drove in silence for a couple of miles before Valkyrie spoke again.

"Peter, do you think those visions are real?"

Peter shrugged and shook his head. "I haven't seen anything, but the idea scares me. Have you?"

"I might have seen something once, but it could just have been a few kids in one of the farm domes."

"I'd go with that."

She rummaged in a small backpack and produced a bottle of pills. She tipped a couple into her palm and downed the two capsules. "You did know he found the Lightning Seed and sent it to sacrifice Vegas?"

"I'll be long gone before that happens."

"I think he wants you to stay. See the New Dawn with him."

"No way," Peter turned the big steering wheel, taking the truck around a long, wide bend. "Why are you here? I thought you liked to be alone."

"Sort of. I don't sleep well. You know I'm an insomniac. That's why I'm not around much." Valkyrie tilted her head. "I'm sure it's the medical implant the last doctor put in to control my fears. It gives me headaches and terrible nightmares. It's been getting even crazier these last few months; you must have noticed. It made me feel worse, and I couldn't bear it. Even these don't work," she shook the little bottle. "I had to get away. You won't tell him, will you? You're the only normal person I know. I can trust you, can't I?"

Peter stared thoughtfully at the bare, snow-swept road ahead. "Of course."

"Thanks. You're nothing like his last doctor. I wonder what happened to him?"

"I never met him," Peter said.

"I like you, Peter." She arched her back and stretched upwards. Turning her wrists, she caressed the soft felt on the top of the cab, then collapsed back and pulled a bar of chocolate from her bag. Breaking it in half, she handed him a piece. "What did Shiva do to you?" Her hand shook as she took a bite from the chocolate.

"Something horrible," Peter said.

"Oh."

The truck's insulated cabin muffled the growling of the steam-fusion engine and drone of the eight pairs of great wheels bearing through the snow-dusted road. Beyond the windscreen, the barren landscape lay exposed to the elements, robbed of all life and colour, abandoned by a heartless, distant Sun.

Behind them in the Winnebago, Plotinus was adding to his diary, the words appearing on a screen as he spoke. "Today, I witnessed the work of Shiva for the first time. Although I can awaken her with a simple instruction, I have no control once her presence is manifest—she is driven to fulfil her tasks wherever she incarnates, and so it is that she awakens those who stray from the renunciation and fall prey to the consequences of their selfishness and worldly yearning. And by her wisdom and compassion, she absolves one to bear witness to her power.

"So it is with a brightened heart that I journey to witness the first purifying and glorification of this America and see the handiwork of His instruments, my horsemen and their wrath."

Chapter Fifteen

"Okay, Al, ready to camo up and climb?"

Graffiti, religious symbols, quotes, sayings, prayers, curses, warnings, and blessings covered the surface of the fortress doors towering up in front of them.

"Do I have a choice?"

"You asked for this, Al."

Alister responded with a resigned nod.

"The waste furnaces are along the wall on the left. That's where we go in. The chimneys will give us some cover. We climb up and onto the roof. Then we split up and meet back there."

She hooked a rope on the edge of the wall and climbed up. It took her several minutes to cut through the razor wire mesh, and Alister climbed up.

Virtually invisible in their camo outfits, they crouched against the two stocky chimneys. Magpie checked the time. "Okay, see you back here at twenty-fifteen. I've set timers to detonate at twenty-one. An hour thirty should be enough time to do this and get back to the Jeep." Magpie pulled the face mask down. Her outfit fluttered like light dancing across rippling water, and she disappeared.

Alister's Soft-Machine bled into the combat gear and spread over his head, forming a gauze across his face. A dull flash of the wristband told him his path was a triangular route around the fortress. First location, twenty metres away, the outside wall of the grain supply room.

He set out along the corridor towards the grain room. A scuffling inside had him press against the wall. Angels or demons again? He leaned round the open door. A narrow path stretched through piles of sacks and barrels. A skinny boy with scraggy black hair held an old canvas bag under a large barrel at the far end. He shifted his weight from one leg to another as grain drizzled into the bag. The poor kid, dressed in oversized cord trousers and a long cardigan over a baggy grey T-shirt, looked shrunken and drained.

A man's head appeared at the window. "Hurry, Amir, fill the bag."

"Dad. I'm scared. Can't we wait until the other Followers

leave?"

"No, they might take a lot of the food here with them."

Amir frowned and, knotting up the top of the bag, waddled over to the window with it. He struggled to lift the sack high enough to reach his father, who, arms outstretched, struggled and failed to get it.

Nothing more than a shimmer of darkness in the shadows, Alister crept in and, putting his hand under the bag, gave it just enough of a lift to enable Amir to raise it to the window.

The father grabbed the bag, "Good boy; wait there." The bag disappeared through the window, and the man's arms reappeared.

"Come on, son, grab my hand."

Amir clasped his father's hands and clambered to the window just as an overweight Follower with a long beard over a grim and ugly face walked into the room. Seeing Amir, the Follower sneered and raised his rifle. Alister snapped the gun from the guy's hands and whacked the flat end of the butt against the man's temple, so he fell unconscious to the ground.

Alister looked down at the man and shook his head in disbelief.

"Amir, what's going on in there?"

Amir looked over his shoulder. "A Follower, Dad. I think he fell and knocked himself out." Amir disappeared through the window.

Alister dragged the body into the room, checked the hallway and closed the door behind him, planting a flashbang at the base of the external wall.

He was halfway along a cold, damp alley covered by a rain-splattered sheet metal roof when a sharp whistling cut through the noise overhead, and he stumbled sideways. Hand sliding along the wall for support, he fell through a door into the toilet and laundry block. The whistling turned into a soft wind, and a warm golden-white glow bloomed in his mind, and then he phased out.

The gentle folding of waves dragged back over pebbles on the beach behind him. A warm sun eased the tension from the back of his neck and head, and he stepped into a cave. It widened as he went further in. Shadows flickered on walls, illuminated by a satin-flamed fire. Three creatures resembling ancient Japanese royalty sat chatting. Dressed in colourful, flowing robes with wings of black, red, and gold feathers. All three had long, pitch-black hair tied back tight in ponytails. Each creature held a feather fan in one hand and a staff with a rounded top where several metal rings hung, reflecting the fire's glow.

"I can feel it in my bones, Saruta, 'tis more than winter and rough weather." The tall, thin creature twitched its head.

The creature to his left pursed his sky-blue lips and shook his head. "Ah, Tengu," he said, "the Lightning Seed. Our solitary time here may be drawing to a close. More company would be welcome."

Tengu spotted Alister. "We have a guest. I do believe it is the one Raguel spoke of."

"What are you?" Alister said.

The third creature twitched his head, looking at the others, and scratched the side of his pointed brown beak so hard the rings on the staff jangled. "We are kami."

"Yokai, please," Tengu said, "a little more courtesy."

"What should we do?" Yokai said.

"We wait." Tengu grasped his staff and pulled himself to his feet.

Saruta raised a hand. "'Tis not our place to act or judge." He nodded. "This mortal's sojourn here is brief and his peregrination ardent. Verily, his mottled memories, bound by nought but smoke from the fume of sighs, doth spur him on a course that will not yield so tenderly." He smiled at Alister. "Fare thee well, sir."

"Come, brothers," Tengu said, "we shall depart and let this man be." He then turned to Alister, "Beware Plotinus, he who the Nightmares have chosen."

The other two kami stood up, their fans disappearing into their robe. Staffs in hand, they bowed to Alister, who instinctively bowed back.

The Kami stepped past him out of the cave into the sunlight and stood momentarily to look at a clear blue sky. Then they spread their wings and stepped off the short ledge in a spray of radiant dust. The rings on their staffs tingled in his ears, leaving a jangled mess of vibrations humming through his body that sent him back into the fortress.

Alister rubbed his eyes. This was the weirdest yet. He

dragged his thoughts back to what he was meant to do and took a from the backpack. After a quick look around, he stuck it under the window above a line of washing machines beside a pile of army uniforms, blankets, and baskets. Next, he smashed the lock on the door to prevent anyone from getting in. He climbed out of the window that took him onto an adjoining low roof and a downpour that splattered around him and filled the streets and alleys below with streams of water. He headed over wood boards and metal sheets covered in thick, transparent tarpaulins to the next target.

Lamps hanging off cables hooked over poles cast rain-drenched light across the maze of alleys and roads. In some towers, guards hunched in rainproof ponchos stared out over the fortress settlement. Sticking to the walls, he stuck a flash-bang under the guttering of a rooftop.

The storm pummelled the tapestry of tiles, wooden boards, corrugated iron, and thick plastic to gather in splattered pools around him. He splashed down onto the cold stone ground of a narrow alleyway, repositioned his backpack, then set off again, planting flash-bangs at twenty-yard stretches around barracks, weapons stores, officer's cabins, and guardrooms. With just a handful of explosive smoke bombs left, Alister turned to the last stretch when, from one of the houses across a small square, a smashing noise punctuated the angry snarls of a man swearing in a foreign language. Then he heard the short, fearful cry of a young woman.

Keeping to the shadows of a rough stone wall, he splashed across the narrow path, rounded a corner, and stopped under an awning. Wiping the rain off his face, he peered through a half-open window into a short hallway. He climbed through and approached the half-open kitchen door at the far end, where someone was sobbing. Matt-grey metal storage shelves held stacks of plates and cups, several cooking pots, frying pans of different sizes, and cutlery trays. Another shelf had plastic jars of grain and pasta surrounded by small bottles of herbs and spices stacked in no particular order. In the centre of the kitchen, a burly, unshaven man with a red headband sat at a thick, stained and worn table. He had a pistol and a small cup of black coffee in one hand. A large dining table stood through a far door with a dozen chairs around it in the middle of a gloomy room.

A dark-skinned teenage girl with long black hair hanging in a bedraggled mess crouched in a corner, her feet pressed against a heavy, upturned barrel serving as a waste bin. Her tear-lined face was covered in cuts and a large bruise. She glared at the man through sad, angry eyes.

The smashed contents of a make-up bag—a crushed tube of lipstick, a flip dish of mascara, a shattered bottle of nail varnish, and a messy pile of metal, plastic, and broken glass covered in powder and gel, all surrounded by a small, muddy pool of liquid—lay beside her. The man's pistol had the same stains. The guy must have used it to destroy the bag of make-up.

The man put the cup down and stood up, pushing the chair back. He said something Middle Eastern while unbuckling his belt, wrapping the end with the holes around his hand, and letting the buckle swing freely. The girl raised her arm over her face.

Alister stepped into the room, the Soft-Machine morphing to gather around his chest. "Excuse me."

The man was faster than Alister expected. He raised the gun and pulled the trigger. Alister turned his head and winced, but the weapon, damaged by its use as a hammer, exploded. The man cried out, staggering back, tripping over the chair and falling. His head struck the wall with a loud thump, so he slid to the ground, unconscious.

The girl jumped to her feet and stared in confusion at the man before turning to face Alister. She pointed a small pistol at him, "Who are you?" She sniffed back tears and glanced from Alister to a Medicaid box on a shelf to her left.

Alister ignored the stubby pistol and the fact he recognised the black barrel of the Beretta Viper. "Followers have stolen a WMD and have my friend hostage. They're heading for Vegas to set it off. I'm going after them. I heard someone scream."

Underneath his clothes, the Soft-Machine coiled around his limbs. He twisted sideways, sprang forward, grabbed the young woman's wrist, and disarmed her. She took a few steps back and looked up at him, shocked. "Okay, okay," she gasped. "Don't hurt me."

"Don't worry," Alister placed her gun on the table, resting his hand on it. "Are we cool?"

She eyed him suspiciously.

"I'm taking my hand from the gun, alright? You can take care of that guy if you really want to."

She nodded and took down the medic-aid box. She tore open a sterile wipe and tended to the man's hand. "What are you doing here?"

"Planting distractions so we can get through without a fight."

The young woman flicked her head so that her long, wavy black hair slipped back over her shoulder. She reminded him of someone...his sister.

"Will you be alright?"

"Yes. Thank you. I'll just do this and go."

"You should hurry."

"No," she said in a simple, matter-of-fact way. "You think my dad was like this all the time?" A few tears trickled down her bruised and hardened cheek. "We used to have so much fun when I was a kid."

Family, Alister thought, what kind of religion takes people away from feelings like this?

"What is it?" the young woman said.

"Nothing. You should get your stuff before the fireworks kick off."

"Fireworks?"

"Explosives where people won't be, well, not at first."

"How long have I got?"

"Not much, I'm running late."

"You said Vegas. That's where my boyfriend is."

Alister nodded. "A lot of other people, too. You got transport?"

She shook her head. "I can drive, I'll steal something." Dropping the bloody wipe onto the floor, she unrolled a bandage and wrapped it around her unconscious father's wounded hand. "Wait, I'm going to the car park. You can plant some of your things there. They'll hate that."

"Good idea, but please hurry."

"Okay. It's almost done. I'm Sophie. Who are you?"

"Alister." He checked the time on the wristband. "You called him your dad?"

"He turned all religious when," she hesitated, "he still worries way too much about me." She choked back tears and finished bandaging her father's hand. "He found a picture of me and my boyfriend, Suresh. Now he's in a Vegas hospital with one kidney and a couple of cracked ribs because of him." She nodded towards her father. "I came back to say goodbye for the last time." She sniffed and winced when the strip contracted over the wound, stopping the last thin drizzle of blood.

"Okay." She pocketed her gun, picked up a large holdall from the shadows between the fridge and cupboard, and slung it over her shoulder. "I'll warn people when I get there."

Sophie knelt down and kissed the unconscious man's cheek, then picked up a photograph of a small girl, arms wrapped around a man's neck, the two beaming with broad smiles. She stroked the image with a finger. "Sorry, Dad, but I'm not coming back." She laid the picture on her father's lap, stood up, swallowed deeply, and, with a nod to Alister, said, "I'll check the alley."

Alister looked down at the man and shook his head, then turned to leave. Behind him, the man groaned and came to. Alister glanced back to make sure he didn't have another weapon, but the man's eyes were on the picture of him and his daughter.

"Where is she?" He didn't look away from the photograph.

"Your own daughter," Alister said. "She remembers how happy you all were when she was a kid. If only you could."

"I do."

"And you treat her like this because of some crazy religion?"

The man's head dropped, and he began to quietly weep. Alister checked his wristband and left.

Sophie was waiting for him at the door into the alley. They hurried through the shadows, turning corners to avoid detection, their whispers and footsteps muffled by the rain clattering on various sheets covering holes in rooftops.

"It's a long drive. You're not scared?"

"Scared?" Sophie shook her head. "You should try living round here, talk to some teenagers and kids. We've seen too many families and friends die here these past few years. It does something to your heart," she paused. "The Freeze took our grandparents, my Mum, and my younger brothers. Dad and I scavenged for food. It broke him and made him easy prey for Plotinus. Dad believed all the crap about it being our punishment." She blinked several times.

"I'm sorry," Alister said.

"There," she said as they turned a corner towards an opening where several vehicles stood unguarded.

"Thanks, good luck, Sophie."

"You too."

Sophie disappeared between vehicles, many of them just junk with their insides torn out and salvaged. She took care of her dad even after the way he's treated her. Connections nothing can break. It was like that guru guy said emotions are real.

Alister moved around the vehicles, planting flash bangs on four of them, then set off to meet Magpie. A flash of lightning lit up the car pound, then thunder rolled across the sky with a rumble that drummed through him. The Lightning Seed; what were they doing to it now? He tried to get a sense of where Suzie was but felt nothing. Was the Seed messing with whatever quantum thing they had going? Maybe she was asleep or knocked out.

Alister slowly walked along dark, rain-drenched alleyways and arrived at the rendezvous point. He had a little under a minute to spare, but Magpie wasn't there. He waited a few minutes, then, staying in the shadows, edged along the side of an aeroplane's body. Voices of men arguing came from inside, "That truck shouldn't have come through here. It carries an abomination. It's wrong."

"Plotinus knows what he's doing." Another voice snarled, "Sacrifices must be made if the world is to be saved."

"We have families nearby."

Alister dashed across the road in the direction Magpie should have taken on the way back.

Further up the road, two Followers rushed towards a Portakabin. Their rain-soaked, bearded faces and plated hair illuminated by the light from a window. The first man banged on the door, and it quickly opened, "Caught her prowling around," he said, then nodded down to the ground. "Neb, alert the others. She probably isn't alone."

Neb nodded, slung the assault rifle over his shoulder and strode off, heading towards Alister. The other Follower walked into the Portakabin, looked down, and sneered. As Neb ran past the alley, Alister yanked him in and swung him face-first into the wall. There was an ugly crunch, and the man fell to the ground. Neb groaned and tried to turn. Alister grabbed his head and slammed it into the hard, wet tarmac, knocking him out, then dragged him further into the alley.

Keeping to the shadows, Alister made his way to the Portakabin. He took the outside light out with one shot, and the space fell into darkness.

He edged along the wall and glanced through the window. Magpie was on the floor, bound and stripped down to her underwear. Wearing only her bra and light-green boxers, she lay slumped against a wall, her hands and feet tied. A short rope around her neck stretched and knotted around a rope binding her wrists and ankles. If she moved, she choked. Blood covered the side of her face and jaw. The bearded man and another Follower leered at her while a tall woman soldier examined Magpie's outfit, turning it in her hands.

The storm intensified, and rain splattered noisily against the walls. Alister leaned back and shook his head. "Bloody hell, Mag." He thought for several seconds, then murmured, "Stuff it. I ain't got time for this, not in this pissing rain."

The world slowed, the Soft-Machine swarmed across his body, and he kicked the door open. He saw everything: the woman by the door, the terrorist to his left, and another on the other side of a table. Slamming the door shut, he shot his fist out into the side of the woman's head. Before she'd even hit the floor, Alister was halfway across the table, pivoting on his arm. He kicked the bearded guy in the face, sending him crashing against the wall. The third terrorist stepped back, and Alister lifted a chair as he landed and swung it so the edge crushed the man's nose. The man dropped to the ground, and the room fell silent except for the rain pummelling the roof.

Alister sliced the ropes binding Magpie, and she fell sideways. He tore a headscarf from one of the terrorists and used it to wipe Magpie's face and mouth. Most of the blood had come from a cut over her ear. She moved her head drowsily and opened her eyes.

"Hullo,"

"Yeah, hi." She slurred, got to her feet, wobbled, and fell against him. The shock of her firm, smooth, semi-naked body pressing against him took his breath away. She was in more than pretty good shape for someone almost twice his age.

"Sorry," she mumbled, stepped back, wobbled, and stared at him. "Pleased to see me?"

"What?"

"Nothing. What's that noise?"

"Heavy weather. You alright?"

"Will be," she rubbed her eyes. "Jeez, kill the lights, will you and watch the door." She staggered over to her outfit. "Could do with an aspirin." She looked down at her semi-naked body and then smiled up at him. "I guess this makes us even."

Alister smiled back, "Nearly," he flicked the light switch.

"You wish," Magpie said in the dark as she dressed quickly. "How'd you find me?"

"People acting strange, talking." Alister stood with his back against the wall, peering out through the window. The rain had turned to heavy hail. "Great," he murmured. "What happened, Mags?"

"Some girl in a four-by-four hit something on the way past. These guys ran out straight into me. I wasn't expecting it. They got lucky."

"Must have been Sophie."

Magpie strapped on her boots and pulled down the ends of her trousers till they reached below the laces. "Who's Sophie?" She picked up her weapons and got to her feet. She slung her arm through the rifle strap and holstered the pistol.

"Caught her dad beating her up. She's on her way to Vegas to meet up with her boyfriend. She'll warn people."

"Good girl." She checked her wristband and tilted her head to the hail battering down outside. "No one's going to be out in this."

"The Seed must be on the move again."

They hurried through alleys to the outer wall, ran along it and through the gates. Once outside, they headed up the muddy path to the Jeep.

"Get behind the wheel and wait for my signal to fire up the engine as soon as the show starts."

"Right." Alister climbed into the cold driver seat and closed the door. The infra-red dots Magpie had fired up onto the sides of the watchtowers were visible through the windshield.

"Why won't the missiles hit the same targets?"

"Target lights will blink at different rates."

Magpie took a cagoule from a small box and put it on as the rain slid off her camo-uniform underneath. She then hauled out the shoulder cannon and a Hydra FM-FPA missile. Kneeling a short distance from the Jeep, she loaded the Hydra, set the launcher on the small stand, and adjusted the sights, picking the targets—the four watchtowers a couple of hundred yards on either side of the wide-open thick metal doors leading into the fortress. She punched the launch button and turned away, hands pressed against her ears. The launcher fired with a resounding, dull thump, blasting out a wall of air that shook the Jeep while the missile disappeared into the black sky. The Hydra came into view when smaller projectiles with their own propulsion burst out of the shell and spiralled down to their targets. Magpie threw the cannon and its stand into the back of the Jeep.

Alister shook his head, "This'll kill us," he murmured under his breath.

"Stop mumbling, start the engine, and bring her round."

He bit the inside of his lip and shoved the gear stick.

"Pedal to the metal, soldier!"

The Jeep sped down the hill toward the crack and boom of explosions. Ahead of them, the towers buckled and tilted, the tops blazing defiantly against the rain and sweeping wind. Alister shoved the gear, and the Jeep snarled angrily and leapt forward. It skidded several feet until the jagged tread clawed into the wet gravel, then surged towards the fortress door. Mud and stones sprayed up and smashed either side of them, and they hit a rock that knocked the Jeep sideways, so it tilted onto two wheels before crunching back down onto the gravelled track to bounce through the fortress entrance. Bullets peppered the windscreen and front and sides of the bonnet.

Several yards into the fortress, the adhesive coating of the secondary Hydra gel that had slowly bled down the tower dissolved away, and the watchtowers flared up like giant beacons while explosions erupted around them. Flashes of light chased by plumes of smoke burst over the low rooftops.

A long, deafening crunch, broken by a string of booms, ripped across the fortress, and for several seconds, the entire area lit up like daylight as, one by one, the towers collapsed. Shadows rose, spread, and deepened across the low buildings, filling with shouting.

"Shit, RPG on our ten!" Magpie yelled. "There!"

A terrorist ran across the flat rooftops on their left, heading for a space between a short row of satellite dishes. The Jeep charged down the wet and muddy road and shot past him. Magpie punched the viewing plate between them, and the rear view appeared. She moved the camera and zoomed into the terrorists on the rooftops, hand steady despite the chaos.

"Hold on." Magpie yanked the steering wheel, and the Jeep smashed right, scraping along the side of a wall and demolishing lines of soft plastic poles supporting a long cable of lights. The road fell into darkness. Behind them, a furious surge of soil, gravel, and mud exploded a dozen feet into the air, spattering debris over the vehicle.

"That was too damn clo—" The pierce of loud cracks resounded through the vehicle, ringing in their ears. "Hell," Magpie said. "They've got high-calibre longshots. We won't be able to take many more of those hits. Another cannon. Twist the wheel, Al."

Alister shot a glance in the mirror. The terrorist crouched on a roof, turning as he tracked them along the road. "Can't," he shouted. "Gotta slow to take the corner. Oh crap!" Another figure had appeared behind the first. Sophie's father.

He swung his assault rifle against the head of the terrorist with the shoulder cannon, then waved to Alister and disappeared into an alley.

The wipers flashed furiously across the mud- and rain-splattered windscreen, spreading and clearing a thin brown layer. Magpie flicked a switch, and the mud slid off.

Alister weaved the Jeep left and right, accelerating and decelerating along the soaked, sodden, uneven road, splashing through hard-edged potholes, skidding and slipping across metal plates covering larger ditches. The heavy-metal rattling of the boxes in the back merged with the hail and sound of bullets crunching into the glass and metal.

"What the hell just happened, Al?"

"Sophie's dad just saved us," Alister shouted over the noise.

"Great," Magpie shouted back. "Then there's hope for these motherfu—"

A figure landed on top of the Jeep with a loud bang. Alister braked hard, and the terrorist crashed forward onto the bonnet, arms waving furiously, then rolled off. The Jeep bumped over the body and squeezed out a gargled scream followed by a long, agonising crunch as the man was squashed face down into the mud.

"Not all of them." Alister grimaced, his voice barely audible over the snapping of gunfire and explosions.

Another figure landed on Magpie's side of the Jeep. She wound down the window and smashed her fist into a teenager's face, knocking him onto the road. Closing the window, she clambered over the back of the seat.

"What are you doing?" Alister shouted.

"Payback."

Magpie snapped the shoulder cannon onto the tripod and flipped it upright. A second later, she'd slotted a shell into the barrel. The sound of the hailstorm increased, and cold air rushed in when she flipped the rear window open. She fired, and the distant explosions silenced the shooters. Magpie yanked the window shut and crawled back.

"That thing's bloody quiet."

"Grandpa," she said, "silent and deadly."

A thin red beam from a shoulder cannon flickered through the rear window of the Jeep, dancing over the windscreen and dashboard.

"Hold tight." Magpie yanked the steering wheel, and the Jeep careered sideways across the road.

"What the...? Magpie!" Alister shouted. The missile flew past them and struck the metal gates ahead. A spray of shrapnel and debris crunched onto the Jeep's body and tore across the windscreen.

Chapter Sixteen

Go," Magpie screamed through the clattering of shrapnel and gunfire. "The gates!"

Alister slammed the gear stick into reverse, and the Jeep hissed and growled back in anger. They could almost feel the liquids shift and counter-flow while the pistons and valves snapped round, and the Jeep veered off the sidewalk back onto the road. Alister punched the gear stick forward with the base of his palm, and the car shot through the gap.

He drove furiously, swerving left and right through and around explosions of frozen soil, stone, muddy gravel, and snow blasting around them. Neither of them noticed that the hailstorm had passed. Alister breathed in short, hard bursts as he shifted gears and yanked the wheel one way, then the other.

"Go left," Magpie yelled. "Get as close as you can to the fence on the other side. They won't risk hitting the community."

He gritted his teeth and curved towards the fence on the far side. Spotlights lit them up from both sides of the buffer zone, and the shelling stopped.

"Don't slow," she said, looking over her shoulder.

"What? Oh, hell!" Two vehicles had appeared behind them, cutting through sweeping spotlights, headlamps slicing sharp flashes off the rear-view mirror into his eyes and closing in fast.

"Can't you—?"

"No," Alister interrupted. "I'm going flat out already."

A bright trail of red smoke shot into the sky and exploded, lighting the night.

"Flares," Magpie said, "Keep going. Buffer zone veers left half a mile ahead between the Community and wind farm."

"They're getting closer, Magpie. Don't think we'll make it."

"Pull over," Magpie shouted and clambered into the back of the Jeep and pulled an old XM25 grenade launcher from one of the boxes.

"Are you serious?" Alister shouted back.

"Just do it!"

Alister braked hard, and Magpie jumped and rolled across the muddy ground to come up in a crouch. The laser rangefinder danced over the approaching Jeep, and Magpie pointed it at the ground just ahead of the oncoming jeep and fired. The Jeep met the grenade and launched sideways to crash upside down into several inches of mud. Alister, firing at the second Jeep as he ran, rushed to Magpie's side. The Jeep exploded, rolled forward, trailing small pools of sizzling green and blue nano-fuels, and stopped in a muddy, colour-fizzled heap.

Another shot of the XM25 demolished the metal gates that led out into the wilderness. Magpie got to the jeep first, dropped the launcher into its box and jumped in, "Move it, Al, before reinforcements arrive."

Alister climbed in and clipped the seat belt.

Magpie punched the gear stick. "Conscience got you again?"

"I'm not a soldier."

"Good thing I am."

The route of the Lightning Seed, now traversing rough terrain, had sliced a long, narrow gash through the sky, leaving a deep, churning scar of black clouds that stretched towards the distant horizon and crackled with pure white explosions of electricity. Thick columns of rain and hail bled along their path. On either side spread a black sky shimmering with stars.

"Nothing's the way it should be."

"Welcome to my world." A flash of lightning lit up Magpie's grim expression. She shoved the gear stick up a notch, and the Jeep jolted and shot forward, rattling the boxes in the back. "My guess is they'll hit the outskirts of Vegas just before we do." She shifted gears, and the engine growled up through the revs to rest at a steady roar.

***

They turned off the Veterans Memorial Highway, and Magpie pulled up on the outskirts of a dead forest. A curved road was signposted 'Las Vegas Paiute Golf Resort'. Taking out a pair of binoculars, she zipped her jacket and stepped into the chill wind. Alister followed and stood beside her. They were barely visible against the grey and white background of the sky and snow-swept hilltop. In the distance, a glimmering patchwork of lights and towers thinned out into the grey landscape.

"So that's Vegas?" Alister said.

"Yep." Magpie continued to gaze down the hill through the binoculars.

"Can you see them?"

"There, one o'clock." She passed him the binoculars and

pointed to the right side of a road that circled the expanded suburbs of Las Vegas. "That's about two miles away."

Alister scanned the maze of buildings, rigged and repaired with thick plastic sheets and tarpaulins. The remains of the original suburbs were patched with settlements of caravans, bucky dome homes, and greenhouses. Threads of rivers, beaded with large shimmering pools, wove through the ruins between long strips of greenhouses, the land between them linked by bridges and plastic-steel walkway tunnels. To the east of the city, overlooking the spread of agri-domes, were the hive farms—glowing towers of fruit and vegetable plots, over which dots of workers scurried like ants, tending and harvesting all year round. Distribution centres were dotted around the perimeter of the farms. Beyond them, a forest of vast wind turbines hummed beside a steam-fusion power station barely visible under the frost-white skeleton of scaffolding and a steel frame.

"So that's where the food comes from?"

Magpie nodded. "Where the architects and farmers first worked together. Stripped down the apartment blocks and knocked up the first hive farms. They're all over the world now. Those smaller domes are personal plots."

"What are all those flashing lights? Looks like there's some kind of festival going on. The road cuts right through it."

"The Christian Aid Peace settlement, getting their Easter Fair ready."

A wide road circled the settlement perimeter and curved towards the main city, where the Strip glowed dimly in the distance.

"They're back on the road," Magpie said. "Stop the Seed shaking up more crazy weather. C'mon."

***

The Jeep slipped and churned through a winding mud track flecked with snow, splashing through a wide stream onto rocky terrain.

"How are we going to stop them?" Alister said.

"Not alone, that's for sure." Magpie concentrated on the road ahead, hands tight on the steering wheel. "As soon as we hit

Vegas, I'm going to call on a few friends, and together we're gonna kick the shit out of those crazies before they frazzle Vegas under the biggest lightning storm in history."

"And get Suzie out on one piece."

"And that. Grab the map and find the PI barracks. I've marked it."

Alister opened up the map and examined it.

"What's taking you so long?" Magpie asked.

"The mess of sketches and pencil lines all over the place meant to show where the ruins, new-builds, and roads are. Hang on." He glanced out of the window, then down at the map. "We're here, barracks are there. I think this is where the Easter event is happening. Okay, take the second right after we turn down the road the Followers took. I'll want to see the layout of the roads for myself from there in case anything changed. What the hell?"

A crack on the Jeep's roof was followed by the chink of something falling onto the weapons. Magpie craned her neck sideways to look up out of the side window. Above them, a small airship dropped out of the sky, buzzing furiously.

"Get out!" Magpie slammed on the brakes, shoved the door open, and jumped.

Alister got as far as the edge of the seat, facing outwards with the door open when the explosion blasted him several yards from the vehicle—along with parts of the seat, door, the Jeep's body, and the dashboard.

Covered in the Soft-Machine, he slammed through the snow into the frozen ground and rolled downhill. A hard crunch against the trunk of a long-dead tree stopped his fall and shook clumps of snow down onto him. Coughing and spitting out powdered ice, he tried to catch his breath. The buzzing in his head seemed to have an echo that zigzagged around up in the sky.

"You really should get up and hide," Zen said.

He staggered to his feet and stumbled into the icy skeleton of a forest to see Zen zigzag through the trees and swirling haze. The Soft-Machine crackled across his flesh and out through the combat uniform, making him invisible, but he was still making tracks. Branches snapped above him, and shards of frozen wood blasted over his head. Alister swore under his breath. Several shuriken struck branches and exploded, sending thousands of fragments down over him. The shock sharpened his senses, and the forest came into crisp white focus. Thick chalk outlines of trees scraped into twilight grey. Ahead of him, bat-like wings had sprouted from the demon's back, shooting skywards into a white blur.

The buzzing grew louder, and more branches blasted apart in jagged intervals. Arms raised to protect his face, he smashed through bushes, and the noise overhead circled away.

Alister stumbled forward and dropped down an incline. Falling through thin ice into a freezing stream, he jumped up to gulp in deep gasps of cold air. The Soft-Machine squeezed out the water and made itself waterproof as he waded to the bank and out into the acrid smoke from the burning Jeep. Hell, he'd been forced around in a circle. Whoever it was flying around in that thing was making sure Alister would end up back here, exposed with no cover. He was being played. Where was Magpie?

The Soft-Machine stretched and swarmed to form insulating gloves as he thrust his hands into the deep, smooth layers of snow. Clawing at clumps of ice-encrusted roots, he scrabbled up the shallow bank. Setting off round and back into the woods, he headed for a large log surrounded by crushed saplings and bushes, then dived into the bank of snow piled against one side. Lying in the snow pit, the Soft-Machine bled out through his clothes and spread across the hole to form a covering the same colour and texture as the snow he had fallen into, connected to him by a thick thread that wound down around his wrist.

He shivered and tried to catch his breath, safe from the light snowfall and swirling wind that dropped more clumps of snow from the branches and swept away his footprints.

The buzzing grew louder and merged with a hissing and sliding. The sound stopped some distance away. The plane must have landed. The blazing roar of the Jeep reached him, and then the closer sound of footsteps crunched through the snow. Alister gritted his teeth and pushed back a crazy notion of jumping up at whoever was trying to kill them. With this guy, it would be fatal. The crunch of footsteps stopped a few feet away.

"Hey, hombre, where are you?" A whiny, nasal voice called out from the other side of the log. "Come on, don't waste our time, English. I have thermal goggles. You lose."

No time for hide and seek. This could be the only chance to take the guy by surprise. The Soft-Machine swarmed back and slapped into the fabric of his combat gear. Spiralling around his muscles, it accelerated his leap over the log so fast that everything was a blur, and he almost lost his balance.

Jesus-Ernesto was faster. A knife appeared in his hand, and he swung it down at Alister, who instinctively took a step left and parried the attack, driving the blade into Jesus-Ernesto's thigh—a perfect Kenpo 'Raining Lance' defence. He followed with a powerful elbow thrust to the horseman's chest, sending him to the ground.

The little man howled and pulled the thin knife from his thigh, hobbled several steps back with an ugly, pained grimace, and threw a shuriken needle straight at Alister's heart while dragging himself away to the centre of the clearing.

Alister slapped the needle aside, swinging his hand up to knock the second needle with the back of his hand, and strode towards Jesus-Ernesto. "Not so easy, eh?"

He stopped several yards from Jesus-Ernesto. The air stilled, and they faced each other in the eerie silence.

The Soft-Machine receded behind the combat gear and wrapped around his skin, keeping him armoured and insulated. He stared grimly at Jesus-Ernesto, aware of the tension in each muscle of the man's body, reading the barely visible impulsive flickers in the near-motionless face. The man's left hand lingering over a belt of blades and shuriken stars couldn't have been more obvious.

Zen reappeared and sat on a log to watch them. He held his tail in his hand and spat flecks of flame to whack them with the forked end of his tail. The little fiery balls flew out to snap and sizzle in the snow a few feet from him.

Jesus-Ernesto glanced to where Alister was looking, peered more closely, and, with a shudder, stood up, two shuriken stars in each hand. A second later, Alister stared at them buried deep across his chest.

"Oh." Alister staggered back, staring bewildered at a red patch across his jacket. Then, with his eyes widened in some strange realisation, he fell sideways into a mound of snow.

"Your devil friend has come to collect you." Jesus-Ernesto

produced a small sachet from an inside pocket, tore the end off, and squeezed the grey gel over the hole in his thigh. He emptied the tube and glanced over at Alister, who lay motionless with his face buried in the snow, then across to the empty space where the demon had been. Teeth clenched against the pain, the horseman grunted and wobbled to his feet. With most of his weight on the uninjured leg, he looked all around and made the sign of the cross over his head and chest, then hobbled back to the airship and hauled himself in. He started the engine and let it idle while he treated the wound on his thigh.

***

Alister turned to his side, bringing the log into view. Zen had swung one leg over the other to rest his ankle on a thigh and leaned forward, peering at Alister.

"He fell for it. Not bad, kid."

"Thanks." Alister carefully pulled out the shuriken blades and examined them, shuddering at the sensation across his chest as the particles of the Soft-Machine reverted back from blood red to black and repaired itself. The blades had penetrated just enough to draw blood. The knives were intricately crafted weapons, etched with swirling patterns on one side and geometric designs on the other.

Zen disappeared. In the field beyond the treeline, a thin, dark thread of smoke curled up from the idling one-man airship. Alister set off towards it in deep strides. He reached the open hillside as the rotors whirred into a haze, and the airship rose slowly. Alister weighed the shuriken in his right hand and threw it as hard as possible. And missed.

"Damn," he muttered. "I need a level up…oh, hello."

The Soft-Machine coiled around his arms and upper body so that he could barely hold back the force and acceleration being added to his throw. The second star shot from his hand so fast all he saw was a gash appear along the underside of the opening wing. A loud hissing fed a rapidly growing, thin, flaming streak, and then the airship tilted and curved downwards, cutting a stream of burning fuel into the air.

Jesus-Ernesto threw himself out before it hit the ground. He rolled away from the crash and dragged himself away from the wreckage. Trailing a line of red to spread and dilute through the snow, he wormed towards the cover of the trees.

"No, it's not possible," he cried. "We are chosen."

Alister walked up to him. "So your god says it's okay to murder innocent people?" He kicked the horseman hard in the ribs. The horseman cried out in pain as he rolled over and reached for his needle armband. Alister stomped on his hand, "Any excuse to slice people to death? That's all you really want, isn't it?"

Kneeling down, he tore away the armbands and lifted one of Jesus-Ernesto's knives. He spun it through his fingers, "Did your god plan this for you, too?" He sliced through the belt of blades across the horseman's chest and waist and ripped them off. The horseman lifted off the ground, then fell back as Alister tossed the belts away.

The man stared up at Alister with an ugly grin on his face. "Only the pure will—"

"Shut it." Alister yanked him by the collar and smashed his fist into the horseman's face.

Jesus-Ernesto gargled and, reaching round his back, said, "The flames of righteousness will—" His face knotted in pain, and he groaned.

A burning ran across Alister's hand. The Soft-Machine reacted instantly and swarmed around his torso and arms. He dropped the horseman and stepped back. Jesus-Ernesto's body flared yellow, then orange, then washed over in a thick layer of blue-white flames. The man screamed and stumbled back into the wreckage. Alister dived away. Behind him, the mix of whatever chemicals were in the man's outfit combined with the burning plastics and fuel to produce a deafening explosion that blasted a searing wave of vaporised snow across the hilltop.

Ears ringing in the silence, Alister stepped into the brown circle of charred grass spotted with clumps of green and the fleshy, scorched remains of Jesus-Ernesto's bones.

The punk angel appeared beside him. Time stopped.

"He blew himself up," Alister murmured in disbelief.

"Death was always a greater part of his life than yours."

He followed the angel's gaze to the blackened, charred skull that used to be Jesus-Ernesto. "He saw Zen, too. What happens when you die?"

"It's complicated. The best thing you can do is remember that the outside world is not the same as how you put it together in your head or how you think about it."

"Brilliant, that'll really help, thanks."

"Be mindful of that, and everything else will fall into place naturally."

"Sure," Alister knelt by the skull, "What kind of man would do that?"

"A fanatic who values his life less than his beliefs."

"This is insane," Alister stood up. "I need to find Magpie, save my friends from these people. This world is totally screwed up. These guys just enjoy killing people."

Alister gave the angel a sideways look. "Does it really matter what we feel or think?"

"More than you realize. You are more than this moment, this body-mind."

"Whatever," Alister sighed. "There's a massive universe with you lot and all these other universes out there, and I'm worried over wanting to rescue a girl."

"You love her. Sometimes, the wake of our intentions marks the greater purpose."

"You what?"

"The motives you believe drive your actions are trivial compared to their consequences and impact on the world around you and beyond. A spark can ignite an eternal flame."

"You're saying that wanting to save Suzie is part of something bigger, like stopping that Lightning Seed?"

"Your past actions have changed the lives of generations. Each action along the way, no matter how trivial, leaves a resonance in the lives of others and affects many lives other than yours and Suzanne's."

"What, is this some kind of fate?"

"No, there is no fate—simply the change brought about by the choices you make, actions that determine which of the possible futures will unfold in this reality and which will be left to others."

"Others?"

The angel was gone. A cold wind struck his face. What could he do? He was just one guy who… "Magpie!" He ran around and down the hill towards the scattered remains of the Jeep. Zigzagging through the wreckage, he found her half-buried in a mound of snow piled against a large bush someway down the hill.

"Damned visions." He looked up and shouted, "You could have told me where she was!" He swore under his breath and scooped away the snow. There was no blood. "Magpie, I'm going to feel for any broken bones, okay?"

She didn't respond. Nothing broken. He held her close while the Soft-Machine swelled out, cocooning them in a thick, fibrous layer. They slowly warmed, and she eventually regained consciousness. He relaxed.

The fabric receded back into Alister's clothing, and Magpie made to lean away from him but instead almost fell sideways. Alister grabbed her, and she flopped onto him.

"You okay?"

"What?" She raised her hand and wiped it over her face until it bumped against her helmet. "Oh, the Jeep, did it blow up?" she asked woozily.

"I'll say."

He made to take his arm from around her shoulder, and she nudged him, "Don't move. We need to keep warm until my head clears. Were your hands over me awhile back?"

"I wanted to make sure you didn't have any broken bones."

"Haven't heard that one before," she managed a smile. "What happened?"

Alister gave a cut-down version of his encounter with Jesus-Ernesto, leaving out the demon and punk-angel.

"The horsemen."

"Horsemen?"

"Plotinus must have sent the four horsemen after us."

"The who?"

"Four horsemen of the apocalypse, you know?"

"Uh, not sure. Something to do with the end of the world? He hired them?"

"What? No." She grimaced and, reaching into a pocket, produced a strip of pills. She tore one out and swallowed it. "Four guys, mercenaries, calls them after the four horsemen of the apocalypse. They're all psycho."

Alister shook his head. "That's all we need."

Magpie nodded. "We need to get in touch with the PI's in Vegas. There's no way we want to face those psychos alone. C'mon." She got to her feet and fell against Alister. "Whoops."

She leaned on him for a few seconds, then headed unsteadily towards the wreckage of the Jeep strewn across the hillside and spotted the charred ring beyond. "You weren't kidding about the fireball." She stepped carefully through the scattered remains. "Let's see what we can salvage."

They walked around in the snow. Alister found a pistol and threw it over to Magpie,

"We used to scout and camp around here," she said, examining the pistol. "Me and Paulie and a bunch of the guys from town." She threw the gun away and, after a few minutes of scavenging, found a thermal blanket and threw it over her shoulder as she walked to the edge of the hill. "We came up here for the training exercises before we set off for the Korean Ice War."

"Ice War?"

"In China, The Big Freeze started the Winter Revolution. The counter-revolutionaries against the changes retreated to North Korea. That started the Korean Ice War between North and South Korea. The US helped the South in the early days of the Freeze. Two years in space suits was hell. Come on, we're on the outskirts of Vegas. The PI Vets have a base at the old elementary school."

Huddled together under the blanket, they set off down the barely visible road towards the city's outskirts.

"Space suits?"

"Yeah, The North Koreans were heavily into chemical warfare. We lived in igloos and dressed in weird spacesuit outfits for the better part of two years. It's where I met Falcon. She saved my neck more than once. Me and Paulie learned a lot those two years."

"Falcon?"

"My partner."

"Parter, you mean?"

"Yeah, gay."

"Oh, Anyway, bet you were glad when it was over."

"No, I stayed gay after the war."

"Oh, haha. How did the war end?"

"The people who abandoned the Chinese Winter Revolution got pretty nasty with the local North Koreans—raping, stealing food, torture. The North Korean Army started fighting against them to protect their people instead of fighting the South Koreans and the Winter Alliance. Eventually, it was all of us against the counter-revolutionaries from China. The war finished after a couple of weeks, and the single United Korea was formed. It's how the Peoples Infantry and Chinese got friendly."

Magpie smiled. "Falcon and my cousin Nara are with the PI squad at West Sahara. They're the only close family I've left."

Alister nodded. "Hey, we got a lift." A small vehicle was making its way up the hill towards them. "Your P.I friends must have seen the explosion."

Chapter Seventeen

"Thou must atone," I heard them say, "and the Lightning Seed shall be the way

to rid the world of winter's scourge. Restore all seasons thus now deserved."

And of its hiding place revealed, in sacred parchments long concealed.

Once again, now brought to light, time to awaken the Seed's radiant might.

— Plotinus II, The Path to Order, Chapter One

Alister and Magpie sat in the back of an old Tesla. Two Peoples Infantry soldiers sat in front. The road to the barracks took them over a fast-running stream that disappeared into a large tunnel under the main road, busy with people on bikes and mopeds. A slow, winding journey around wrecked houses, Portakabin settlements, dome-homes, and over streams and storm tunnels led to the makeshift barracks across from the Centennial Hills Hospital on the opposite side of Deer Springs Way.

The car pulled up outside a building at the far end of the barracks, and a soldier took them to Colonel Rogers' office.

"Take a seat. The colonel will be with you in a minute. Alister sat at a small wooden table and looked out across the training ground towards the remains of Vegas gleaming under dark skies while Magpie examined a city map. Colonel Rogers strode into the room, followed by a private, and Magpie immediately stood at attention.

"Relax," the colonel said. "Take a seat." He gestured to two chairs and went round the table to sit in the wide leather seat facing them. "So, Magpie, with all these rumours flying around, maybe you can explain what the hell is happening." He paused. "And tell me why a civilian has been sent out on a mission."

The colonel leaned back and listened while Magpie explained the Lightning Seed, Suzie sand Nehir, and the horsemen.

"There are two other convoys out there, and you convinced Cape to send you and a civilian after this one?" He looked across at Alister, "Your girlfriend huh?"

Magpie put a hand on Alister's arm and gave him a look

before turning to Rogers. "Sir, His girlfriend's Suzie Emerson."

"I know of her and her uncle," Rogers nodded.

Magpie continued. "Alister has provided us with accurate situation-critical intel on several occasions. He also helped save over fifty hostages and found and rescued a key asset."

"Really? Sounds like Emerson picked a good one." He turned to Alister. "How'd you get to know so much?"

"I don't know, sir. I lost my memory back in Halfbeak. It's coming back slowly."

"Let's hope you get it back soon," Rogers said. "Magpie, do you have a plan?"

"My guess is the Seed is going to the Crown, sir."

"The tallest building in Vegas, that would make sense to a psychopath who wants to put on a big show for the end of the world." Colonel Rogers turned to the map on the screen behind him and gestured to magnify one area with his hands. "The Crown Tower." He touched the image, and a pop-up box appeared. "Sixteen hundred and fifty feet high. A blacked-out bus arrived there a couple of hours ago. Parker, go find the messenger who brought the latest intel on Crown activity. Call a meeting, we'll have to start planning an evacuation."

"Yes, sir."

Rogers sat down. "Over five hundred Follower families live in the Crown. Plotinus's Martyr Army and a Hindu sect, followers of Agni, took residence there last week. We did suspect it was in preparation for his arrival."

"Sir, he'll kill everyone in the city, including his people," Alister said.

"Son, I'm well aware of what Plotinus is capable of," Rogers said. "Magpie, what are your orders from General Cape?"

"Make contact with you, sir, for backup and any support you can give to protect civilians and prevent Plotinus's people from detonating the Lightning Seed. Then, as soon as comms are up, radio in for further instructions."

"Plotinus's men will use residents as human shields. Mounting an assault to get the Seed is out of the question. A small tactical team might have better luck." Rogers fell into a thoughtful silence. "We might be able to get our hands on building design and floor plans. There's not much time to plan. Do you have camo outfits?"

"Yes, sir," Magpie said, glancing at Alister. "We both—"

A flash of lightning exploded over the city. After a few seconds of silence, another blinding explosion released a torrential downpour of rain and hailstones that shattered across rooftops and crashed onto vehicles, mottling them like golf balls.

Magpie raised her voice. "We both have, sir."

Alister was staring at the tower and thinking about what Raguel had said. "Anything could happen. And it all will," he said out loud without realizing.

"You alright, son?" Rogers said.

"What? Sorry. Yes, I'm fine." Alister nodded. Suzie was up there. "Magpie and myself are the only people in town with the camo-outfits and any chance to get close enough to shut that thing down."

"There are other soldiers who can wear your gear."

Magpie and Alister exchanged glances."

"Is there something I need to know?" Rogers said.

"I have nanoparticles in me that can shut that Armageddon bomb down."

"Nanoparticles?"

"My family worked for Centauri in the nanotech labs."

"You had some kind of Spider-Man incident?"

"Something like that."

"I see." Rogers sighed, "You've brought him this far, Magpie. I guess you're the best person to..."

Shock waves thumped through the building, and the lights went out, the blast knocking them off their chairs. The viewing plate and pictures fell off the wall to shatter on the floor. Sirens rose to wail through the darkness while lightning crackled across the black sky.

"We're under attack," Rogers said, "Stay down."

Small explosions fell along the tarmac road outside, sending up a spray of stones and rainwater. Alister scuttled to the wall while Magpie and Rogers crawled to the window and inched their heads up to peer over the edge. Several buildings around the far-side perimeter were in flames. Soldiers rallied to turrets, shelters, and armoured vehicles. Alister crawled over to the others and caught a glimpse of something in the remains of a broken window that had swung out. He raised his head over the edge of the window frame to get a better look. At the far end of a long, straight road, beyond a red 4x4, a large quad-bike glimmered in the haze of the downpour. A man stood beside it, tapping on something in his hand, probably a remote control for all those mini-missile launchers on the bike.

"There's some kind of weaponised quad-bike by the entrance sentry box with a guy controlling small missile launchers. It looks like your people can't see it."

"That sentry box is a hundred and fifty yards away in a dark storm," Rogers said.

"Sir," Magpie said. "I'd be inclined to go with Cloud on this."

The door swung open, and Private Parker and another soldier staggered in. "Sir, the main gate has been breached by an unknown vehicle that just smashed through under covering fire, coming in from somewhere nearby. One passenger in the vehicle."

Rogers looked from Magpie to Alister, then turned to Parker. "There's a stealth-armoured vehicle by the sentry box. Spread the word, tell people to stay out of the line of fire and target everything they've got to the entrance. Miles set up a perimeter and get some firepower in that direction ASAP."

"Yes, sir," Miles said and disappeared.

"Stalin's in the truck, sir," Magpie said. "The quad must be Omar."

Rogers shook his head. "Strife and Famine, Plotinus's horsemen? He really wants you dead." He gestured to Magpie. "Cloud, stay here with Magpie. You two need to stay alive and finish this. Parker, you look injured."

"Just bruises, sir, I'm fine."

"Good, let's move out," Rogers said, leaving with Parker.

Magpie turned to Alister. "Seeing in the dark—what other tricks can you do, Al?"

Alister took a deep breath. "I've got this Soft-Machine outfit that can do weird stuff like change shape, change colour, armour up, even make me invisible, somehow blends through what I'm—"

The chink of metal falling onto broken glass was followed by the dull thud of an explosion, and gas filled the room. Magpie swore and fell onto him, unconscious.

"Magpuu, wha…?"

A fist demolished the remains of reinforced glass and hauled him through the window, hurling him across the road. Barely conscious, Alister flew several yards through the storm, the Soft-Machine swelling around him. He smashed into the side of a building and crumbled to the ground. If not for the cushioning of the Soft-Machine, the impact would have broken most of his limbs.

The particles inside him triggered an adrenalin rush, along with immune instructions to produce an antidote to the gas. He recovered enough to see an enormous hulk of a man striding towards him while a long line of explosions fell around them.

Towering over Alister, Yuri wiped the rain off his tattooed face and waved to Omar before resting his fists on his hips. He was different, eyes manic, whole body vibrating with energy. This guy was fully tanked with who knows what kind of psycho-physical stimulants.

"You?" the man snarled.

Alister feebly inched his head up. Yuri smiled down at him. "How did you survive my mighty throw? I will try again."

The Soft-Machine blended into his combat uniform seconds before Yuri leaned down and grabbed Alister. His arm slipped out of Yuri's grip. Yuri tried again and failed again. He wiped his hand on the leg of his trousers and grabbed Alister's wrist. As he did so, Alister swung his leg, catching Yuri on the ankle, and the giant dropped to one knee. Alister slipped his hand free, rolled away, and jumped up. This time around, Yuri was fast, really fast. Alister barely had time to react before a punch to his chest hurled him back to crunch against the wall again.

How the hell was he going to take this guy down? Yuri was going for punches, as there was no way he could get a grip on Alister. Alister ducked, and Yuri's fist smashed a cavity in the concrete wall.

At the far end of the road, Omar was adjusting the controller.

"Only two of you?" Alister said, rolling away and taking several steps back.

"What?" Yuri said, striding forward. "You can see Famine?"

Stuff this. The Soft-Machine curled and spiralled around his body, and he jumped into Yuri with such force the impact cracked the giant's chest plate and sent him staggering back.

Alister pushed away and landed crouched, curling his left

arm up and rubbing his left shoulder. "That's going to leave a mark."

Yuri reared up and, spreading his arms, roared, "Now!"

A wide ring of heavy splats fell around them and, finding each other, turned into a solid ring of white flames. The burning seemed to feed on and climb the downpour, turning water into fuel. "Now I have you," Yuri said, the rest of his words lost in a torrent of explosions beyond the searing wall.

"What the hell..? Alister breathed in warm air and gaped at the ring of fire that rose almost fifteen feet around them. He squinted and turned away from the curtain of shattered flame, disorientated by the furious light.

The first punch came so fast that Alister barely dodged it. He twisted and sidestepped Yuri's assaults, who seemed immune to the rain and lights. When Alister did fall, a kick hit him square in the chest. The impact lifted him off the ground and sent him flying through the thick wall of flame. Covered from head to toe in the Soft-Machine and drenched in a thin sheen of flaming rain, he fell into the pool of sizzling liquid. Yuri was already bearing down on him. There was no way he could take that hulk out now. The guy had done something to himself—drugs, gear, both. Whatever it was, it was deadly.

Alister staggered to his feet, a blazing wireframe figure. Rain landing on him ignited and covered him with thin, fiery streams that hissed and exploded. He sprinted away from Yuri towards the shimmering outline of Famine and his quad-bike.

Omar swivelled a short, stubby turret gun and released a hail of fire at the burning demon approaching him. Alister dived sideways into a path between two Portakabin barracks and hit the ground heavily. Damn, he should have known Omar would see him. He had to think straight; if only those particles could take away the pain for a while. The Soft-Machine tightened around his torso and ribs, and the pain subsided. Breathing easier, he waited a few seconds for the flames to fade off his body.

Invisible but for the thin lines of rain streaming over him, he dashed across the road into the opposite alley and clambered up a pipe onto a low roof. Below him, Omar had shut down the assault of explosive bullets and the fire wall and swung the mounted machine gun around in small circles, looking for him.

Yuri strode towards Omar and the ring of micro-interceptors, motion sensor mines and incendiaries keeping soldiers away.

Then the rain stopped, and an abrupt silence fell across the barracks, leaving the city heavy with charged air. In the distance, under folds of thick, dark clouds, slithers of lightning clawed wildly at Crown Tower.

Unable to reach Omar, a group of soldiers ran towards Yuri with their weapons raised. Yuri gestured to Omar, and Omar snapped the machine gun into its slot and clambered onto the quad-bike. A flick of a switch had all his defence mechanisms shoot back into slots on the quad-bike, and still invisible to all but Alister, he hurtled down the road towards Yuri with the soldiers in his sights.

Alister sprinted across the roof and hurled himself off the edge, heading for a point several feet in front of Omar's weaponised quad-bike thundering down the road. Time slowed again. Omar's quad decelerated, and Alister had yet to land. He'd hit the road and probably get crushed by the quad.

The Soft-Machine spread between his arms and legs, trapping the air and slowing his fall, so he swooped and flew straight at Omar to crash down at an angle into Omar's side. They flew off the bike onto the sidewalk. The bike accelerated along the road and struck Yuri head-on, shoving him several yards back into a parking lot beside an old fuelling station.

Alister pulled a pistol from Omar's holster and pressed it against his shoulder. Omar began to sneer. Alister didn't hesitate. He simply pulled the trigger. Omar screamed in pain, only to snap his mouth shut when the end of the pistol jabbed hard into his forehead.

"Shut it," Alister snarled. "It's over."

"Hardly, pal. You think that would hurt Yuri? He can handle more than—" A chemical-fuelled explosion ripped open the night and sent a burning mushroom into the air. The quad-bike had taken Yuri with it straight into the filling station. Alister staggered back with his arm raised, leaving Omar clutching his shoulder with his back hunched against the inferno.

"No!" Omar screamed.

By the time Alister got to his feet, he was surrounded by soldiers. He left them to secure Omar and returned to the office and Magpie.

Magpie was on the floor, leaning against the wall woozily like she'd just woken up. Alister fetched some cold water from the cooler and handed it to her.

She took the drink and threw it into her own face. "That's better. Did I miss much?" She took his hand and pulled herself to her feet, wiping her hand across her face.

"Not really," Alister said, smiling.

Outside, a furious wind had picked up. Beyond the shattered window, smoke was shredding over the smouldering wreckage of cars and motorcycles, creaking and groaning in the strong wind. "Not really, eh?"

"I had a run-in with Omar and Yuri."

Magpie's eyes widened.

"Omar's quad hit Yuri and took him into the car park."

"They both dead?"

"Not Omar. I knocked him off the quad before it took Yuri out. Your people have him."

"That leaves Death, the final horseman. I guess the outfit kept you alive?"

Alister nodded. "Keeps changing shape to protect me. It armoured up a couple of times, and when Yuri threw me against a wall, it padded out and went all squidgy."

"And it makes you invisible, too?"

"Yeah."

"You should have a comic book hero name. Cyber Nuts, maybe."

"Shut up."

Magpie laughed, and it made her grimace and raise a hand to her ribs. "C'mon," she grunted, "let's find Rogers. We got work to do and not much time to do it."

Several buildings away, lights came on, and a door opened. Parker came out and waved them over.

"Great," Magpie said. "Someone's got the lights on."

A stiff wind blew through the compound. It gathered pace and rain and howled around them as they ran down the road, dodging crates and boxes that tumbled across their path and crashed into vehicles and buildings. Soaked tarpaulins thrashed through the air to tear over cars, slap into walls, or wrap and flap noisily around lamp posts. Streaks and knots of lightning flashed and swirled over Crown Tower, shattering into thousands of shards across black clouds.

Magpie and Alister strained to push the door shut against the wind at the Medic building. In the reception area, a soldier wrapped a bandage around another soldier's arm. Beside him, a woman carefully squeezed a tube of plasti-skin over a long scar across the back of another's shoulder. People sat or lay on half a dozen gurneys lined down a corridor.

Parker appeared at the door. "This way." Magpie and Alister followed him down two flights of stairs and into a long tunnel. "The colonel told me to take you as close as possible to the Crown. He's sent snipers ahead and will launch a diversionary assault on the main and underground car park entrances. They'll try and keep your route clear once you're inside. PI will put up a perimeter fifty yards out from the building and checkpoints a hundred yards beyond that. There's still no comms, so you'll be alone until they're up. He's sending a squad to target the security cabin. That'll give us control of all access, elevators, and security cams."

Alister nodded. "How far away is the Crown?"

"About a mile and a half. Until the PI is in place, you'll be running a gauntlet the last half mile."

Alister and Magpie exchanged glances. "There has to be another way," Alister said. "What about service tunnels?"

"Impossible. Followers have them heavily guarded and booby-trapped, but…" Parker hesitated. "…there is a storm drain system under the entire city, big enough to handle any flash flood."

"Really?" Alister said. "Big enough for a boat?"

"A boat?" Magpie said. "You're kidding, right?"

"No," Parker said. "The storm drains are big enough for a small boat. In fact, the Crown has its own run-off and storage tanks to collect water, along with filter chambers to provide water for the toilets, indoor gardens, and car wash. You could get into the building that way."

"Those tanks must be flooded," Magpie said. "Can't see those extremists worrying too much about flushing, fish, and flowers."

"Nope," Parker was shaking his head. "The families there, some are pretty smart. They've turned the gardens into an indoor farm, and the aquarium is now a regular food supply."

***

Magpie and Alister eased the paddles into the slow-flowing waters, and the dinghy slipped through the gloom. Magpie adjusted her goggles and glanced at the small map on the glowing wristpad. "In half a mile, we'll hit a lower drain."

Her whisper echoed and faded into the occasional slaps and splashes. "We'll moor there and make our way up."

"What do you think, Magpie?"

Magpie replied with a terse nod. "It's doable. Just remember, slow is steady, steady is swift. Nothing rash or reckless. Keep your eyes open and watch your back."

"Yeah," Alister said uncertainly.

"Too late to worry, Al. Besides, we have the advantage. My camo gear, your outfit, sniper support. Those guys won't know what's hit them."

"We've handled some pretty nasty situations and cleaned up, haven't we?"

"Oh yeah, we're badass."

Turning a corner, they moved into the area directly below the tower and continued in tense silence, the paddles barely distinguishable from the gurgles and splashes of the flowing water. A light flashed around the corner, and Magpie brought the assault rifle up. Alister raised the paddle when voices echoed through the tunnel.

Alister pointed to himself and then the direction of the voices. Magpie nodded, and he slipped out of the canoe while she waited.

Pressed against the wall, he waded through the waist-high water, hesitated at the corner, and disappeared. Ahead of him, the storm drain continued for several yards, then sloped into a deeper arched tunnel. A metal ladder fixed to the arc's right wall led up to a narrow path along the top with a door at either end and one in the centre with a sign reading 'Great Basin Highway'. Beneath the sign, two Followers in black urban combat gear argued in harsh whispers, their echoes filling the drain tunnels. One pointed a gun at the other's face.

".... you chicken-shit coward. I should kill you now for bringing those families down here, Joel."

"Do it, Avi. At least I've saved some lives. Plotinus has lost his mind."

Still invisible, Alister climbed out of the water and up the ladder, wincing at the sound of water dropping from him to splash into the water and narrow path.

Avi glanced over his shoulder, and Alister froze, even though he was invisible.

Avi squinted and inched round to see better when Joel interrupted him.

"You either kill me now, or I'm going back up to guide the other families down here and away from the slaughter."

"Fine." Avi pushed the pistol into Joel's chest, and Alister whacked him. Avi tilted and toppled off the path. Cracking his skull against the narrow path below. He splashed into the water and sank, carried away into the darkness. Alister appeared beside Joel and grabbed his arm to prevent him from falling.

"What are you?" Joel's voice echoed down the tunnel.

"A friend. Did you mean what you said about getting other families away from the Crown?"

"Who are you? Where did you come from?"

"I'm here to stop the bomb going off."

"On your own?"

"No. Mags," he called, "we're good."

The dinghy came round the corner with Magpie, her assault rifle raised. "You okay, Al?"

Alister glanced at Joel, who nodded back slowly.

"Joel here wants to get some families out."

Magpie steered the dinghy to the ladder and climbed up. "Good, then you can help us get into that place."

"But—" Joel began before Alister interrupted him.

"You help us in. We help you get people out."

"Clock's ticking, Al," Magpie said.

Joel seemed uncertain and examined Magpie's face and finally said. "Okay, this way."

He led them along a narrow corridor, past small utility and store rooms, and into the laundry room. Their flash-light beams slid over dusty machines, ironing boards, rails, and cables. A rat scuttled along the side of the wall, quickly followed by another.

"Through here." Joel said, and they followed him out of the laundry room, along a narrow corridor, and into a gloomy and damp, low-ceilinged, underground car park. Pools of muddy water covered the ground, and a thin, fast-flowing stream curled down along the access ramp. About a hundred and fifty people—elderly, women, and children—formed a long, scraggy line along one wall.

"We have to hurry," Joel said.

"Not all of these people are Jewish," Alister said.

Joel shrugged. "Mostly Muslims, Sikhs, and Christians. The Jewish families are upstairs. Militants have forced one of our rabbis to hold a gathering to prepare for the purification. When they refused, the militants threatened to kill the tsaddiks."

"The who?" both Alister and Magpie asked.

"Righteous ones, mediators between the Divine and humanity. They're all in a conference hall. Plotinus is speaking to them. I was going to go back for the families, for them."

Magpie grabbed Alister's arm. "I know that look on your face, Al. Forget it. We need to reach the penthouse and stop the Lightning Seed. A city of people could get killed, maybe the whole damned planet."

"You hear what he said? Plotinus is here, Magpie." When Magpie didn't respond, Alister continued. "He won't see us coming, no one will. What if he gets away? What was it you said? Take them out now, don't give them another chance?" Magpie still didn't reply, and Alister turned to Joel. "Where are your people?"

"That door has the stairs leading to the fourth-level conference room where the Jewish community is."

"We can do it, Magpie. We'll have to go past Joel's people anyway. We can just give them a chance to get down here."

"He's a Follower, Al."

"Plotinus may have John Dee's library and other sacred texts," Joel said, "but a donkey carrying a load of holy books is still a donkey."

"Al," Magpie snapped. "We're running out of time. Do you wanna save a couple of hundred people or the planet?"

Joel shook his head slowly. "I can't tell you what to do, but I'm going to do what I can to save those people. On my own if I have to."

"You don't have a chance," Alister said.

"I've even less of a choice," Joel replied, checking his watch.

"They say the Seed will release its full force in under two hours."

"Sync me." Alister took Joel's hand and synced the countdown, touching his watch to Joel's.

Magpie shot a look at Alister. "Plotinus, eh?" She sighed and nodded. "Damn, Al, you are one stubborn sonofabitch. Get these people out," she said to Joel, nodding at the crowd. "We'll try to send the others down."

"Thank you. Tell them Joel Klein sent you," Joel said. "Most other families have locked themselves into their rooms, too scared to come out."

"Don't push your luck, kid," Magpie said.

"Joel," Alister said, "I'm sorry. We'll go for the people in the conference room, but that's it."

"I understand," Joel swallowed down his sadness. "Please don't fail." Without waiting for a response, he gestured to the line of families to follow him into the storm-drain access tunnel.

"Right," Magpie said, "let's camo up and see what's waiting upstairs." She opened the shoulder rest of the assault rifle, pressed a button, and the weapon faded from sight. Then she pulled a cloth mask over her face, slipped on a pair of thin gloves, and clipped together the buttons that initiated the pulse through the camo-dye in her combat outfit, and then she disappeared.

"Okay, Al, let's do this."

Guided by a thought, the Soft-Machine spread over his face and hands, leaving the camo-dye in the combat outfit to do the rest. The remaining Soft-Machine swarmed over his torso to form a layer of body armour and weaved around his back and arms, adding strength and speed. Passing instructions to the Soft-Machine was getting easier and smoothing out the buzz.

"Goggles are tuned, I can see you, Al."

"Same here."

"Right." Magpie pushed through the grey metal door into the stairwell. Graffiti covered the walls, sprayed and painted over the years since the Big Freeze. Prayers, threats, accusations, gang tags, declarations of friendship and love.

On the first landing, through a long, thin window, flashes of jagged white and electric-blue scars ripped through the thick, swirling grey sky, the silences in between broken by occasional crescendos of hail shattering against the walls outside.

A jab of Magpie's stun blade silently dropped a terrorist to the ground. They left him slumped on a chair in the corner, leaning against the wall, and went into a stale-smelling hallway leading to the conference hall. A dirty carpet, its soft gold patterns long lost under years of stains and the footfalls of heavy boots, covered the floor. Thin layers of brown- and green-mottled fungal growth marked the frayed wallpaper. Several times larger than the originals, stuck out like ugly boils, light bulbs emitted a pale-yellow glow and illuminated flaking silvery paint around door frames. All the apartment doors were shut. Walking past the cries and murmurs from behind some of them was tough.

Alister and Magpie turned a corner to find themselves at the end of another long hallway, which led to a curved glass wall beyond six feet of carpeted space, then another wood-panelled wall. Doorways stood at intervals around the glass wall, each with an ornate clock face, in the centre of which was a single large number. Every other door was guarded by a tall, heavily built Follower in green-brown combat gear armed with pistols and assault rifles.

Magpie gestured to Alister, and he followed her round the corner. "It stinks. They should open a window or something."

"Okay, Al. You got the better invisible armour, so take them out one at a time. I'll go through door 3', recon the conference room, and take down Plotinus. You come in when you're done. I'll wait."

Thunder rumbled overhead. "Got it," Alister took out the stun blade. "Good luck."

Alister set off anti-clockwise. He took down two Followers, and Magpie slipped into the conference room. He took out four more terrorists, leaving half of one side of the conference hall unguarded. It all seemed to be going like clockwork. He continued around the outer wall to the last Follower and stumbled sideways against the wall, head spinning. His mind felt like it had just done a flip, and he reached out to steady himself. Hail crashing against the windows of the small meeting room to his left shuddered through him, and then he saw the Follower. The burly, clean-shaven man cowered up against a doorway, his face an ashen grey expression of terror. Gibbering in some East

European language, his muscular left arm stretched up, the spasms of his fingers searching for the door handle several inches beyond his reach.

Alister struggled to breathe the foul air around him that stank and pulsed in short punches against his senses. He stumbled out of the putrid stench and into a pool of thick, morbid silence that ebbed and bled into him, spreading a fear that engulfed his mind until there was nothing but pitch black.

***

London, Ruya's Apartment

The screen faded into a soft grey, and Janus's voice came from the speakers. "Mr Ruya, the Wrychun probe is passing through the Kuiper belt. At its current speed and trajectory, and factoring gravitational adjustments as it passes the orbit of neighbouring planets, current estimations put arrival within range of detecting Earth in nine hundred sixty hours."

"What is Alister's condition?"

"Networks in the USA are still down. I am unable to connect with the nanoparticles in his system. The last neural connection I established showed evidence of partial memory recovery. I will commence establishing a direct neural connection in preparation to channel his link with the Seed."

"I want that connection made as soon as networks are live."

"The connection will take less than a second, sir."

"We're running out of time, Janus," Ruya said.

"Sir," Janus said, "Even a partial detonation could open a portal."

Ruya ran some calculations on his wristband. "Until communications are back up, we must assume Alister can still reach the Seed. In the meantime, begin work on breaking the Wrychun probe's programming language and encryption codes. I want you to decrypt its transmissions and analyse the structure of the broadcast signal. Hopefully, we can shut it down before it detects the Seed."

"Yes, sir."

Chapter Eighteen

She approached Alister, drifting through a vast space-dark place saturated with fear that swept through him like a relentless tsunami. Indifferent to it all, she closed in with exquisite freedom and effortless grace; gliding around him, he shivered from inside out with each passing. Alister strained to suck in clumps of air out of the darkness. "Help, help me," he rasped.

"Oh, Alister," she sighed. Her soft whisper caressed his senses and sliced into him like a slender blade, peeling back the tender flesh around his soul, exposing memories like raw nerves, warm emotion slowly bleeding out of him.

"I am Shiva, Destroyer, Transformer, your final, most intimate." Each word carried on a sweet, gentle breath, each elegant syllable another painless, deep cut. "My gift. For you."

A slow drizzle of soothing memories, formless until sparked by consciousness, burst through the fog of amnesia into vivid images and emotions. It all came back. His mother, father, sister, school, his dog, childhood summers, friends, college, Kenpo, holidays, his father's funeral, waking with Suzie beside him, her warmth, soft skin, the fading, spicy fragrance of her perfume and perspiration in the morning.

"Nothing lasts," Shiva said. She was right, of course. A cold, dark odour trickled through him. Shiva had given him one final sense of what he was: how he connected to Suzie, emotions, memory, everything. Then she'd somehow made it all fall from him, for good, slicing that one link he had to every recollection that made his past a part of him, more than just a memory.

All he'd experienced, owned, felt, and any connection he had to his past was just made up so he could be somebody, for his existence to have purpose and meaning. He'd spent his whole life reinforcing that connection, and now he could finally let it all go, stop it.

"Let it go, Alister, stop holding on. It was gone long ago."

She was right. It had always been worthless, meaningless stuff that had once happened. She'd broken the link, leaving nothing more than junk to fade and drift away. Alister didn't fight it. Alister, did that sound, thought, or name really mean anything anyway? No need; it was happening to someone else— or was that him, who he had been, or was becoming, or both.

Horror rose from somewhere deep inside him.

"Death, dear Alister, the nothing you came from, it never leaves you. From the day you were born, it is there. The vast spaces within the atoms of your DNA, your being. You are nothing but uncertain traces. Death, that final nothing, lingers behind every out-breath. It is the release and slide into sleep, the cushion of each surrender to a lover's embrace, giving grief and sorrow their substance. And, in the end, this is how you leave it all behind, the waste. Everyone dies gradually."

He was losing himself. A tangible sense of nothing rising to engulf him like a great ocean swell, carrying him up and down, then just down, deeper and deeper, darker, more silent.

"No," he heard himself say. "No, I'm not going anywhere."

Her soothing voice brushed away what little resistance remained in his tired soul. "Dear, Alister, resisting will only make it worse, far, far worse. Resistance is a knot. It will only lead to rebirth and more suffering. Do you still really want that?" Her voice caressed his fear with a teasing comfort and lifted him into absence.

She was right. All these years, he'd been associating with stuff that wasn't him. It was never him; he'd made that connection all up. He started to let go. This feeble, desperate grasping at petty fragments of memory began to fade away. Keep letting go. It wasn't so bad; eventually, he'd be gone into effortless, painless nothing. Heart slowing, breathing coming to rest, the rush of blood settling down. He was alone. She was gone, her work was done, she had nothing to stay for; there was nothing to stay for.

"Alister?" That was Suzie's voice.

Silence.

***

Magpie, still invisible in her camo outfit, stood pressed against the wall and scanned the scene in front of her, relieved by the silent vibration of her radio. Communications were back up. Alister wasn't replying; she was on her own.

Plotinus stood on a wide crescent dais facing a large crowd of men, women, and children of all ages scattered in groups around the conference room. Those unable to sit on the ground sat on plastic grey chairs. On the wall behind Plotinus hung a viewing plate declaring 'Plotinus II', and underneath in gold lettering, 'The Purification and Revelation'. Above the viewing plate hung a long banner, 'Mankind is Poised Midway Between the Gods and the Beasts'.

Plotinus was speaking. "...so I tell you again, look at yourselves, see that you are yet to be prepared. Soon, the purity of the Lord's lightning will beautify you. He will discard your animal nature, enlighten you to perfect your true, other, purer face and thus reveal his work. Be prepared to surrender, renounce, cut away all that is excessive, straighten all that is crooked, bring light to all overcast, labour to make all one glow in beauty, and do not retreat. Then there shall shine out from you the godlike splendour of virtue, and you shall see the perfect goodness surely established in the stainless shrine. Your sacrifice will restore the seasons."

There were no guards inside the room. A young man stood to one side behind Plotinus. The man had Plotinus's large cloak slung over his shoulder and was tapping on his phone, probably texting someone. He'd cast a cynical look at Plotinus every so often, then turn his attention back to his phone. He'd unlikely come to Plotinus's rescue if anything kicked off in here. Magpie wasn't going to get a better chance than this. She raised her rifle, aimed at Plotinus's forehead, and fired.

The bullet struck the reinforced invisible steel glass with a crack that resonated around the room and lost itself in the screams and loud bustling from the audience. Plotinus, driven by the exoskeleton, disappeared through a door in seconds. His PA did a strange thing. He rushed to the dais, pressed a button by the microphone, and dashed after his boss. At the end of the stage, by some steps, a door misted over and swung outwards.

"Thanks, pal," Magpie murmured. He must really hate his boss.

Before she could go through, a door across the hall opened, letting in a wave of fear that had everybody, including her, cowering. Magpie instinctively pointed her rifle and fired. A scream was followed by a rippling of light, and a figure in black appeared and fell to the ground, bleeding from the shoulder.

Magpie switched off her camo outfit and headed to the end of the stage by the steps. Opening the door, she approached the dais and spoke into the microphone. "Listen up, I'm part of a rescue team. Joel Klein is downstairs waiting to lead you to safety. Go through that door over there and straight down the hallway. Stairs through the door at the end will lead you down to Joel."

People rose to their feet and stood around in small groups. The room filled with a fearful murmuring. Then, several older men and women rallied the families to follow them, and a few waved their thanks and began to shuffle out.

Magpie crossed to the elevator, speaking into her mic as she walked. "Al, do you copy? The families are on their way out. Al, are you there? Shit." Magpie knelt down and removed the black face mask from the person she'd shot to reveal the face of a young woman. "Who the hell are you?"

A phone vibrated in the woman's pocket, and Magpie pulled it out. The screen displayed a column of unread text messages.

'Where are you? Your father is boring all these people to death. :-)'

'If you don't get back soon, we're all going to fry here. I'm not leaving without you. xx'

'Okay, now I'm getting scared, everybody is.'

The texts must have been coming from the guy behind Plotinus; by the look of these messages, this girl had to be Plotinus's daughter. Magpie smiled. Now, she had a bargaining tool.

The woman wore a wide belt with rows of small plastic spray canisters and a holster with a long-barrelled pistol. "I'll be damned, Shiva and her pharma."

Unclipping her knife, Magpie tore open the sleeve of the injured woman. She took out a thin tube and was about to squeeze a blob of plasti-skin over the wound but stopped to stare at what lay under Val's skin. "Well, you are a bag of surprises, aren't you?"

Magpie applied a dab of anaesthetising gel, sliced a thin line down the woman's upper arm and removed a drug capsule linked to an electronic release chip. She slid the malleable chip out of the silicon protective cover, then carefully removed the cover itself, guiding out the thin tube feeding into the vein. She then applied the antiseptic plastic skin. From the slither of electronics, it looked like the implant could be wirelessly controlled. Someone, probably Plotinus, was switching this girl on and off. What a bastard— his own daughter, the poor girl.

Magpie pocketed the device. "Come on, girl, up you get."

The young woman got to her feet without arguing and stood drowsily against the wall, spaced out.

"What's your name, girl?"

"Huh?" The woman's eyes remained motionless and unfocused.

"Your name?" Magpie shook her head. "Jeez, what is it with me and amnesiacs?"

Magpie took her hand. "Come with me."

Val nodded. Her phone buzzed again; it was another text. 'Val, we're heading for the truck, can't get away, will try tho', sorry.'

Magpie pulled the mask down over the woman's face and switched their camo outfits on. She adjusted her eyepiece to modulate between Val's and Alister's signals, then led the girl around the external hallway to find Alister.

Alister lay beside a tall, muscular Follower pressed against the wall in a foetal position, blubbering incoherently. "Wait here." Magpie let Valkyrie slide to the ground and rushed over to Alister. He wasn't breathing and had no pulse. This didn't make sense; he had no visible injuries, wounds, head injuries, or signs of choking or suffocation. Maybe he'd been poisoned, though there were no visible signs on his hands, face, mouth, or eyes. She glanced back at Val. Poor kid, manipulated to murder by her father. What a mess. She touched Alister's shoulder, "You did good, kid." Magpie checked the tracker around his wrist; it was transmitting. She swallowed hard and got to her feet. "Someone will come for you, Al, I promise." She took a deep breath and turned away.

Her headphone crackled. "Magpie, do you copy?" It was Parker.

"Yeah, I copy."

"Seed's in the penthouse balcony. We got sight of Suzie and some other captive with her."

"Copy that." Magpie grabbed the young woman propped against the wall and led her into the elevator. "On my way." She jabbed the penthouse button, and the doors slid shut.

"Alister's got a static tracker, and you're not together. What's going on?"

"Alister's down," Magpie said. "He didn't make it."

"Oh," Parker murmured, and the line fell silent until Magpie spoke.

"What's the situation out there?"

"The Panthers arrived, all wearing camo outfits. Stealth'd up and engaged the Follower reinforcements flooding the lower levels through the linked walkways. They're heading up, but it's slow. Most of the families are on their way out. Followers aren't stopping them. Seems they're more keen on giving Plotinus a clear exit."

"Outstanding,"

Parker replied, "Samurai marksmen are supporting our snipers and engaging with the Followers on the higher levels. They're pinned down on the south side. You should have a clear run up the north side to the Seed. Hang on, there's another message coming in." The line went dead for several seconds, then he came back on. "Magpie, the PI are in the security cabin and control all access and elevators."

"Roger that," she said. "Give me a clear run on the elevator I'm at."

"Already on it. We have your location."

"Great, oh, one more thing. I've got Shiva here with her utility belt of cocktails. Taking her up with me. She's a real softy."

"Shiva? Unbelievable."

"Yeah. Listen, there's some guy called Joel Klein. He's okay. He's coming through the storm drain with a couple hundred people."

"We found them already. They're all being escorted to one of the underground bunkers until this ends."

The elevator slowed. "I'm going in. Magpie out." She turned to Valkyrie. "Stay here."

Valkyrie nodded dreamily and slid back down to the floor.

Magpie readied her assault rifle. She'd have to deal with whatever was out there on her own. She slid her hand along her knife belt, then smashed the elevator light before the doors hissed open. A simple knife twist snapped open the metal plate over the elevator control panel, and she jabbed the 'Emergency Stop' button.

Chapter Nineteen

Beyond a wall of sliding glass doors, the penthouse balcony, the size of a basketball court, extended out of the Crown Tower under an ocean of curling black clouds. A domed observatory stood in the centre of the balcony. The invisible nano-weave glass plates curved down through the brown rock-wood floor and continued to a point underneath. From a distance, it resembled an ice cream cone.

With Val invisible on the elevator floor, Magpie edged out against the wall. Far below, a mesh of lights glimmered in the rain-soaked air. Bare freeways, patched with transparent plastic steel sheets, gleamed and weaved through the cityscape. Las Vegas disappeared into the distance: Dull outlines of long abandoned hotels and casinos surrounded by a mosaic of trailers, dome homes, and fields of Portakabin settlements stitched together with streams and rivulets.

Three Followers struggled to open one of the sliding doors, and Magpie raised her rifle to engage when a sudden, momentary silence stopped them dead. A serpentine beam of black light, three feet wide, rose up from the centre of the dome to suck at the swirling mass of clouds. The final stage had begun, and from the look of the mess in the observatory, there was no way to switch the damn thing off. The sky slashed with flashes of jagged silver-blue bolts bursting through broiling black chaos. She was too late; the city, maybe the world, would fry, and Alister had died for nothing.

*****

Not one of us is lost or forgotten; we are just led from the path of truth and revelation.

The leaders of the world's nations doth prostitute themselves to the very industries that continue to rape the world and corrupt Truth. They are drunk and blinded by power and wealth borne from the blood and toil of my brethren and sisteren and all those who succumb to false promises of happiness and security.

Thus, my brethren and sisteren doth strive desperately for favour and endlessly yearn for transient pleasure. One half of all human life did the Cursed Winter take as toll for the suffering wrought on the sacred Earth. Yet even so, the effluence of industry continues to intoxicate mankind and blind them to the Truth behind reality.

The Revelation of the One guides us to gather here, blessed as the bearers of instruments, revealed to me by sacred visions, destined to cleanse this realm of greed and decadence to reveal the timeless Truth to one and all. The Absolute Awakening in Radiant Truth and Light is soon to be upon us, and the Sacrifice will deliver a new world, a new spring, and infinite seasons perfect in harmony and grace in one Faith.

The Confessions of Plotinus II, Chapter 4, verses 11-13

Chapter Twenty

The padded bench curled halfway around the interior wall of the observatory where Suzie sat. Beside her, Nehir leaned back unconscious, a large blue bruise across his face.

The glass dampened the rain and hail noise, leaving the observatory strangely silent. A streak of lightning lit up the grim expression of the Follower sitting opposite Suzie as he flexed his fingers.

"Don't say the name again, whore," he said in a deep Southern accent.

Something had happened to Alister. She could sense it and had involuntarily called out his name. Suzie glared at the man and quickly turned away when he raised his hand to strike her again. Having lost his one punchbag after knocking out Nehir, the man had turned his attention to Suzie.

"Hah," he said, "now you are learning." The man pushed back his grey-green combat helmet and scratched his bald head.

The egg-shaped Lightning Seed stood on a pedestal that once held a large telescope. Five small speakers placed around the Seed pulsed rhythmically. Suzie had watched the Seed expand from a football-sized object to the size of a barrel. Each pulse triggered a glowing ring to spiral up around the Seed.

Two Followers stood by a small table, watching an old laptop computer closely. Wires from the laptop trailed across the ground to the speakers. On-screen, a thin yellow line blinked and undulated across five red columns that rose and fell in line with the pulsing lights increasing in luminosity and frequency. Outside, the clouds thickened, darkened and melted across the skies, releasing more explosive shards of lightning. One of the men pushed back his long black hair and spoke in a foreign language to the other man. Suzie's guard turned round and snapped, "What did the moron say?"

The other man began to reply, "He's a scienti—"

The Follower snarled and jumped to his feet. "You wanna argue with me? Now? We're gonna die anyway, so why should I put up with your crap? Just tell me what he said before I gut you."

"He said it won't be long now, around fifteen minutes, maybe less."

The knife disappeared from the guard's hand. He leered at Suzie and lumbered in an arrogant, rolling walk to the edge of the observatory, mumbling, "Lead us from temptation; deliver us from evil." He stopped to pull out a piece of paper and read from it.

"From Majliz Al Jinn, across deserts, forests and oceans.
City to city, the coming storm,
A hurricane hunts across the heavens.
Thick clouds that bring darkness and death,
Wild winds rising to cast gloom over the bright day.
Imkhullu, the evil winds forcing their way,
The flood of Adad, mighty destroyers.
In the height of heaven, lightning flashing
To wreak destruction with gleaming blades.
In the broad heaven, the home of Anu, the King, righteously do they arise,
and none to oppose."

He turned to Suzie. "You hear that, bitch? None to oppose."

Suzie looked away and felt a buzz run through the building. Something had changed. A little broadcast light blinking red by the door had turned a steady green. She shot a glance at the Follower as he returned to his seat. He hadn't noticed.

"Nehir," she hissed under her breath and, using her heel, kicked him.

Nehir moaned and turned his head. Slowly opening his eyes, he pushed himself up to a sitting position and rubbed the bruise on his face while looking around, the confusion turning to despair.

Suzie mouthed, "The radio's up again."

Nehir stared past her to the Seed, where thin lines of rainbow colour spiralled furiously around its surface. The three Followers, Suzie and Nehir, shielded their faces with their hands when a radiant layer of mist bloomed out to surround the surface of the Seed, then expanded to engulf and shatter the speakers, absorbing them with a noise that sounded like glass in a food blender.

Covering her eyes, Suzie squinted through thin gaps between her fingers. The three Followers had retreated out of the observatory back into the penthouse. Glittering particles swirled through smoky streaks streaming around the Seed. The lines merged and rose to form a boiling cloud several inches above the Seed. Thin tendrils of lightning whipped out to shred the laptop into more particles and suck them along the crackling thread to merge into the gas cloud. The observatory filled with screeches, crackles and sharp sizzling like crows being burned alive.

A black spike sliced upwards from the Seed into the centre of the hovering cloud, which burst and flattened out into rings of metal, glass, and plastic particles, all racing around a small fireball. Suzie and Nehir stared, mesmerised, as each ring collapsed and began to cluster, the particles gathering to form planets and moons so that, for a few seconds, a perfect solar system appeared above the Seed. The fireball 'Sun' bloomed into a supernova, swallowed the planets, and shrunk into a shadowy ball. The black spike rose again from the Seed, lanced up through the ball and beyond the observatory to break into three points, and clawed at the thick clouds. The point swayed around, slowly tearing at the dark plumes until it caught a lightning bolt and shattered it into thousands of electric shards that rained down across the city, setting off bolts of lightning that hopped across the rooftops, setting off explosions and fires that defied the downpour.

The explosions and sirens across the city failed to penetrate the dome.

"Is that it?" Nehir whispered in the silence.

"Well if it was we…"

A deep hum filled the room. The Seed dulled to a grey stone and released a broad, black serpentine line as wide as itself, laced with wire-thin electric blue veins flowing with some eldritch energy. The column rose into the heavens, releasing a deep resonance through the building, making the foundations shudder.

Suzie grabbed Nehir and pulled him up. "We have to get out."

Barely feet away from the door, they were both thrown back by the force of an explosion. The crackling of gunfire and shattering glass filled the surrounding air.

A figure staggered out through the shadowy penthouse towards them, and Suzie called out in relief, "Magpie, thank God."

With a grim expression, Magpie stepped through the rubble and debris and rushed around the Seed to help Nehir, who was trying to get Suzie to her feet. In a daze, Suzie pushed his arm away.

"Where's Alister?" Suzie asked.

"I'm sorry, Suzie," Magpie said, "he's gone."

"No."

Her head cleared, and all the objects, including Magpie and Nehir, appeared to be a perfect hologram—a perfectly replicated model—more polished, deeper, and sharper than reality. Suzie grabbed an overturned chair and got to her feet. She stood, wavering for a moment, then, guided by a graceful presence, she pushed past Magpie and Nehir to cross over to the Seed.

***

"Mr Ruya, radio and network frequencies have been restored. However, I am unable to connect with Alister. There is no communication at all from him."

"What information do you have, Janus?"

"Information is fragmented. The PI and Panthers have surrounded Crown Tower, and the Seed is operational. Suzie and Nehir are still with it."

"Nothing on Alister?"

"No, sir, he is either dead or no longer has the particles inside him."

"I see," Ruya gazed along the frozen Thames towards Parliament and the London Eye. "Amplify the nanoparticles in Suzie."

"Sir, may I remind you, Alister passed into her only twenty-eight per cent of the particles before his dosage was supplemented. Miss Emerson does not have sufficient particles to channel the energy from the Fae Realm or allow clear telemetry with the Lightning Seed. I would need to utilize her neural resources to accurately interface with the Seed's processes and shut it down. Draining that much neural energy for the connection could prove fatal."

"I'm aware of the risk, Janus. Do it. There's no alternative."

"Very well, sir. Mr Ruya," After a moment, Janus said, "I have Suzie's cooperation. She's aware of the risk."

"You told her?"

"Yes."

"Why?"

"It is her life to choose."

"Are you developing morals and a conscience, Janus?"

"It appears so, sir."

"We'll discuss this later. Please proceed. Be as careful as you can."

"Of course, sir. I have engaged neural and motor control and am attempting to minimise the drain on her central nervous system. The monitoring and calculating of two point five petabytes of neural data through that amount of nanoparticles require all my processing resources. I'm afraid I will have to temporarily disengage from corporate activities."

"Do what you can to stop the detonation and keep Suzie alive."

"Yes, sir."

Janus prompted Suzie towards the Seed while numbing the pain spectrum across her spine and head.

***

"I know what to do," Suzie whispered. Stepping closer to the Seed before either Magpie or Nehir could stop her, she pushed her hands on either side of it. Her hands seemed to sink in a few inches before they touched something solid. She closed her eyes, and when she opened them, they seemed made of the same stuff as the black, electrically charged column. Nehir screamed and grabbed Magpie's arm, pulling her back.

Unable to loosen the grip, Magpie and Nehir stumbled and fell. Suzie's electric black eyes turned back to the Seed. She touched the surface, and the nanoparticles in her system reacted immediately. A soft, warm energy swarmed into the device. Suzie nodded. There was phenomenal power hidden in that warmth, a warmth that felt like nothing she'd experienced.

In London, Raymond concentrated on a screen displaying the flow of lines across a grid, tracking Suzie's neural activity and measuring the copper, potassium, and sodium integrity in her system. When she connected to the Seed, the lines jumped into the red.

"Mr Ruya, the neural link is established."

"I see it, Janus. Try to keep her alive."

The warm energy wove into the patterns shaping the Seed's

processes, creating the perfect conditions for the deadly lightning storm. Like a sponge, the energy absorbed the knots of dark energy spreading across the city to interact with the electrons in the clouds.

"My God," Ruya said, his eyes on the undulating spectrum of lines on the screen.

"Mr Ruya, I have to disengage the protective sequencing from Suzie to match the energy required to neutralise the Seed. There is an eighty-five per cent probability that the feedback will trigger a rapid degenerative neural cycle within Suzie."

Ruya hesitated.

"Sir," Janus said, "Suzie was aware of the consequences when she agreed. Earth will be destroyed if we do not proceed."

Ruya nodded, "Do it." He turned from the screen and slumped onto a chair to stare blankly at the floor. "Suzie, I'm sorry. I'm so, so sorry."

In Las Vegas, the dark beam silently expanded and disappeared, leaving a single white line shining into the dark, churning blooms. The beam struck the clouds and fragmented into a jagged web of lightning bolts that sizzled through a black mass, releasing deafening explosions across the sky. The feedback occurred in Suzie's brain as Janus had predicted, despite his attempts to channel the stream out.

"Mr Ruya, it is done. The frequency re-modulation of the Lightning Seed did not reach the critical point, it is shutting down."

"What about Suzie? How is she?"

"It was impossible to attenuate or direct the feedback stream through the nearest compatible polarisation plane. Prognosis is poor, neural activity may continue to deteriorate."

"How long does she have?"

"I estimate ten days, Mr Ruya."

"Make arrangements for Suzie to be taken to the Neurological Centre in London." He let out a deep sigh. "It's the best place for her."

"Shall I arrange accommodation for her mother and sisters?"

"Yes, of course, spare no expense."

Ruya left the small meeting room and made his way along the corridor, indifferent to the screens on the walls displaying slide shows of the happy, smiling faces of children, families, and communities around the world—people his foundation had helped.

***

In a motionless trance, eyes glazed over, Suzie's body shook violently as if electrocuted, and she fell to the floor. Magpie and Nehir rushed over to kneel beside her.

"She's trying to say something," Nehir lowered his head, put his ear near her mouth, and then looked up, his eyes moist. "She wants to know why Alister is so quiet. What did she mean?"

Magpie looked from Nehir to Suzie and shook her head.

Tears formed in Suzie's eyes. She grabbed Nehir's collar, and he leaned forward again.

Nehir sat up, an expression of confusion on his face. "She said he's alive."

Suzie lost consciousness, and her hand fell from his collar.

***

"Mr Ruya, reports are coming in that Alister is dead."

Raymond Ruya stared out of the window. "His father was a good friend and one of my best scientists. I promised I'd look after Alister, and I let him down. Does his sister know?"

"She is on her way to formally identify the body."

"Did the probe detect the artefact?"

"I believe so, sir. It is analysing the signal and will notify Wrychun Prime. Fortunately, the precise location of Earth was not transmitted."

Ruya nodded and, taking a large slug of whiskey, stared silently at the half-empty bottle for almost a minute. "Contact the Mechanic."

For the first time in its operation, Janus paused before responding. "Another Mechanics ship is refuelling in the Termination Shock, sir. Are you sure you wish to take this action? The Mechanics are impulsive, unpredictable, and do not respond to authority beyond their beliefs and values."

"They are the only ones with the technology to prevent a Wrychun Invasion. Make the call."

"It is done, sir."

Raymond emptied his glass and poured himself another. "Heaven help us," he said, downing it in one.

Chapter Twenty-one

The Panthers—now visible and imposing, big and strong enough to wear full-combat body armour and carry tri-barrel rifles like toys—stood guard over the captured Followers huddled in one corner of the Crown building foyer.

"Boss," Ben said, "I need a piss. Where the hell are those PI lock-up trucks?"

E spoke without moving his gaze or the direction of his rifle from the prisoners. "Forget the trucks. Just use the toilets like ordinary people, Ben."

Steve let out a loud laugh.

"What? Boss," Ben said, heading for the toilets, "that's the kind of joke you should save for your kids."

"I thought it was funny," Steve said.

"Well, you got the brain of a seven-year-old anyway," Ben said and went through the door.

A few minutes later, Leroy touched his earpiece. "Trucks are coming into the drive now, sir. Lucky for them, Ben went before they arrived," he said, setting them off with laughter that just got louder when Ben came out of the toilet, shaking his wet hands.

"What?" he asked. He looked from them to his hands. "There's no damned towels for crisssakes!"

***

The Centauri Foundation ambulance made its way through the bright, rain-drenched streets. The Sun had broken through the clouds for the first time in weeks. In the back of the ambulance, Nehir sat in a wheelchair, his arm in a bandage and another wrapped around his head. Suzie and Alister were laid out on either side of him. He'd insisted on travelling in the same ambulance as his friends. Suzie lay with a drip leading into her arm. Alister was in a body bag on the other side of Nehir. A plastic tube extended out to the air purifier and monitoring system, tuned to detect the release of any toxic fumes or substances.

Nehir tilted his head and, scratching the wispy growth on his unshaven face peered at the heart monitors. Only Suzie's was beeping. If not for the oxygen mask over Suzie's mouth and nose, it looked like she was simply sleeping. The last thing she said was Alister was alive, and he believed her. Holding her hand, he thought he felt a strange tingling run through his hand and up his arms. She'd been saying weird things since they'd been kidnapped, and it had all turned out to be right—though all that stuff about seeing angels and demons was pretty odd. He leaned across, pulled down the oxygen mask from the kit above Alister, and slipped it over Alister's mouth, carefully stretching the strap over his friend's head so his hand ran over Alister's hair. Again, that feeling of something passing into him made him pull his hand back and stare at it. There wouldn't be static in an ambulance, would there?

"Alister, if you can hear me, Suzie needs you. They're talking about getting her back to London, the neurological hospital. I think..."

"Hey," a voice sounded over the speaker behind him, and Nehir jumped. "Can you see us? The screen at this end just blanked out."

"Sorry, no," Nehir replied. "I thought Centauri had the best technology in town. I mean, look at all this equipment you have back here, and half of it went all funny as soon as I sat down when we set off from the Crown. Don't you people do regular checks? Why, even when I was in my kitchens, every day I used to—"

"For heaven's sake, Dan," another voice said. "I got out of there after five minutes of his non-stop chatter. Give it a rest."

The ambulance stopped, and Nehir quickly removed the oxygen mask from Alister's face seconds before the doors opened. The ramp whined to the ground, and several porters wheeled the gurneys out. They rattled over the mesh grill onto the raised concrete deck on one side of the ER entrance. Nehir made sure the wheelchair brake was on and stepped out to wait under the awning of the hospital entrance for the two gurneys. He followed them through wide doors into a brightly lit, square reception area and the disinfectant's crisp, sharp smell. To the left was the public entrance and several rows of seats. Directly ahead stood the light blue and yellow reception desk. Two corridors stretched past numbered treatment rooms into the distance, the floor lined with differently-coloured stripes leading to various departments. Four wide elevators lined the wall to his right.

Most of the seats were occupied. Several soldiers sat slumped in wheelchairs with long poles slotted into the backrests and drips attached.

"Go register at the ER over there. There's a queue for the walking wounded," the ambulance operator said.

Nehir shook his head. "I want to stay with—"

"You can't. You need those injuries treated. Now go."

"Where are you taking them?"

"Ms. Emerson is being taken to the intensive care unit. Mr Cloud's body is going to the morgue. Now, if you would excuse us, please."

Nehir crossed over to the reception desk and watched the two ambulance men hand the gurney with Suzie over to four medics, who then disappeared down the bright hallway.

Several porters in short white jackets arrived a few minutes later, lifted Alister's body unceremoniously onto another gurney, and wheeled it into a waiting elevator.

"Fill this form in, please, sir," the ER receptionist said.

Nehir turned to the desk and stared at the thin screen, then took another look at the elevator just in time to see the silver doors closing. That was it. He was alone. He bit his bottom lip, swallowed, and blinked back the tears, looking around at the room full of disinterested faces. He completed the form and handed it back to the receptionist. A nurse was now behind the desk, and she took the screen.

"You were one of the people close to the WMD?"

"Yes."

"Come with me, please."

Half slouched on plastic seats, several weary people looked up when the nurse came out from behind the reception area and nodded for Nehir to follow. Nehir gave them an awkward shrug and mouthed 'sorry', then turned to quickly follow the nurse down the hall.

The nurse took him up two floors and down a long hallway to a doorway beside a window where a yellow and green blind concealed the room beyond. The nurse knocked and then opened the door without waiting for a response.

"Wait in here, please. There's a buzzer on the wall over there if you need anything. We're swamped, so try not to use it."

Nehir stepped into a cream-coloured room. A thin grey carpet covered the floor. Magpie sat on one of four chairs around a low sky-blue plastic table. She gave him a single nod, glancing at a seat beside her. The TV cracked and fell dark when Nehir wished it would switch off.

"Some drinks over there. If you've lost your sense of taste, I'd stick with plain water."

A filtered water dispenser with hot and cold water stood beside a narrow table with jars of powdered coffee, powdered tea, and milk substitute. These were lined up behind several small stacks of red plastic cups.

Nehir filled a cup with water and sat beside her. "Why are we here, Magpie?"

"Centauri scientists want to check us out at their research clinic."

"Why...I...is it radiation from the Lighting Seed?"

"Probably. They're running tests on people who've had close contact with it. How do you feel?"

"I feel fine, well apart from this fractured arm, and my face hurts every time I move my head around, and I think I may have gone deaf in one ear. How are you?"

"Never felt better. Where have you been?"

"I came straight down with you. After you went off with the soldiers, I waited in the Tower reception with Parker for the ambulances, and then a large security truck arrived with guys in spacesuit-type outfits. I guess they went up to get the Lightning Seed. Then the ambulances arrived. A couple of soldiers drive one. They took that woman and the Followers who were around the Seed; the other ambulance took me, Suzie, and Alister. Do you think we've got radiation poisoning? We were in that truck with the Seed for a long time. I feel a bit...'"

"Damned TV," Magpie said, "I was watching for any news on what's going on out there."

"Oh," Nehir felt a tingle run through him. He'd been feeling strange since he'd held Suzie's hand. He glanced up, and the TV came on again. Nehir crossed over to the window to get away from the news stream.

A Japanese pebble garden had been built in the small park beside the hospital.

"My neighbour had a pebble garden on her roof terrace. I

helped her build it before I left for the…oh," Nehir paused and squinted, rubbing the glass.

"What?"

"Jinn and an angel, kind of." Nehir nodded and lifted a feeble hand to wave back when the angel waved at them. They weren't so foggy to him. In fact, they seemed pretty solid.

"That seed must have done something to you," Magpie said

The taller, thin jinn spotted Nehir and tapped his temple.

Nehir listened to the voice in his head, nodded and glanced at Magpie. When he looked back, the park was empty.

"Magpie."

"Yeah."

"The jinn says we must find Alister and put him in water."

"Forget it," Magpie said, "I'm not going anywhere, not until I get the all-clear from the Centauri people. They better have something to—"

"The jinn said."

Magpie gave Nehir a look that silenced him for a few seconds. He wrung his hands with a pained expression. "Please, Magpie, just let me tell you what he, it said. I can't keep this to myself."

"Fine," Magpie sighed, "Get it over with."

"The jinn said if we can put him in water, then they can use the particles inside him to—"

"You taking advice from hallucinations?"

"Serif said—"

"Serif?"

"The jinn who spoke to me."

"So, they got names now?" Magpie shook her head slowly. "You don't get it, do you?"

"Serif said your sister…"

Magpie turned to Nehir with a stony expression and spoke through clenched teeth. "You mind what you say."

He winced like she'd slapped him. Looking away, he mumbled something and sat down.

"What was that?" Magpie said.

"Alister helped us all. We should help him."

"He's dead, Nehir. Trust me, I've seen dead people before. It's not nice." Magpie went back to the window. "Take another look, kid. Whatever you were imagining out there is gone. It's

Plotinus' drugs or the radiation from that Lightning Seed thing. The Centauri people will sort us out, don't worry."

"I worry about my friends, so should you."

Magpie continued to gaze down at the park. "What did he say about my sister?" Nehir didn't hear her.

"Nehir."

"What?"

"My sister, what did he say about her?"

"When you were trying to pull her from the rubble on the riverbed, she was already gone."

"If I'd found her sooner, she would have survived."

Nehir shook his head slowly without looking up. "He said the debris broke her neck in the rapids."

"Wait, how did you know she.." Explosions shook the building, and Nehir jumped to his feet. Magpie dropped and leaned against the wall.

"Get down, kid." Magpie snapped and went to the window. A thick, grey cloud hung over the car park to their far right. "Someone's shelling the damn hospital."

Nehir crawled to the opposite wall and crouched under the window by the door.

Magpie pulled a small pair of binoculars from a side pocket and scanned the distance. "There," she said, "it's a truck with a remote-controlled cannon mounted on the top. There's a small army of Followers guarding the line and pushing forward. Shit. These guys never give up."

Parker burst into the room. "Follow me."

"What's going on?" Magpie said.

"I'll tell you on the way," Parker said. "Nehir, you too."

"Where are we going?" Nehir said, rushing after Parker into the noisy chaos of the hallway, now bustling with nurses, doctors, and porters heading into wards and recovery rooms.

Parker raised his voice over the fearful shouts and commands around them. "Other side of the hospital. We're moving all critical patients to the paediatric hospital across the road. This way." He pointed towards the stairs. "Everyone else is going to the Palace Casino farther away along the block."

"What about Suzie?" Nehir said.

"Military unit's moving her back to the barracks to get her to the airport ASAP."

The elevator doors opened, and soldiers in fatigues appeared and joined groups of hospital staff and patients pushing hospital beds or wheelchairs towards the elevators and stairs.

"It's Plotinus," Parker said. "He's got a strange notion about Alister not being fully dead."

"See," Nehir said.

"Shut it," Magpie snapped.

Parker led them downwards, leaving behind the other evacuees surging out of the ground-level exits. Pushing through large swinging doors, they emerged into a dimly lit yard. People's Infantry soldiers lined up beside Jeeps and APCs, checking weapons and maps. Two large grey-green army trucks and a military ambulance with a big red cross on the side were parked by the service delivery ramp. The open rear of one truck exposed rows of assault rifles, grenade launchers, and other weapons Nehir didn't recognise.

Magpie headed straight to the open ammo truck, where three men stood at a metal table handing out weapons and ammunition. One of the men recognised her and waved.

"Nehir," Parker called over the noise, "get to that ambulance. You're going to the Centauri Foundation Clinic."

Nehir was crossing to the ambulance when he spotted the sign for the morgue and pathology laboratory. He looked back. Parker was standing over a map with Magpie. Nehir darted around the side of the Jeep and then stumbled through the door marked 'Pathology: Staff Only'.

Fluorescent tubes stretched along the ceiling of a long, bare corridor. A sign on the left indicated the direction to the pathology laboratory, and a pink line led to the autopsy suite. Nehir nodded to himself. He just needed to get Alister into some water.

Several times, he snuck into small offices or crouched behind filing cabinets to evade hospital staff and soldiers. The corridor intersected with another where a wide metal door bore the sign 'Hic Locus est ubi mors gaudet succurrere vitae'. Heavy footsteps bearing down from the right were followed by gunfire and shouting. Nehir dived into a large reception area and slipped behind a desk. A photograph and a couple of ornaments—a duck and some other plastic thing that looked like they were made by a child—stood neatly beside a computer screen. He waited, then ran through another pair of double doors into the autopsy suite. A naked body on an examination tray, not Alister's, lay under a scanner. Then the lights went out, and Nehir screamed.

Chapter Twenty-two

Nehir breathed a sigh of relief when the backup generators kicked in, and a dim light filled the cold room. Dropping to his knees, he scrabbled around the equipment tables, reached the wall on the right and pushed through a door. Three gurneys were lined along one wall. He recognised the PI My body bag with Alister on the gurney closest to the door. Nehir took a deep breath and hesitated before pulling back the zip. The shout from the reception area beyond the autopsy room stopped him.

"Nehir!"

That was Magpie. Nehir stared at the door, back at the body bag, and steeled himself. He hunched for a second against the snapping of gunfire, shattering glass, sharp clangs, and shouts from the hallway. Then he stumbled against the trolley, and it rolled back to clang against the wall of drawers.

Two explosions quickly followed by another shout: "Nehir, get your ass out here now!"

Face scrunched in confusion, he gripped Alister's trolley and sized up the door leading into the autopsy suite. "I can do this, I can do this, I can do this." He moved around the gurney, steered it towards the door, then leaned forward and pushed it open. The dimly-lit room was empty, and he manoeuvred the gurney over to the shiny metal preparation area, moving it alongside the large sink and metal hose. He looked at the body bag and, without hesitating, yanked open the zip, wincing and looking away.

Followed by another woman soldier, Magpie rushed into the room before Nehir could pull the metal hose over to Alister and fill the bag with water. Magpie gave him a confused look and then slammed the metal door shut. The other soldier pushed a cabinet full of instruments to fall across the entrance. "Good thinking," Magpie hauled the examination tray with the body on it to slam against the cabinet while bullets splattered the door and wall outside.

With the hose still in his hand, Nehir froze, caught in Magpie's glare. Defiant, he turned the water on and stared incredulously when nothing came out.

"Damn you, Nehir," Magpie said. "If we get out of here alive, I'm gonna…"

Something heavy slammed against the door. Magpie leapt

across to the long X-ray arm stretching over the room and swung it round to thump against the door while the other soldier turned the wheel, controlling the pivot. With the arm wedged against the door, the two women retreated to where Nehir stood against the preparation area.

Magpie glanced down at Alister's body, then up at Nehir. "Is there another way out?"

"I don't know."

"Plotinus is out there with a couple of his goons."

"Is there help coming?"

"Yeah, right," sneered the other soldier, a tall, slender woman with a short, thick Mohican of blonde hair. "Be a damn miracle if they get through the wreckage of the elevator and stairs. It's us against a pair of tooled-up die-hards and some fat guy with an exoskeleton and body armour I'd sell my mother for."

"Easy, Falcon." A thin smile momentarily crossed Magpie's features.

"Plotinus?" cried Nehir. "We're going to die."

"Maybe." Magpie gazed at the door. "But not without a fight, kiddo."

After almost a minute of silence, Falcon spoke. "What the hell d'ya think they're doing out there, Mags?"

Magpie shook her head and shifted the strap of her assault rifle. "What's through that door over there, Nehir?"

"It's a cold room where I found Alister. There are two more bodies and a wall of long trays where there might be more bodies."

"Good," Falcon said. "Wheel those stiffs out here and wedge them with the other one between the door and this operating table thing. Give us a bit more time."

"Nehir, pull yourself together, you heard the lady," Magpie said. "Get to it."

Nehir nodded, and soon, three trolleys were squeezed behind the door with the wheels locked down and angled holding bars pressing into the floor.

Nehir, Falcon, and Magpie leaned back against the trolley with Alister's body on it.

"We're trapped," Nehir said.

Magpie peered around the gloomy room and was interrupted

by a hissing noise from the barricaded door.

"Acid," Falcon said.

The hole expanded, and Falcon raised her rifle, aimed, and fired. A scream came from the other side, and Falcon smiled. "Talk about dumb."

After several seconds of silence, a thin nozzle emerged through the hole, and the sound of metal grinding against metal came from the other side.

"Oh, shit," Magpie looked around and pointed at the air vent on the wall above the preparation area.

"Get that vent open, Falcon. I'll cover the door. Nehir, you're going first."

"But Alister."

"Let us worry about him."

"Should have thought of that sooner, sister," Falcon said. Climbing up onto the tray on one side of the sink, she pulled out a knife, prised open a gap between the vent and wall, and then pulled off the cover with a loud snap. Grabbing Nehir's outstretched hand, she hauled him up to the sink, then cupped her hands. "Step up."

With one foot on Falcon's hands, Nehir grabbed the end of the vent, and Falcon pushed him up so that he disappeared head-first into the dark metal tunnel.

"Just keep going as far as you can and look before you get out anywhere."

"Okay," Nehir's hollow voice called back.

"So," Magpie kept eyes on the door, "do we let this body burn or try to get him out through the vent, too?"

Falcon shrugged. "What the hell, Magpie? We've come this far. Let's go for it. The kid deserves a decent burial."

A broad spray of liquid showered over the cabinet, and cadavers rammed against the door, then blue and yellow flames flared up from the bodies, blasting a pungent odour of hot, sweet, coppery burning flesh across the room. Sprinklers spread across the ceiling, burst into life, and a spray of water showered across the room and over Alister's body, slowly filling the body bag.

"Screw this," Falcon leapt up, grabbed the edge of the vent and hauled herself up. "C'mon, Mags."

Water poured over Magpie as she clambered onto the tray.

She swept away the bottles and instruments on the shelf and climbed onto it.

"Can't do it, Falcon," Magpie called back. "Damn shelf's slippery as ice." She wiped her drenched face with her forearm and jumped to the ground.

"Hang on, Mags, the shaft splits up ahead. I'll turn around, come back and pull you up."

The sizzling of bodies merged with the snaps and metallic groans of the X-ray arm and gurneys bending away from the door. Two large hands pushed the door ajar through the shower and flames, then arms reached through and effortlessly lifted a gurney to tilt it away from the door, impervious to the fire that still danced across the corpses despite the shower.

The heavy arm of the X-ray machine crashed onto the bodies with a gruesome spongy crunch, splattering globs of burning flesh across the room, then smashed onto the floor. Two Followers barged in, blind-firing into the flames, smoke, and downpour. Falcon, lying in the shaft, took them both down.

Magpie slipped to the ground to find Alister's body; it must have somehow rolled off with the weight of the water in the bag.

An enormous figure encased in white armour swept the door aside with one blow and stomped into the room. Shimmering red and yellow flames reflected off the drenched armour. Plotinus stood astride the two dead Followers in the doorway. There was a click as a microphone came on. His electric voice, amplified through his helmet, roared over the chaos. "You killed them, whores of Babylon, you take them."

Massive arms scooped up and hurled what was left of one body. Magpie dodged, and the corpses flew past her to hit the wall and then drop to the ground between her and Alister. The shots from Falcon and Magpie's pulse rifles slammed into the body armour, leaving nothing but shallow dents. Plotinus didn't budge; he thrust his fist through the charred carcass on the twisted trolleys, toppling the cadaver to the ground, and splashed heavily into the room. The flames reflected over his transparent helmet, so his head seemed to be on fire. He stopped momentarily to look around and headed straight for Alister's body. He tore open the bag and lifted Alister by the ankle, turned, and swung out his free arm to extend a long plate from the forearm to whack away the assault rifle Magpie had pointed at him. The plate shot out to strike her chest, and she flew back onto the floor.

Plotinus let out a laugh and threw Alister's body across the room. Alister struck the wall so heavily that the impact boomed over the noise of sizzling and spitting flames. Lifting the tray Alister had been lying on, Plotinus raised it over his head. "I don't need all your body." Stamping across the room, he swung the edge down Alister's neck so violently that the steel tray's end buckled several inches inwards.

Shocked and confused by the tray buckling, Magpie, holding her broken arm, scrabbled to her feet. She staggered through the wreckage and into the reception area, heading for the smouldering rubble and hole Plotinus and his two Followers made. Using a steel beam, she hauled herself onto the ramp, and the precariously balanced metal collapsed, pitching her forward onto her arm. She cried out in pain, the chilling boom of Plotinus's voice behind her.

"Your destiny is mine to decide now." He raised his foot to stamp on her, and Magpie rolled away. It missed her chest by inches and crunched through the slab of concrete she lay on, sinking into the rubble, where it stuck. Plotinus twisted and pulled, snarling like a trapped animal.

Magpie rushed back into the autopsy suite and found her rifle. The sprinklers had exhausted themselves, and Falcon waved to her from the ventilation shaft. "Magpie, grab my arm."

Magpie leapt towards the tray and reached up with her good arm. There was a loud crash from the hall outside. Falcon caught her wrist and crawled backwards. "Damn, he's free,"

"Dammit, girl, pull me up," cried Magpie.

Falcon swore under her breath and then said. "I don't believe it,"

"Falcon, I'm hanging by my one good arm here. What are you doing?"

Falcon let go, and Magpie barely managed to land on the tray with one foot and jump to the floor. Falcon pulled herself forward and dropped to stand beside her. They both pointed their weapons at the empty doorway and reception area. From beyond, there came a horrendous crashing of metal and stone, broken by Plotinus's agonised screaming and the loud creaks and smashing of metal. Then the noise stopped, and the hallway fell silent but for the occasional crumble and fall of rubble.

"What the hell's going on out there, Fal?" Magpie said.

A tall, thin figure, covered from head to toe in black and looking like a solid shadow, appeared and leaned against the doorway. Falcon raised her rifle, and Magpie pushed down the muzzle.

Magpie mumbled something under her breath. Falcon glanced down at her with a smile and whispered, "I'd love to, but this time, it'll really have to wait."

"I could do with a drink," the figure said.

Chapter Twenty-three

Alister sat alone in the treatment room, speaking with his sister on the phone while Magpie was in the next room, having her broken arm seen to. He had his clothes back and was dressed in his thin, black-hooded sweatshirt, grey jeans, dark-grey-washed canvas jacket, and red-gold skateboard shoes.

"No, all I remember is being on a bright beach, crowded with demons, genies, angels, and all these other weird creatures. Thousands and thousands of them. The beach seemed to go on forever. Then the whole vision shattered into billions of fragments, and I saw what must be the particles, like squids but with only five tentacles. They were transparent and sizzling with tiny electrodes. Then I woke up.

"Doc said I somehow came back around. Said I had, how did he put it, 'complete central nervous system dysfunction and paralysis'...I know it does, doesn't it? No wonder they took me to the morgue."

A receptionist came and knocked on the window.

"I gotta go, Jules. The lines out of town are mostly down, and there's some kind of phone jam. Other people need to make calls... Yes, I'll call as soon as I arrive at the airport...I will. Remember to ask Graham about Dad's notes, won't you?... Okay, you too. Bye, sis."

He handed the phone back and returned to Falcon, sitting by herself. "How you doing, kiddo?" she asked.

"Pretty good," Alister said with a nod.

"Okay." Falcon stood up. "Wait here for Magpie. Tell her I have one last job to do. I'll be in the ward down at the end across the hall." She pointed to a set of green doors.

"Will do."

A few minutes later, Magpie emerged, examining the mesh cast over her arm. "Three weeks I have to wear this while the biosynth repairs the broken bone. So, did you speak to your sister?"

"Yes."

She fell into the seat beside him. "Hacked into Plotinus's outfit with your neural nanoparticle things," she tapped the side of his head with a finger. "And shut it down, eh?"

Alister smiled and nodded. "Where is he?"

"Locked up," Magpie said. "You are one lucky sonofabitch."

"I know, that nutter would have ripped me apart, but I woke up remembering everything."

"Where's Falcon?"

"Oh yeah, she's down the hall through those doors. Said there's one more job."

"Come on then," Magpie said, and they set off down the corridor.

"So how did you survive Plotinus ripping into you, let alone come back to life?" She poked him with her good hand. "Look at you, still alive and all in one piece."

"I came round when Plotinus was laying into me. It's all a bit hazy, I remember him whacking me with the end of a big metal tray.…but by then, the Soft-Machine had kicked in and converted into full-armour mode."

"Like I said, you are one lucky S.O.B."

"Yeah."

Magpie put her arm around his shoulder and gave him a hug. "Don't worry, Centauri have the top surgeons and equipment. They'll put her right."

Alister nodded.

Falcon emerged from a treatment room with another PI. Beside them stood an unhappy-looking young man in his twenties wearing combat fatigues, clearly not a soldier.

"Hey, babe," Falcon said to Magpie, a broad smile on her face. She gave a nod towards Magpie's arm. "Another biosynth fix. You sure know how to collect them."

"At least I was where the action was and not stuck in a hole."

"I'm glad you said that and not me, Mags."

Magpie returned the smile, then nodded at the other PI. "Hi, Stan."

"Hello, Magpie. Glad to see you in one piece."

"Who's this guy?" Magpie said.

"Valkyrie's boyfriend, Peter Grace, Plotinus's PA. He is willing to tell us all he knows. He's coming back to base with us for a debrief."

"Then I can join Valkyrie, right?" Peter asked. "She's innocent. I found the drugs he was giving her."

"Not up to me. Take it up with the boss, Cape," Falcon said.

"Falcon, we need to go, there's a drive waiting for us," Stan said.

Falcon nodded. "See you back at the barracks, Magpie." She turned to Alister. "Thanks, Al."

Alister nodded and stepped aside, letting the others pass them to head towards the exit and ambulance bay.

They were the only people in the elevator, large enough to take two beds. Magpie sighed and leaned her head against the wall behind them.

"This has been one crazy week."

The elevator stopped on the fourth floor, and the doors opened to the intensive care unit. A sign and small arrow on the wall opposite instructed all visitors to sign in at the reception desk.

"Nehir's already signed in," Alister said, putting the pen down. He stopped at one of the observation units and tapped on the window. A young Asian man with a backgammon board open on his lap sat up in a bed. Sitting beside him, Sophie smiled and waved to Alister, beckoning him in.

"Hi, Sophie. How's it going?"

"We're good now. First, that storm and then the attack on the hospital. I've never been so scared. What are you doing here?"

"My girlfriend, Suzie, is just down the hall."

"The girl in a coma?"

"Yeah." Alister nodded.

"I'm sorry to hear that. Oh, this is Suresh, my fiancé."

"Hi," Alister said with another nod.

"Hi," Suresh replied. "I hope she recovers soon."

"Thanks. Sophie, you should know your dad helped us get through the settlement. Have you heard from him?"

"Yes." Sophie smiled. "A rabbi from the Semite settlement helped him get out; he's on his way."

"That's good." Alister turned to Magpie, tapping on the window. "I'd better go."

"Good luck," Sophie and Suresh said in unison.

"Thanks, you too."

There were two beds in Suzie's room. Suzie lay in one, with rubber tubes going into her nose and a drip attached to her arm. A small mesh cap covered in micro-thin wires transmitted signals to a neurological monitor. Nehir sat on the empty bed, looking across at her. He jumped to his feet and gaped at Alister as they came in.

Magpie smiled. "This is the first time I've seen you speechless. How is she?"

"Uh." Nehir continued to stare at Alister.

"Nehir, I'm okay. I was never dead, just really, really close, okay?"

Nehir slowly nodded.

"Should I slap him or something?" Magpie said.

"No, I'm fine," Nehir said. "Suzie, she's been like that since I got here. The nurse said she's stable. They're going to take her to…" He pulled his phone out, tapped on the screen, and read, "The Centauri Wing, Neurological Hospital, London."

Alister fell into the seat beside Suzie and touched her face. "I have to do something."

"I'll come with you," Nehir said.

"What?"

"I'll come with you to London."

***

Foss and Keasha stopped eating when the emergency message from Raymond Ruya scrolled across the screen.

"So much for our honeymoon," Keasha said. "Guess we were in the wrong place at the wrong time. I'll send a message back to base and set a course for Earth."

Foss pushed the empty plate aside. "Trust our luck."

"Maybe we can have a bit of a break on Earth," Keasha said, "have a look at the super-massive tank. How much time do you think we'll have?"

"Earth time?" Foss asked. "About a month before the Wrychun cyborgs arrive. Taking down the blood-sucking killers will be easy. Finding their cloaked asses while they stay invisible is going to be the tough part."

THE END